The Battle *for* Eliza

MISSES OF MELBOURNE

BOOK 1

VICKI MILLIKEN

Bonnie May Books

Published in Australia by
Bonnie May Books

ABN 23 005 104 640
PO Box 937
Williamstown
MELBOURNE VICTORIA 3016
AUSTRALIA

vicki@vickimilliken.com
www.vickimilliken.com

First published in Australia 2020
Copyright © Vicki Milliken 2020

All rights reserved. No part of this publication may be reproduced, stored in a retrieval system, or transmitted, in any form or by any means without the prior written permission of the publisher, nor be otherwise circulated in any form of binding or cover other than that in which it is published and without a similar condition being imposed on the subsequent purchaser.

National Library of Australia Cataloguing in Publication entry

 A catalogue record for this book is available from the National Library of Australia

ISBN: 978-0-6487849-7-5 (paperback)
ISBN: 978-0-6487849-9-9 (epub)

Cover photography by Darya Komarova (Couple portrait)
Cover layout and design by Tri Widyatmaka
Layout and typesetting by Sophie White Design
Printed by Ingram Spark

This is a work of fiction. Names, characters, places, and incidents are either the product of the author's imagination or are used fictitiously, and any resemblance to actual persons, living or dead, business establishments, events of locales is extremely coincidental.

*To
Andrew
with love*

HISTORICAL NOTE

In 1925, Australia played host to a visit by a total of fifty-seven vessels and approximately twenty-five thousand officers and men of the United States Navy.

Melbourne, as the official capital of Australia and temporary seat of Federal Parliament at the time, received the largest contingent, including the flagship USS *Seattle*, and three battleships, USS *Pennsylvania*, USS *Nevada* and USS *Oklahoma*, which docked at Princes Pier in Port Melbourne on Thursday 23 July.

The city was gripped with a joie de vivre. The plans of the female population included ensuring a reserve of sleep in the weeks before and then cramming all they could into the daytime and dancing hours of the fortnight that followed. *The Battle for Eliza* is the story of one Melbourne Miss ...

CHAPTER 1

Saturday 11 July 1925

'Mmm.'

The soft, low-pitched moan stopped twenty-five-year-old Eliza Sinclair in her tracks. Placing one hand on the backstage curtain of the ballroom, she took stock. Her first assignation. Not something to boast about. At her age.

More moans and husky murmurs filtered through to her, followed by a throaty chuckle.

Damn, she thought. *Timing.* Timing was everything. Why couldn't the couple have gone someplace else? Why did they need to ruin her tryst? No one needed the practice more than she did. She didn't aspire to be a femme fatale, but life was short, and she wasn't even out of the blocks yet.

'Mmm, you're good.' There was a gasp and the sound of lips moving over skin before the smack of lips meeting lips. 'But we can't continue here ...'

A gurgle of feminine laughter sounded. 'No, darling, not here, not yet ...'

Finally, someone's coming to their senses, thought Eliza, then quickly realised she couldn't be caught eavesdropping.

Even if it was accidental.

Too late. The curtain's edge was wrested from her fingers and she found herself standing face to face with Queenie Nolan. *We're the same height*, observed Eliza to herself with some surprise – an absurd thought under the circumstances. A lithe five-foot-ten frame wasn't a deterrent to men when packaged with bewitching curves.

'Eliza, what a surprise. Spying? Or ... maybe looking to pick up some tips?'

'S-sorry, I didn't know anyone was here,' Eliza stammered, tucking her hair behind her ear.

'Derek and I were —'

But Eliza didn't register the rest of her sentence, as Queenie's Derek, whom she'd thought to be her Derek, emerged from the shadows performing some last-minute adjustments to his trousers. Eliza and Derek Fisher were dating. Or so she'd imagined after he'd taken her to the theatre last week, the movies the week before, not to mention his attentions earlier tonight during the waltz. Evidently, the dating wasn't exclusive. It wasn't even real.

Eliza managed to swallow the lump in her throat. 'You and Derek were —'

'Testing the equipment,' Queenie purred, casually stroking her hand down the front of Derek's pants where he stood at her shoulder. Derek stepped behind Queenie, smiling ruefully, but not before Eliza noticed the growing bulge in his striped satin trousers.

'Awkward. Sorry, Eliza,' Derek said. 'We're still friends, though, aren't we? We had some fun. It isn't as if we were serious ...'

'We're not friends. We're not ... anything,' spat Eliza.

How stupid, gullible or naïve did he think she was? Thank goodness she hadn't confided in anyone other than her best friend, Rebecca – Bec – Cross, about her interest in Derek.

Queenie pouted, tipped her head to one side and patted her bejewelled bandeau. 'Eliza, sweetie, don't make a fuss. There's no harm done. Derek here was looking for some *real* fun.'

Eliza opened her mouth, then closed it, her voice deserting her. What would have been her defence, anyway? Queenie had raised the stakes. Derek wouldn't be satisfied with a few kisses now.

'He's a fast learner … shows some promise,' Queenie added, with a tinkling laugh that could have broken crystal.

'Oh!' Mortified, Eliza turned, head bowed, heedless of where her feet took her as long as it was away. Away from handsome men with Valentino looks and fickle interests, and bewitching women wearing gold starburst heels.

'Eliza,' called a voice. 'Eliza, wait up.' The voice was louder this time and accompanied by a familiar hand wrapped around her arm.

Eliza lifted her gaze, then promptly collapsed with a sob into her best friend's arms.

'Bec, I'm so naïve. So foolish.'

'Shh.' Keeping an arm around Eliza's shoulders, Bec led her to a sturdy bench seat that had been abandoned alongside a set of backstage props at the rear of the ballroom's main hall. After carefully dusting the area with a black satin glove, she urged Eliza to sit.

From the ballroom, Eliza could hear Birmingham's Danse Palais band break into a foxtrot, 'Yes Sir, That's My Baby', the swing-time melody seeming to mock her. She'd always loved the song because it never failed to bring a smile to her face, but not tonight. It was a favourite with the crowd, who no doubt had packed the dance floor. Idly, she wondered if enough time had passed for her brother, Daniel, to notice she was missing – he was her chaperone for the evening.

Bec, her brow etched with concern, pressed a scallop-edged handkerchief into her hand and rubbed her back. The quiet attention was soothing.

Eliza dabbed her eyes, took a deep breath and sat up straighter. 'I was supposed to meet Derek. A few innocent kisses ... maybe something more ... But when I arrived, I heard another couple, you know ...'

Bec nodded and Eliza continued, 'And then Queenie and Derek emerged. She was so blatant. So confident. So ... damn sexy. There was no way Derek was going to settle for a few kisses after that.'

'A work of art, our Queenie. Her motto? To "never die wondering". It must be a Sydney thing. Not that she'd have had too much pushback from Derek. He's a dolt, though a good-looking one, I admit.'

Eliza winced, studying the tips of her dancing shoes.

'Sorry, I know you went out a couple of times, but he's self-absorbed, always looking for the next chance – be that racehorse, sporting match or woman.'

Eliza raised her eyes to Bec's.

'It would be a real test of our friendship if you hooked up with him permanently.' Bec shuddered for effect.

Eliza shook her head. 'He seemed nice enough. Maybe I just don't have what it takes to hold a man's attention. I haven't even been kissed properly – Derek's first attempt last week fell flat when I headbutted him.'

Bec burst out laughing. 'You didn't?'

'Nothing serious. He didn't get concussion or anything. I pretended I'd lost my footing.' Eliza covered her face with her hands, leaving the balled-up handkerchief in her lap. 'In days gone by, I would have been considered "on the shelf", dreary, fussy or comic and shipped off to some great-aunt as a companion for her final years.'

'You don't have any great-aunts,' quipped Bec, her grey eyes luminous with scarcely suppressed humour.

'Finally, some good luck.'

They lapsed into companionable silence. Eliza fidgeted with the fringe of her skirt, while Bec worked to remove the dust cemented to her glove.

'It's more than just Derek, isn't it? You've been out of sorts for months.'

When Eliza yielded nothing more than a shrug, Bec continued, 'You cut your hair, although I grant that the style suits you. I could never get away with it. Your fringe seems to flirt with your eyebrows and those bangs draw attention to your glorious cheekbones. But, I'm not sure your mother will ever forgive you. Is she still asking whether you paid good money for it?'

Eliza gave a rueful twist of her lips. 'She didn't understand that I was trying to be less dull.'

'I don't agree that you're dull. I bet you haven't lacked a dance partner since we arrived this evening.'

'That's different. Dancing is one of the things I am good at.' Eliza paused. 'This might sound silly.'

'Try me.'

'I want men – actually just one man – to notice me, be attracted to me, and fall in love with me, for myself. Not for my father's connections, or my mother's cooking, or my ability to hold a tune, keep a beat, dance without treading on men's toes, for being biddable or easygoing ...'

'Or for your great taste in friends.'

Eliza giggled, then hiccupped. 'Or that,' she agreed, quietly reflecting how thankful she was for Bec's friendship, and her dry humour. They enjoyed time together most days – either on the train to the city or at the YWCA where they were both employed. Eliza providing tuition in dance, singing and drawing, and Bec being engaged in the employment office.

'And what are you going to do with this man?' asked Bec, interrupting her musings.

'You'll declare this is old-fashioned, but I want to get married. And I want to be courted and kissed ... and petted.'

'You have hidden depths. Petted indeed. Don't you need a car for that?' Bec asked.

'You're asking me?'

'Good point. Got anyone in mind for your wanton intent?'

Eliza shook her head.

Bec's lips curved. 'Well, I have.'

'Who?' asked Eliza, feeling her eyes widen. 'Anyone I know?'

'It's a surprise. He hasn't even realised it himself yet.' And with that, she grabbed Eliza's arm, and skirting the public areas, marched her out of the venue. They ignored all offers to dance – and the disappointed faces of the men they passed – pausing only to collect coats, hats and handbags.

'They've left. Did Eliza say anything to you? Or Bec?' demanded Daniel of his best mate.

'Nope. Bit early, isn't it?' returned Alex Heaton, casually

THE BATTLE FOR ELIZA

surveying the evening's crowd. They were standing beside one of the floor-to-ceiling columns, on the steps leading down to the Palais' dance floor. They'd retreated there as it provided one of the best vantage points of the venue without having to climb the stairs to the balcony.

Daniel's brow wrinkled with annoyance. 'Yes. Something's going on. Harry at the door said it would have been easier to stop a steamroller than those two.'

'What?' asked Alex, watching a smile chase the frown from his friend's face.

'Then again, it means we're off the hook.'

'What do you mean *we*? She's not my sister. I was never on the hook.'

'I promised on your behalf. Mum asked, and I knew you wouldn't be able to refuse, so I agreed we'd chaperone Eliza and Bec tonight. But it's damn annoying the way they took off without a word.'

Alex would wager that Bec had led the charge, Eliza trailing, tucking a strand of hair behind her ear in consternation. Daniel was fortunate that his sister hadn't embraced the more forward behaviour of others her age. Not that she was dull, just lacked a bit of self-confidence. It would have greatly impinged on their entertainments if they had been interrupted to rescue her from one escapade after another. He knew it was selfish of him to think of it in that light, but twenty-six-year-old bachelors did not wish to waste their evenings engaged as nannies.

Ah well. Good to have the formalities of the evening over with early. Saturday nights always teemed with possibility. Alex used his six-foot frame to scan the floor for golden curls dressed in emerald green. 'Have you seen Queenie?'

'Not for half an hour, at least. Wait, there she is entwined with Derek Fisher in the far corner,' Daniel said with a lifted brow.

Alex pursed his lips as he studied the couple, briefly surprised at his lack of anguish, despite he and Queenie having been an item for the last six months since her appearance in Melbourne, from Sydney. So, he was being punished for turning her down last night – and last week – was he? Two could play that game.

'No matter. Let Queenie have her fun; it might invest some additional spice in our arrangement. Derek wouldn't have been my choice. Handsome but shallow.' Alex shuddered before straightening and turning on his heel.

'First Eliza and Bec, now you. Is anyone going to tell me what's going on?'

Alex stopped short. 'I'm off to enjoy myself further afield, having developed an interest in the colour pink, blonde curls and a large you-know-what. Don't wait around for me. Usual time tomorrow for lunch?'

Daniel nodded. 'Good luck. You know Queenie hates Beth.'

'I'm counting on it!'

CHAPTER 2

Sunday 12 July 1925

Sunday lunch seemed like it would never end. Eliza mentally ticked off the topics covered so far and calculated that she and Bec had another half an hour before they could escape.

There was neighbourhood news, otherwise known as gossip, from her mother, Eleanor. The headline? A camel washed overboard from a visiting freighter and found clambering across the rocks on the foreshore. Then there was the nuisance created from wandering cows and horses on the beach, which, Eliza concluded, had probably strolled down to marvel at the camel.

The weightier suburban news was led by her father, William, or Bill as he was popularly known. Eliza listened with interest as the conversation drifted from the absurdity of council funding decisions, to house prices, before touching on the lack of life-saving equipment, which all agreed wasn't the highest priority in Williamstown in winter, when only the hardiest of the population braved the sea. Eliza nodded as she watched the rain batter the kitchen windows – hardiest and foolish.

Spearing the last of her green peas one by one, she waited for the usual questions about what her mother called – since she and Daniel were eight – 'the children's news', despite both now being in their mid-twenties. Nor were Alex or Bec spared, her mother shameless in her interest in the lives of her children's best friends.

'Now before you say anything, I was the one who asked Daniel to chaperone you girls last night. I know you think you're grown up, but you're both young, attractive and single.'

Eliza focused her attention on placing the tines of her fork beside her knife and pointing them to twelve o'clock. Table etiquette had been one of life's early lessons.

'It wasn't too hard,' said Daniel. 'Thought we'd lost them for a bit, but they turned up eventually.'

Eliza lifted her gaze and found Alex watching her, an amused smile playing across his lips. She wondered if he was going to elaborate on Daniel's comment. It was all right for Daniel and Alex, they weren't fettered by conventions. Alex had his pick of women, parties and other entertainments, and no parental interference since his parents had moved to London late last year. A regular 1920s pin-up boy. She returned her attention to the position of her cutlery, turning her knife's edge to face inwards.

Bec was looking Daniel straight in the eye with an arched brow, as if daring him to continue the story. When he didn't, Eliza breathed a sigh of relief. Although Eliza was innocent of any wrongdoing, her mother would not have been pleased to hear of her daughter and Bec escaping Daniel's vigilance and journeying home alone.

'I know Dick and Nola Birmingham run an upstanding

establishment, but you can never be too sure. Was there a big crowd?' her mother asked.

'The usual,' replied Daniel. 'It wasn't a crush. But I'd expect once the Yanks arrive, it'll be chock-full.'

'Are they holding dance lessons this week, Eliza?'

'Wednesday and Thursday, before the evening social, and then all teaching classes are suspended for the fortnight. Birmingham's is going to open every night. Even Sunday.'

'Those Americans,' said her mother with a shake of her head. 'You girls need to be careful. I remember the visit of 1908 as if it were yesterday. They had a way about them they did. Brash! Loved anything in skirts.'

Eliza intercepted a shared glance between her parents before her mother continued. 'Just last Thursday, Maureen Butler was talking about her Jenny. Such a sensible girl and yet she said her head seemed to be crammed with talk of nothing else.'

Little did her mother know, but Eliza, Bec, Jenny and most of the female population under the age of thirty had spent the last month talking of little else. Initially, they had pored over newspaper headlines reporting the daily progress of the fleet's journey across the Pacific. Then, armed with information published on the many balls, sporting events and other entertainments planned, they'd organised their time and were looking forward to an exciting two weeks.

'The city could use an injection of cash, Mum. Big spenders, those Yanks. Yesterday ...'

Eliza stopped listening as Daniel launched into a soliloquy on economics and returned to her musings. Ten thousand men – give or take – in uniform. And not just any uniform, but an American naval uniform. Navy-blue jackets with jaunty flap collars, bell-bottom trousers, all topped by pork-pie hats. Splendid dancers, the sailors, or so the tabloids had said – jazzers and foxtroters!

There was work, of course, that couldn't be avoided, but the opportunities to fill the evening hours and those of a weekend were endless. And with ten thousand men wandering the streets of Melbourne, there were plenty to go around. She'd heard they weren't as conservative as the homegrown variety, they were generous with compliments and money, and knew how to show a girl a good time. It made her giddy just to think of the possibilities. It would be an experience of a lifetime – one in which the word 'sensible' had no part to play.

'Being so far away from home, I'm sure all they're after is a home-cooked meal and a bit of company,' said Bec with a smile.

Eliza swung her leg, connecting with Bec's shin. But even Bec's baleful glare and surprised 'Ouch' could not deter Eliza's mum from climbing back onto her soapbox.

'And that's the other thing. Jenny's badgering her mother to host a couple of sailors for dinner and maybe an overnight stay. Some initiative that she feels she should support in her role at the YWCA. Humph! You modern girls, just be careful, I say.'

'It's been in all the newspapers, Mum. The YMCA and even the prime minister's department are calling for families to billet a sailor,' said Eliza, hoping the mention of government endorsement would allay her mother's concerns.

'If I had my way, you'd both be grounded from the hour they land till the hour they set sail,' said Eliza's father.

Eliza turned a dismayed face in his direction and his tone

softened. 'I understand you'll be well chaperoned during the fortnight. I expect your mother has everything well in hand, don't you, Ellie?'

'Daniel, and Alex, are happy to help keep an eye on these two,' said her mother. 'Aren't you?'

'Of course, Mrs Sinclair. Always happy to help. I was thinking of buying two pairs of leading strings. Any objections?' said Alex, pretending to give the matter some careful thought.

Eliza scowled at him, and he grinned.

'Great idea. We could tether them to a fence or lamp post, to stop them wandering off,' said Daniel, warming to the idea.

'I'm glad that's settled, then.' Eliza's father came to his feet. 'Don't frown, Eliza my dear, the lads are only joking. Your mother and I survived the last visit, maybe ask her for a few pointers.'

Eliza's frown deepened. *Ask her mother for pointers?* But she had no time to quiz her father further. As he passed behind her chair, he dropped a hand onto her shoulder and gave it a reassuring squeeze. 'Now if you'll all excuse me, I have papers to review ahead of council tomorrow.'

Under cover of the bustle by Eliza's mum to put on the kettle and make tea in the kitchen, Daniel leaned towards Eliza and Bec, and hissed in his severest big-brother tone, 'No more disappearing tricks like last night, huh.'

'I would think you'd have more to worry about than us,' rejoined Bec smartly. 'Queenie,' she said with a cautionary look at Alex, 'and Evelyn,' this with an ominous look at Daniel, 'will need close supervision with all those lonely sailor types parading around Melbourne. Knowing Queenie, she's probably already signed them up to host a sailor or two.'

Eliza studied the two men's responses to Bec's prediction – she wouldn't be sorry if Daniel's latest crush married a sailor and moved far away.

Daniel pursed his lips as if giving the matter some thought, before shaking his head and punching Alex's shoulder. 'Not Evelyn ... who could guess with Queenie, though, she's become wilder lately and her aunt isn't exactly vigilant of her comings and goings.'

'That has its advantages, mate,' said Alex with a wolfish smile which quickly dissolved as he realised where he was and in whose company. 'My apologies. Tell me why we are discussing this with you both, anyway?'

'Therapy. They say confession is good for the soul,' quipped Eliza, tipping her head and giving him a flirtatious smile. *She might as well get some practice before the twenty-third, when the fleet was due to arrive.*

Alex seemed stunned for a moment, before he shook his head and said, 'A gentleman never tells.'

Damn Alex's personal code of behaviour. She could have used a few tips.

'It's called "deflection",' said Daniel. 'You and I know it in engineering terms as the degree of displacement under load, but these girls make a science out of keeping us off course and working to turn us inside out.'

Eliza shook her head. Daniel enjoyed relating engineering terms to everyday situations.

'Stuff your fancy name, it's called pointing out the obvious,' said Bec as both girls rose to help clear the table.

CHAPTER 3

Monday 13 July 1925

'I have a plan,' announced Bec as she bounced into the YWCA's tiny staff room, where Eliza had toed off her shoes and was massaging the soles of her feet.

'A plan for my poor aching feet?'

'No, for your transformation from *dull* – your words not mine – to fascinating, compelling, attractive, intriguing.'

'Oh, Bec, I don't know ...'

'You haven't even heard it yet!' complained Bec.

'You have form. I'm still recovering from your last plan. Remember —'

Bec waved her hand dismissively. 'Your hair style is glorious, as I said the other night. But it's being let down by your clothes. You're too *beige*.'

As Eliza started to protest, Bec held up her hand. 'Look at you. Brown from head to toe apart from a white knotted sash. And not an ankle in sight.'

Eliza looked down. She preferred *biscuit* to *beige* but couldn't argue the blandness. 'They're serviceable. And I can't afford a new wardrobe. I'm saving, remember, to move out of home. And with the extra private tuition classes I've picked up at Birmingham's, I'm finally making progress.'

'Pooh! As serviceable as a tea towel. Lucky for you I have a solution. Christine Tailleuse, Mother's dressmaker, is offering to give you a gown for the competition and has a selection of items which Lord ... Someone's wife paid for and then abruptly left the country.' She lowered her voice conspiratorially. 'Seems like she may have been involved in some hanky-panky.'

'Stop. Firstly, what competition? And secondly, why is Miss Tailleuse so interested in helping me?'

'Birmingham's Fleet Waltz Competition that was advertised in *Table Talk*, remember? Where women are partnered with a visiting American naval man to compete for one hundred pounds cash. We talked about you entering.'

'We talked. Briefly. I don't remember deciding anything.'

'That's because you're *dull*,' Bec repeated.

Eliza was already regretting having confided her poor self-image to her friend.

'This is the perfect opportunity for you to conquer your fear of men.'

'But I don't have —'

'Don't argue. It's not that you're unattractive. You're aloof. And men never get an opportunity to get to know you as you're always pushing them away.'

'Are you saying that I'm unapproachable? Unfriendly?'

'No. I mean you're reserved. And the competition is just the right occasion for you to practise your feminine wiles on someone you need never see again.'

'Bec —'

'And if you don't like who you're partnered with, there

are another nine thousand, nine hundred and ninety-nine others to choose from,' said Bec, doing a twirl.

'Bec —'

'And Christine knows that your figure, combined with her dress, will be a fantastic promotion for her designs. You can thank me later. Got to run. Be ready at four-thirty.'

At Eliza's bewildered look, Bec explained, 'Your first fitting is this evening after work,' and with a wave she sailed out the door.

Eliza groaned and then smiled. She was best friends with a jaunty windstorm – undaunted by life – sweeping all before her. Bec was the perfect foil for herself. Eliza was more cautious and circumspect. She still remembered the day they'd met, at Birmingham's, four years ago. The failure of the electric power had led to Eliza dressing by candlelight. It wasn't until the power was restored and she was under the full glare of the ballroom's lights, that she realised she'd donned odd stockings. Mortified, she'd hastily retreated to the sidelines. Bec, recognising her from the office, had sat out a dance to talk with her. After hearing the story, she'd laughed, dragged Eliza to the ladies' room, torn off her stockings and bade Eliza do the same. She'd insisted that no one would notice if they both went without. And no one had. They'd been best friends ever since.

Another thought struck her. How was she going to keep the competition from her parents, let alone her anointed chaperones?

She'd make that Bec's problem, too.

Standing on a dais, under the glare of the lights from a brass chandelier, Eliza watched Christine Tailleuse and Bec circle her like a carnival game prize. They paused briefly to tweak and tease the gown's gorgeous georgette fabric and chiffon overlay before continuing – around and around.

Eliza had fallen in love with the hand-painted material depicting butterfly motifs and embellished with sequins, beads and metallic thread, at first sight.

'The hem will need to be lifted an inch, maybe less,' declared Christine. Bec nodded. 'The handkerchief hemline needs to skim just below the knees, but other than that it looks ... perfect.' And with that final statement, she motioned to Bec for the pins and started on the alterations.

'The colour is exquisite,' enthused Bec. 'Sea green and blue do things to your eyes. I wish I could wear that combination of colours, but I look like a deceased fish whenever I try.' Her impression of a drowning goldfish caused Eliza to laugh.

'Stand still, *ma chérie*,' admonished the dressmaker. 'There will be no dead fish leaving this salon.'

Bec pulled another face, before musing, 'Your sailor will be blown away. And maybe not just him, but a few others as well.'

'I don't have a sailor at this moment, or anyone else,' pointed out Eliza.

'Not yet,' said Bec, peering into the mirror as she attempted to tame a few liberated mahogany curls back into her waved bob. 'First step, we'll visit Birmingham's during our lunch break tomorrow to register.'

'Bec, I'm not sure ...'

'And that's why you've got me,' Bec gushed. 'Because I am. Sure, that is. And Christine here is going to make sure that you look irresistible. You'll have men lining up ... maybe even to dance with you,' she added cheekily.

Eliza had no doubts about the dancing, it was the rest of it she wasn't convinced of. She studied herself in the full-length mirrored glass, which Christine had set before the dais. At school she hadn't been much interested in boys, nor boys in her, she'd been all angles and edges – no curves to speak of.

During the war, she'd been energised by the opportunities presented to enter the workforce – taking an entry role as a postwoman to deliver mail. There had been limited chances for socialising – the long hours, the clumsy regulation boots issued that made her feet ache, not to mention the lack of men.

At Christine's request, she angled sideways to the mirror.

Strong arguments at the end of the war had pitted her lesser physical capability to that of a man's and she'd been forced to relinquish her position. Society's assumption that as a woman she would be anxious to return to pre-war propositions – home duties or marriage – without having experienced dances, parties, theatre and the like, also had worked against her. She hadn't been happy with her limited prospects then or now, nearly seven years later. She wanted to get married – she wasn't that unconventional – but she also had lost time to make up. And the timing of the peacetime invasion could not have been scripted better. Lightning courtships and marriages were not unheard of, according to her mum. Eliza hugged herself. She'd enjoy a fortnight of fun and remain open to the possibility of finding love.

CHAPTER 4

Tuesday 14 July 1925

As Eliza hesitated, a no-nonsense shove accompanied by a loud 'Argh' sent her stumbling into the empty vestibule of Birmingham's Danse Palais. Recovering, she posed a questioning look upon her best friend, who returned without preamble, 'It's a dance competition, you're not applying to run naked down Flinders Street. Come on, we've got twenty minutes before we're due back at work.'

Eliza removed her new cloche, the low brim making it difficult to see in the shadowed foyer. Absently patting her hair, she advanced towards the solitary lamp battling to keep the darkness at bay. Eliza spent a lot of hours here, but normally the light from the many-tiered chandeliers vanquished the shadows and ensured that everyone present could be accounted for. No shenanigans were tolerated. Pausing, she savoured the silence, and the familiar smell of beeswax. Her home away from home.

'Hello?' Her voice reverberated around the chamber, sounding loud to her ears. But there was no movement from within.

'Louder. You wouldn't attract a pixie with that volume,' Bec said. 'And it's freezing in here, hurry up.'

Raising her voice, she called, 'Hello? Is anyone here?' Eliza knocked on one of the sturdy oak doors that separated the vestibule from the dance hall, for good measure. On dance nights, these would be stoppered open, silently welcoming the hundreds of patrons as they streamed into the venue.

Eliza heard the faint sound of staccato clicks across the ballroom's sprung floor. They echoed eerily in the cavernous interior before one of the doors was levered open and the owner of the pair of killer heels appeared, silhouetted in the doorway.

'Eliza ... Bec ... what brings you both here at this time of the day?'

Even at this hour, Mrs Nola Birmingham – Mrs B to most – epitomised glamour. Not a hair out of place, a face that belied her fifty years of living – granted, it had some help from the carefully applied cosmetics – and a slim figure. Truth be told, Eliza found her a little intimidating. Although, she wished the matriarch would update her perfume. Floral scents were so dated.

Eliza smoothed her palms down her skirt. 'Hi, Mrs B. I've come to put my name down for the Fleet Challenge ... um, as one of the dancers ...' Not the most confident appeal, Eliza admitted, adding what she hoped was a winning smile.

'You and half the town, it would seem. There are only fifty places, you realise.' She smiled in that placating way which on others might seem condescending, but on Mrs B seemed to exude charm.

'Yes, I know. Mr B has been hinting since the start of the new year that I enter one of the local competitions. But I didn't have a partner,' Eliza ventured, dancing from one foot to the other. She hoped he'd forgive her use of him to support her nomination.

'Well, dear girl, let me speak with Dick to see what he had in mind and I'll let you know. What about you, Bec. Were you looking to add your name to the contest, also?'

'No thank you, Mrs B. I'm happy to support from the sidelines.'

'Humph. Now, girls, be off with you, I have classes to prepare and no doubt you both should be somewhere else, too.'

'Thanks, Mrs B. We'll see you tomorrow night,' they both chorused, edging out the door which separated the environs of the Danse Palais from the goings-on down Collins Street.

Eliza consulted the large octagonal face of her watch, its straw-coloured gold glinting in the subdued lighting. It had been a present for her twenty-first, an unusual gift, but something her father had fully supported since it was practical and functional. Eliza loved it, despite its practicality. Ten minutes until she and Bec needed to be back at work, which for Eliza meant directing the efforts of twelve excitable girls in the waltz, and for Bec, hunting employment opportunities for the many women who'd found themselves supporting their families since the war. They were now only two blocks away; they'd make it if they hurried.

Grabbing Bec's hand, she tugged her down the steps, almost bowling over two smartly dressed women who were strolling along the footpath. One sniffed and both gave the girls an irritated look, muttering about the manners of the current generation. Eliza issued a hurried apology before she and Bec dashed off, hands on hats, skirts flying, knees on show. More mutterings followed them. Dashing was obviously another offence, not to mention the unseemly display of knees.

A couple of buildings before their destination, they slowed their pace, not wanting to arrive appearing dishevelled.

'Whew. I must be out of shape,' gasped Bec. 'Look at you, wouldn't blow out a candle.'

'Oh, Bec. I'm nervous, what if Mrs B can't fit me in.'

'Mr B will put in a good word. No sweat.'

'And then there are my parents ... and Daniel. How will we keep them from finding out?'

'You worry too much. There is so much planned over the fortnight that it'll be hard to pay close attention to our comings and goings. You can stay at my place on the nights of the competition – my mum isn't as attentive as yours. Or even better, here in the lodging at YWCA headquarters. I can help you with your hair and dress. It'll be swell.'

Eliza grinned. Bec never seemed to bother over the conventions as much as she did. It was going to be fine. Bec was right, she worried too much. With that thought, she hurried into her afternoon's lessons.

CHAPTER 5

Later That Day

Eliza arrived home in the late afternoon to find her mother, brother and Alex settled in the kitchen enjoying tea and fresh scones. Her mum's face was rosy, but whether from the heat of the oven or Alex's flair for compliments, she couldn't tell. She reckoned the latter as scones on a Tuesday were unheard of, but not unappreciated. She greeted her mother and tossed her crushed-style hat onto the benchtop, before she ran her fingers through her hair.

'I'd have been home sooner had I known there were scones,' said Eliza. She reached between her mother and Daniel to secure one from the tea towel they were wrapped in. Daniel swatted her hand and Alex deftly placed the tea towel out of reach.

'Not so fast, sister dear. You can't just come in and plunder our spoil.'

Eliza punched him on the shoulder and advanced on Alex, who easily fended away her efforts to capture the prize.

'Mum,' she pleaded.

'Boys, that's enough. Give her one before she bludgeons one of you with the butter knife.'

Alex reluctantly surrendered the parcel. With a jubilant smile, Eliza coaxed a warm scone from its linen basket, broke it in half and lavished butter on both sides before she took a bite. Melted butter ran down her fingers and she licked them appreciatively, like a kitten lapping milk.

'Eliza!' admonished her mother. 'Not in company.'

'Company? I don't see any company.' Eliza looked up. Alex didn't react. His eyes were glued to her tongue as she sucked the butter from between her fingers. Did he think her uncouth? Shrugging, she poked her tongue out at him, breaking his gaze. He flushed, ever so slightly – maybe from the heat of the kitchen.

Eliza's mum watched the exchange with a curious expression. As her daughter plucked another scone from the tea towel, she asked, 'What brings you home so early?'

'Bec and I are off to see *Girl Shy* at the Williamstown Theatre tonight,' she said between mouthfuls.

'That the one with the hero who can't speak to women without stuttering?' asked Daniel.

'Yeah, the same.'

'A *romantic comedy*,' Alex said, wincing theatrically.

'Have you ever been to see one?'

'No. I make it a rule only to watch pictures with a car chase,' stated Alex.

'How staid of you, making rules at your age,' said Eliza, managing to avoid a kick under the table from her brother. 'You're both welcome to come along if you want. It might broaden your horizons.'

'That would save Bill from having to go out after his

final cuppa to make sure they get home,' said her mum, nodding her approval.

Alex raised a questioning eyebrow at Daniel, and received a reluctant nod. 'Sure. We're always open to having our horizons broadened.'

Bec took the news genially that their party had doubled. Daniel secured tickets, and they climbed the carpeted staircase to the balcony. Selecting a row in the middle of the theatre, Alex chose the seat beside Eliza, and Daniel flanked Bec on the other side. They relaxed into upholstered comfort.

Alex spent a few minutes battling Eliza's left elbow for the armrest. This was conducted silently and without eye contact. It was resolved when Alex retreated and extended his arm along the back of her seat.

As the movie progressed Alex relaxed, grudgingly acknowledging the skill of the comedian, even if the plot was a little contrived. There were eight reel changes. During one, Daniel slipped out to the candy bar and returned with coveted Eskimo pies and Violet Crumbles.

When the hero made a frenzied headlong dash involving car chases with multiple vehicles, including a police motorcycle, a horse-drawn wagon and trolley car, Alex felt Eliza nudge him in the ribs. With her eyes still on the screen, she bent towards him and whispered, 'Who would have thought, a romantic comedy *and* a car chase.'

Alex closed the distance between them and pressed his lips close to her ear, the slight scent of citrus pleasing his nostrils. 'You've certainly helped to expand my tastes.' He also approved of the masterly way in which the hero carried off his wife-to-be at the eleventh hour, saving her from the clutches of a bigamist, but thought it best not to mention that.

While Eliza's face remained resolutely forward, he could see the corner of her mouth twitch. He stopped himself just in time from teasing it with his tongue. *God*, what was he thinking? This was Eliza, and he was her honorary big brother, a role, as part of the Sinclairs' extended family, he'd accepted without complaint. But lately, Eliza had invaded the periphery of his awareness ... ever since she'd bobbed her hair. He could still see the blissful expression on her face this afternoon, her tongue chasing the butter running between her fingers ... God, even his cock had been captivated. He took another lingering look at her smart mouth, before sitting up straight and concentrating on the remaining minutes of the film.

When the credits rolled, he stretched and looked around. It was a full house. Not bad for a Tuesday. They waited, chatting and arguing about the merits of the story until the balcony seats were almost empty, before making a move towards the exit.

Alex, descending the staircase behind Eliza, found his gaze captured. The back of her hair had been cut shorter than her hairline, showing off the elegant curve of her nape. He was instantly taunted by the image of nibbling and kissing every inch of it – from right above where it met her shoulder to just below her earlobe.

The noise from the patrons that had exited the theatre and spilled out onto the pavement, disguised by the floor-to-ceiling glass windows, brought him out of his fantasy.

Pausing in the lobby, Alex made a show of glancing at his

watch. He was keen to remove himself from the object of his increasingly racy thoughts. He hastily made his apologies, using the excuse of avoiding a long walk by ensuring he caught the last train to the city. Daniel assured him, with a sly wink, that he could handle the ladies, offering each an arm as they walked in the opposite direction.

Turning up the collar of his coat, Alex strode towards the North Williamstown station, hoping the cold air would quieten his thoughts. Although, that wasn't the part of his anatomy that needed calming. He couldn't say when he'd started noticing Eliza. Her recent hair style had helped. Short hair suited her. But he'd sensed a more fundamental change in her. As if, after all these years, she'd decided to stand up, having been previously content to sit down.

He'd felt a stirring dissatisfaction in the direction of his own affairs since his parents had sailed. Living away from home had freed him, but also taught him that he was fully responsible for everything in his life. And he'd been toying with the need for some spring cleaning. His relationships had a sameness about them. He'd initially thought Queenie, despite her forwardness, may have been different. She'd made no secret of her desire for him from the first introduction. And he'd been flattered – she could have passed for a movie star. But outside the parties and petting, they had little in common. She never showed an interest in his work or pursuits unless they interrupted his availability to play escort.

Eliza, on the other hand, had spent a full hour a couple of weeks ago drilling him on his latest project – the electrification of the city's trams. She wanted him to lobby his boss to donate one of the old cable fleet to the YWCA as part of their annual fundraising efforts. She had thoughts that they could sell it. Funny girl. That was the problem, he realised. Eliza was no longer a girl. And it seemed he was just catching up on that news.

CHAPTER 6

Wednesday 15 July 1925

'Upton, good to see you. Eliza, good evening.' Alex smiled at the couple leaving the dance floor. 'No need to trouble yourself further, Eliza is promised to me for the next bracket.'

To Alex's annoyance, the man did not relinquish her arm. Instead, he glanced enquiringly at Eliza, as if doubting Alex's word. *Good instinct*, Alex thought grudgingly.

Colin Upton was one of Eliza's set and a regular partner. *Too regular*, if you asked Alex. And his dress sense, for God's sake! The man was a slave to fashion – where did one start? His hair perhaps, heavily slicked – those shares in Brilliantine must come in handy – and combed to within an inch of its life towards the top of his head. And was that a faint red stripe in his white shirt peeking from under his dark-blue worsted suit? The man was audacious, both in manner and dress.

Eliza patted his arm. Colin casually kissed the back of her fingers and murmured his thanks, before he shot Alex an assessing look and strolled in the direction of the lounge.

'I don't remember promising you a dance,' Eliza said.

'Must have forgotten. You have been a little absentminded lately.' Alex sent her his most practised charming look: a small tilt of the head, a slight lift of the left brow, eyes gently but intently focused on her. It was something he'd perfected over the years. He had a version for social situations such as tonight, and a version for ... more intimate situations. The one he'd directed at Eliza was somewhere in between. It was disheartening to discover that other than a slight poppy-coloured hue to her cheeks, she seemed unaffected.

'Alex? You want something.' Eliza's eyes had narrowed to shards of jade green, and her eyebrows had settled into a pronounced frown.

Alex's mouth curled upwards. Delaying his reply, he pulled her into his arms and effortlessly picked up the waltz rhythm. 'As a matter of fact, I did want to ask you for a favour. I've received an invitation to the Lord Mayor's Ball to welcome the officers of the fleet, and I wondered if you'd come as my partner?'

'Really? Me? Why?'

'Why not?'

'Well ... I mean, it isn't as if you're short of options. Queenie, for starters. And then there's Beth, and ...'

'Yes, well ... I'm asking you.'

Alex glanced down to find Eliza drilling visual holes in his waistcoat, her frown still in evidence. Was he such a poor prospect that she had to debate the pros and cons? Most women of his acquaintance would have been pleased to accept his invitation. He'd be lying if he admitted to not feeling bothered by her hesitation.

'Why not.'

'Is that a yes?'

'Uh-uh.'

As acceptances went, it wasn't the most enthusiastic he'd received, but it was a yes. Alex couldn't confess that his boss had been quite specific on who wouldn't be received favourably to the Mayoral Ball. That accounted for Queenie and Beth. And for some reason, it felt right to ask Eliza. If only he didn't feel so off balance in his dealings with her lately. Like a tightrope walker on training wheels.

'Do you think Eliza's changed?' Alex asked Daniel a short time later. They were standing, observing proceedings from one of the balconies that overlooked the Palais' dance floor.

'You mean apart from her hair?'

'Yes. I had noticed that. Your mother's face the afternoon she had it bobbed is etched in my memory. Although it suits her.' *Calls attention to her eyes*, he thought inadvertently, before catching himself and adding hastily, 'Has she said anything about the new skirt length?'

'Tonight's outfit, you mean?'

Alex nodded.

Daniel cracked a smile. 'No, she disguised it under her winter coat, arriving in the kitchen tonight dressed as if anticipating a snow storm. I'm waiting to see what her strategy will be for the warmer months.'

Alex laughed. 'See, that's an example. The old Eliza wouldn't have acted so artfully. She can't even cheat at cards when we play. Something has changed. I just can't put my finger on it,' he said, stabbing his finger in the air for effect.

'Maybe,' said Daniel with a shrug. 'A bit of a dry argument, though, don't you think? Time for a pint. My shout.'

THE BATTLE FOR ELIZA

Eliza was gliding around the floor with Philip Dickson, Dick Birmingham's friend from England. He was a beautiful dancer and amusing to boot, entertaining her with a running commentary on the floor craft being demonstrated, or the lack thereof, and the sophistication of dress. He was a wicked man. Eliza liked him immensely.

'I can only hope that you don't mutilate my fashion sense and dancing abilities while you're circulating with others,' Eliza admonished him.

'*Mon chouchou*, that would never happen. You are very *à la mode*. And I have asked Dick to speak to you about partnering me in a demonstration this Saturday evening. Has he done so?'

Eliza was speechless. Two invitations in the same evening – unexpected but not unwelcome. She wondered if Bec was behind them, but quickly dismissed the thought. Alex was not the type to need dating advice. And Philip didn't even know Bec.

'Ah. I can see from your face, he has not. I will not speak of it again until he has. You may be curious to know it is a little dance called the Baltimore, with some theatrical variations. What you're wearing will be perfect,' he said, glancing down approvingly at yet another Christine design, this one a cyclamen-blue *crêpe joyeux* dress. 'But you probably won't want to wear such a distinctive colour so soon again. No doubt you have other suitable ensembles.'

Eliza grinned. 'Well, I can't talk about it until I've spoken with Mr B, but for the record, I'll be delighted.'

'Very well. I'll take you through your paces tomorrow after lessons,' Philip said, executing a quick turn to avoid a fast-approaching pair – the man apparently oblivious to the swathe of aggrieved dancers in his wake.

'Once I've spoken with Mr B,' Eliza assured him.

'Yes, yes, my dear. We'll make it proper and above board,' said Philip, nodding strenuously, already diverted as he hunted the floor for the socially awkward or flamboyant steppers. It didn't take long.

'My lord! Music obviously means very little to that couple … Look at that *jay walker* – who knows where he'll end up, striding hither and thither …' And on he went until the dance reached its conclusion and Mr Dickson moved off to find Mr B with strict instructions for Eliza to stay put.

Smiling to herself, she dodged behind an enormous potted fern, felt the stirrings of a breeze through the doors that led to the gardens, and drifted out and down the steps. It wasn't as cold as one would expect for a July evening. One of those atypical days in every season that caught everyone unawares.

'Eliza, wait up.'

Turning, she watched Bec skip down the steps towards her. 'Where are you going? I'm not interrupting an assignation, am I?'

'And if you were?' asked Eliza, hands on hips.

'I'd make you promise to tell me all later and guard the door to make sure you weren't disturbed.'

'What would I do without you?'

'Descend into spinsterhood, married to your job, badly groomed and still never having been kissed.'

Eliza laughed. 'Well, as it turns out, my fairy godmother has been active this evening.' She went on to relay the news of the unexpected invitation from Alex and the request from Philip Dickson.

'I wonder why Alex didn't invite Queenie. Not that you're not an excellent choice,' Bec added, giving Eliza's arm a reassuring squeeze.

'I asked the same thing, but he ducked my question.'

'Interesting. A date with Alex. Christine will be pleased with the opportunity to show off more of her gowns, because, as it happens, I too have an invitation.' Bec squealed in excitement.

'Really?'

'Yes. Dad is entrusting his daughter to one of the officers from the USS *Oklahoma* to partner. One of his customers – the local mayor – mentioned they were short of females, but assured him it would be well chaperoned.'

This time, it was Eliza's turn to squeal as she danced Bec in a tight circle before collapsing on a nearby bench. They sat in comfortable silence, until they became aware of the sound of raised voices.

An aggrieved female tone cut through the night air. 'What I understand is that you're punishing me.'

Eliza looked at Bec and mouthed, 'Queenie.'

'Don't be ridiculous, darling. Why would I be punishing you?'

'Alex,' reciprocated Bec.

'I don't know. You're not jealous, are you?'

'Of?'

'Derek, of course. It's not serious, you know.'

'If Derek amuses you, then it's of no consequence to me. He is tolerated only because he happens to be the sole scion of old money. But even money can't buy charm and a modicum of common sense. The man's a pill.'

Eliza and Bec's eyes widened at the tone of Alex's dismissal.

41

'Then why?' This was said in a wistful voice.

Eliza could imagine Queenie gazing up at Alex, a slight tremble on her lips, her eyes shimmering from an unshed crocodile tear or two. Men were so gullible.

'Because I've asked Eliza. And that's the end of the matter.'

'Humph. I wouldn't have thought she was your type.'

'Finally, the conversation turns interesting. I am rather partial to golden-blonde ...'

'Mmm. Distract me all you like, Alex, but we will continue this conversation ... maybe not just now ... do that again ...'

'You mean this ...?'

Eliza felt heat storm into her cheeks. It was one thing to have heard of Alex's reputation, but quite another to picture it in action. Eliza motioned to Bec to move. She'd been caught eavesdropping on Queenie once before, and she didn't want to be caught again.

'It appears all is not well in Camelot,' joked Bec as they moved out of earshot.

'Bec, please. I'm not keen on ending up in Queenie's bad books.'

'It was Alex's choice. You didn't proposition him. Queenie's beef is with Alex, not you.'

'And with me by implication,' sighed Eliza.

'I've told you before, you worry too much. It's Alex's problem,' said Bec as they re-entered the ballroom. 'Unless you don't want to go on a date with Alex?'

'It's not that sort of date! I'm his best friend's sister, remember?'

'For now,' said Bec with a sly wink, before accepting an offer to foxtrot.

Eliza dismissed Bec's statement with a shake of her head.

Alex's invitation was puzzling, since he was clearly still dating Queenie. *Am I being used to punish her? Does he think his invitation to me will serve as a lesson to her?* Queenie would never believe it. Although, one could daydream. Imagine Queenie, the woman who only had to sashay into a room to have men jostling for her attention, jealous of her. It was laughable.

Eliza fingered the leaves of a potted Japanese bamboo. She'd never questioned Alex's intentions before. He'd appeared at their kitchen table one Sunday during Daniel's first year at Melbourne University and been a regular ever since. Unlike many of the men returning from war, Alex wasn't bewildered, bruised or bandaged. He'd been too young to enlist and his engineering studies had guaranteed him a part in the state's investment in its future. His deep brown eyes, the colour of sinful dark chocolate, held a hint of mischief – Eliza had labelled him a player from that first introduction – but they were usually full of mild provocation in her case. She'd trust Alex with her life ... Just not her heart.

CHAPTER 7

Thursday 16 July 1925

'Eliza, before you go.'

Eliza glanced up from unbuckling her dance shoes. 'Yes, Mrs B?'

'About the competition.'

Eliza held her breath.

'Your nomination has been accepted.'

The breath rushed back into her lungs. 'Oh, thank you, thank you, thank you.' And then she hiccupped. 'Sorry.'

'Do you have a gown?' asked Mrs B, repositioning tortoise-shell horn-rimmed glasses and giving Eliza's attire an assessing look. Ignoring Eliza's affirmative nod, she continued her inspection, tilting her head to consider Eliza as one might a particularly difficult puzzle.

Eliza waited, but the moment passed, and Mrs B continued as if satisfied with her musings. 'The fleet will radio the particulars of the young men ahead so that we can make the appropriate pairings ...'

Eliza's stomach did a somersault. *I'm really going to do this!*

'... And we're planning a meet and greet on the Saturday

44

following their arrival. That'll give the men a chance to get back their land legs ...'

Eliza's stomach followed with a double twist.

'... And we'll publish the rules and contestant pairings in our next fortnightly newsletter.'

Eliza's stomach dropped and landed with a thud. She and Bec had agreed to keep Eliza's participation in the competition quiet.

It's only a dance. One American sailor. It's not as if I'm consorting with the whole fleet, she reasoned silently. *Who reads the newsletter outside of the dance studio, anyway?*

'And of course, *Table Talk* is keen for a 250-word article ...'

'Really? *Table Talk*, you say. That's fantastic, of course. Well, thanks, Mrs B, I really must run. See you Friday.'

Escaping out the door, she made a mental note to ensure Bec's plan to keep this from her parents and Daniel included managing Melbourne's social pages.

As Nola watched Eliza's distracted flight, she became aware of the distinctive aroma of leather, tobacco and vanilla. She took a breath, schooled her features into her social mask and turned to greet Queenie, who appeared chic in a pencil-thin navy-blue skirt teamed with a silk blouse splashed with orange. The jaunty sailor collar added a nautical flavour. Where was her husband when she needed him to manage young women obstinate in their vanity, she wondered.

'You wanted to see me, Mrs B?'

'Yes, my dear. It's about your competition nomination.'

Queenie smiled serenely. Nola had to admire the young woman's calm poise. It had taken her years to perfect her own composure and this one, at twenty-two, had it in spades. Ah, to be young again. 'We haven't been able to accommodate you, I'm afraid.'

Queenie's eyebrows snapped together, and she levelled Nola a look of disbelief. 'I beg your pardon. Did you just tell me that I won't be dancing in the competition? There must be some mistake,' she finished with a smile that reached no further than the corners of her Cupid's bow lips.

Nola sighed. The girl did not lack confidence, humility maybe. 'No mistake, my dear. We could have run three contests with the number of nominations we received. It hasn't been an easy choice. But I know you'll accept the decision graciously.'

'I see ... well, I think you've made a mistake, but as you say, it is *your* decision.'

'Thank you, Queenie. I appreciate your understanding. We hope to see you as usual tomorrow night.'

Smiling dismissively, Queenie turned on her heel and sauntered out the door of the ballroom.

'Still in one piece, dear heart?' a familiar voice spoke into Nola's ear.

'Yes, you old coward,' replied Nola.

'I never like to disappoint a pretty lady, present company included,' said Dick, dropping a kiss on her nape. 'You're much better equipped to handle these matters than I.'

'Mmm. We'll need to keep an eye on our Queenie. Hell hath no fury like a woman scorned, and all that.'

CHAPTER 8

Friday 17 July 1925

Queenie was holding court, the centre of a small group that consisted of Alex, Daniel, Evelyn and a couple of others Eliza didn't recognise. Eliza did not want to enter the lioness's den, but since last Sunday, when her mum had appointed him her designated chaperone, Daniel was insisting that he be kept abreast of her movements. She knew she was being unkind, but she was twenty-five, not fifteen. And she didn't see why she needed to report that she was headed off for a quiet drink and then home. They needed to come to some sort of understanding before the next couple of weeks' entertainments began, but until then ...

As she reached the door to the balcony, she heard Queenie disclose, '... and so I said ... "I think you've made a mistake, but as you say, it is *your* decision" and then I left ...' Eliza was intrigued and stepped closer.

'Really, honey, it's their loss,' this from Evelyn, who laid a comforting hand on Queenie's arm. As Eliza noted, however, she quickly returned it to her brother's sleeve and gave him a syrupy smile. Eliza hoped Evelyn never

47

achieved sister-in-law status.

'Oh, I'm not upset. It would have been tiresome to interrupt the next fortnight with such a bucolic event. But I was prepared to make the sacrifice to liven things up,' said Queenie, wrapping her arm tighter around Alex's bicep and giving him a secret smile.

Eliza wondered what had happened to Derek. Was Queenie tired of him already? Although, why Queenie would want any other man when she had Alex's attention, Eliza could only guess. Confidence and wit, the allure of moral and physical strength, yet enough of an enigma to bewitch even the most seasoned gal. *If she were Alex's girlfriend ... What?! Where had that thought come from?* Eliza watched as he stroked his finger down Queenie's cheek, trailing it along her swan-like neck to where it met her shoulder. He bent his head purposefully, replacing his finger with his lips.

She felt Queenie shiver ... or was that her? She must have made a small sound, because Queenie glanced up and fixed her with a self-satisfied look.

Eliza's cheeks burned crimson. Queenie whispered something, and Alex raised his head sharply, his gaze spearing her where she stood. Eliza could feel tendrils of awareness ... everywhere, but centred mostly in her stomach. She couldn't seem to look away. Her palms felt moist, and she appeared to have lost her voice. *What a strange affliction,* she thought. After what seemed like minutes but was only seconds, Alex released her from the searing heat of his gaze. In an instant, his bored social expression was in place and she was left to wonder if she'd imagined his interest.

Eliza realised Queenie had been watching the encounter and was now subjecting her to an inspection.

'Eliza. How ... refreshed you look this evening. Is that a new style?'

If Eliza had hoped for her blush to abate, Queenie's tone managed to recharge it. This time, she felt real heat and resisted the urge to use her palms to cool her cheeks. With her luck, they'd sizzle.

She knew she looked good. The slim lines anchored by a heavily embroidered handkerchief-point skirt showed off her figure to advantage. Christine had clapped when Eliza had tried on the dress after the final alterations, and Bec had danced her around and around the fitting room until she'd been dizzy.

Squaring her shoulders, she smiled and said, 'It's a Christine Tailleuse design.'

Alex was finding it difficult to maintain his nonchalant expression. Eliza looked delectable. The dress's asymmetric neckline drew his eye to the slight pulse above her collarbone. It looked like she had a tiny butterfly trapped beneath her skin. The skirt landed just above her knees, making her legs, sheathed in nylon, appear endless. But it was the colour that was the standout. Aqua blue. From memory, Eliza had never worn any colour other than brown or black or a combination of the two.

Feeling Queenie's eyes on him, he smiled in what he hoped would be interpreted as an approving brotherly way and said teasingly, 'The colour suits you. Your chaperone here will have his work cut out for him.' Queenie gave him a calculating look, which he opted to ignore.

'Are you ready?' A voice behind Eliza interrupted. Bec, looking glamorous in black velvet with a crystal-bead fringe and a sequined bandeau, stepped onto the balcony and put an arm through Eliza's.

'Ready for what?' enquired Daniel.

'A group of us are off for a drink. We'll make our way home from there,' said Eliza.

'Colin has offered to drive us back to Williamstown in his new car, so don't give us another thought,' volunteered Bec.

'See you tomorrow, brother dear,' said Eliza, seemingly taking her lead from Bec and affecting a casual smile. She cheekily kissed Daniel's cheek.

'Goodnight, all.' And with a wave she and Bec squeezed side by side back through the door into the ballroom and disappeared.

'So, ladies, we're now off duty and officially at your disposal,' said Daniel with a wink at Alex. 'I think we've accorded the YMCA fundraiser enough of our time and money, so let's get out of here.'

'What do you have in mind, darling?' purred Queenie in Alex's ear, her tone telling him that she hadn't forgotten the show of awareness towards Eliza, but she was willing to forgive him.

'Daniel and I have secured invitations to a private party in St Kilda for the six of us —'

'There will be dancing, a supper to die for and endless champagne. And,' Daniel directed a searing look at Evelyn, 'a discreet corner or two to re-energise.'

Evelyn giggled.

'Lead the way,' said Queenie in a sultry voice.

Alex shepherded Queenie through the doorway that led back into the ballroom, followed by Daniel and Evelyn and the other couple. Despite his apparent enthusiasm, he didn't feel as eager as he'd expected by the thought of the evening's entertainments. His awareness of Eliza had jolted him. Deeply. And he needed time to examine what had occurred. But it would have to wait. Queenie was too astute to be satisfied by anything other than his one-hundred-percent attention.

He hadn't forgotten her short-lived dalliance with that fool Derek. But he'd forgiven her. It hadn't been that hard. Another surprise. He'd shrugged and reminded himself that they weren't exclusive. He'd forfeited the make-up sex, however, despite Queenie's intimation of some new, inventive positions. He didn't consider himself inexperienced in the carnal act, but he would have learned a thing or two that night had he accepted her offer – the liberated female had become quite instructive. But, as he'd fended off her hands, Eliza's face had barricaded itself in his thoughts – her green eyes enigmatic.

Daniel hailed a taxi and they piled in. He caught sight of a flash of green. Eliza, stepping into Colin Upton's new Standard Six Studebaker, the balloon tyres gleaming in the gaslight. No doubt heading off for that drink. He wished he was joining her. Instead, he gave his attention to Queenie, who had started to entertain them with musings from the evening.

CHAPTER 9

Tuesday 21 July 1925

Eliza paused before a brown leatherette case. It contained one of the YWCA's most treasured chattels, a Decca portable gramophone. It had seen combat in France, but like many of the returned would not talk of its experiences. It had been luckier in that it only bore physical injury – a gash here, a gouge there – not the trauma from memories.

Behind Eliza waited five excitable female offspring of Melbourne's working class – Mavis, Beryl, Betty, Norma and Vera – three reluctant members of the city's finest male specimens in Alex, Daniel and Colin Upton, and Bec and Jenny.

They were assembled in the YWCA's Russell Street headquarters, in what was known as the Connibere room, named after one of the organisation's wealthy patrons. It was beautiful, its walls anointed with a soft lemon that glowed in the mornings and softened as the sun arced westward – as it did now. Eliza placed the record on the turntable and lifted the needle into place. Almost immediately, the sounds of Joe Raymond's Orchestra bounced off the instrument's copper reflector bowl.

'Now remember, girls, concentrate on refining a smooth, graceful walk,' said Eliza as she turned back towards her audience. 'Ready? One, two, three, four.'

Eliza had enlisted the help of the men, Bec and Jenny to partner the girls in a practice session in preparation for the Lord Mayor's Ball. They were being sponsored by the lady mayoress as part of her benevolence work. Eliza had one week to perfect the girls' style. Her assessment based on this evening's efforts suggested a month wouldn't scratch the surface.

'Vera, relax. Trust Daniel to lead. No man wants to wrestle his partner around the floor.' Eliza smothered a smile as Daniel danced past looking like he was manoeuvring a warship.

'Head up, Mavis. The floor will not disappear, I promise you. One, two, three, four.' Bec made a face at Eliza as she did her best to keep Mavis from hunching forward.

Beryl and Norma were trying hard, and Colin and Jenny while not exactly enjoying themselves were having an easier time.

Betty was probably the best of the lot. Petite and light on her feet, she had taken a

shine to Alex. Eliza debated with herself whether to chide her for her limpet-like hold, but decided it was too amusing to watch him try to extricate himself while still maintaining a fluid gait. Another admirer. She didn't know how he managed it. Well, that wasn't strictly true. He was undeniably easy on the eye ... Feeling her cheeks grow warm, she pushed that thought away and concentrated on the task at hand.

The music ended and the pairings dissolved to

stand awkwardly, as if awaiting judgement and possible deportation.

'Mmm, not as smooth as I'd like,' said Eliza. 'Maybe a demonstration would help. Daniel and Bec, would you mind?'

Eliza watched as they claimed each other readily and settled into an easy rhythm.

'Girls, notice how relaxed Bec is. Foxtrot is like walking backwards. Now, you'll see that Daniel has added a couple of side steps, but then it's back to walking. And you can all walk, I assume? Thanks, Bec. Thanks, Daniel.'

As Eliza continued to reassure her audience of the simplicity, she noticed a whispered exchange had erupted between Bec and Daniel. Sometimes they were like oil on water.

'Let's take a five-minute break, shall we?'

Walking over to her best friend, she heard, 'I was not leading. And if I was, it was because you were dancing like a pansy.'

Eliza could see Daniel's nostrils flare and his right eye start to blink, a tic from childhood. She thought he'd outgrown it, but Bec seemed to possess a panache for provocation.

'Everything all right?' Eliza asked.

'Yes,' said Bec.

'No,' replied Daniel at the same time.

Eliza blinked. 'Well, what is it? Yes or no?'

Daniel took a deep breath and glowered at Bec. 'Yes. How much longer will this take?'

'About twenty minutes. I'm going to have you practise some more walking and then add in a couple of side steps and turns.'

'That should be entertaining for you!' he said, before joining Alex and Colin, who stood leaning against one of the casements, talking.

Eliza raised her brows and Bec chuckled. 'Sometimes we're like a match to tinder. Pay us no mind. By the look of it, you've got bigger problems getting this lot into shape.'

Eliza sighed. 'I thought that having actual partners would help. Instead, it's just highlighted their inadequacies.' Then feeling uncharitable, she added, 'Does that sound unchristian of me?'

'No, just honest,' said Jenny, who, having finished guiding Norma once more around the floor, had joined them. 'The battle may be lost, but we won't lose the war. Lead on.'

'Girls,' Eliza called in a voice reserved for high-strung, skittish adolescents and young adults. 'Remember the drill we did with the wooden hoops? I want you to think of your partner as a hoop.' This was greeted with giggles.

Betty gave Alex an assessing look. 'I can think of better things to do with my hoop than dance.' More giggles and gasps sounded at Betty's daring. Alex levelled a bland smile and neutral expression in her direction.

'That's enough. Pair up and show me your dance frame.'

They complied quickly, having correctly interpreted Eliza's tone as not tolerating further impertinence. She walked around and between the couples, adjusting an arm here, a hip there.

'We'll try it without the music. Now, walk. Pretend you're gliding backwards down Collins Street. You don't need to look at the pavement, Mavis, no death grips, Vera or limpet holds, Betty. Norma, that is looking much better, relax your knees. You too, Beryl, you don't walk with stiff legs now, do you? Much better. A couple more turns of the floor.'

After a few more minutes, Eliza was satisfied that the girls were displaying a more natural style. 'That was much better focus, girls. Have a rest. We're going to try a couple of side steps and a turn. Don't look so worried, it is quite straightforward. I'll demonstrate.'

Before she could enlist a volunteer, Alex was standing in front of her.

'Allow me,' he murmured as he slid his hand around her back and secured her right hand.

Eliza checked herself, taking a moment to run her tongue over her lower lip. She felt warm and her pulse was racing. Glancing up, she found Alex poised, awaiting her instruction, his eyes attentive to her discomfort.

'Lead me into a walk, a side step, a turn and then back into a walk,' she directed, channelling her best teacher voice. They moved off, Alex flawless in his execution.

'Once more please, Eliza. A little slower. I'll talk the girls through the steps,' Bec said.

Eliza was relieved Bec had taken control. Her brain and tongue were refusing to communicate for some reason. Thankfully, her legs were on autopilot.

'Breathe,' whispered Alex.

She did as he asked and felt her heart rate return to a regular cadence. *How silly of me, everyone knows you can't dance if you don't breathe.*

Alex danced forward, slower this time. Three walks, two steps to the left, three more walks, a turn and an unsolicited dip, with Bec calling each of the steps, even the dip. The last was performed with a flourish. Eliza had slid one arm around Alex's neck as she'd felt him reposition his hand to the middle of her back and tilt her towards the floor. Transfixed, she watched his gaze drift across her face before focusing it on her lips, as if he were about to kiss her. Eliza's eyes widened. *He wouldn't! Would he?*

'Thank you, Alex. I think the girls have the idea of it.' Eliza registered Bec's voice and started to struggle upright, relieved when Alex smoothly returned her to her feet and spun her out to loud applause.

Eliza took back control. 'Let's try that. Without the dip for now, I think,' she said, sending Alex a censorious look. 'If the men, Bec and Jenny can lead three walks, two steps to the left, three more walks and a turn, please. Ready? One, two, three, four.'

By the sixth repetition, the girls had managed a passable attempt and Eliza suggested they leave it there.

'That's an hour of my life I'll never get back,' grumbled Daniel, as the girls filed out of the room.

'I thought girls were born to dance, but obviously not,' said Colin with a grin.

'Not those girls, anyway. I pity their poor partners,' added Alex.

'Don't be so uncharitable,' chimed in Jenny with a laugh. 'They were really trying.'

'They were certainly trying,' agreed Daniel. 'Although, sis, I was impressed with your patience.'

'And control. But that Betty kept trying to plaster herself against me. During all your instructions, I noticed you didn't suggest she step back a fraction,' Alex complained.

Eliza turned from packing up the gramophone. 'You looked like you had things under control. A case of teenage infatuation.'

'As long as she's not hoping for a dance at the Lord Mayor's Ball,' said Alex as he shrugged into his overcoat. 'I'm not relinquishing you to satisfy a besotted adolescent.'

His words hit Eliza like a sledge hammer. *Breathe*, Eliza reminded herself. *It doesn't mean anything. He's dating another woman, probably two at the same time!* Aloud she said, 'I genuinely appreciate the hand this evening. Your performances were far beyond any hoop.' She raised her hands defensively against the good-natured noise and howls of disbelief.

CHAPTER 10

Wednesday 22 July 1925

Alex was riveted as he watched Eliza's lithesome body. It was in constant motion, coiling in one direction before uncurling and seeming to corkscrew into another. He couldn't deny an intense longing. Desire. He'd dreamed of her, and not just once. At first, she'd appeared with a flirtatious smile ... but things had swiftly escalated.

His eyes flicked to Daniel, whose attention he was relieved to see was also fixed on the couple gliding across the floor, despite the bored expression he took pains to cultivate on his face. Alex breathed a sigh of relief, schooled his features into an appearance of nonchalance and felt his heart rate return to a steady, unobtrusive cadence. Best friend he may be, but as her elder brother, Alex wasn't certain Daniel would be pleased by his latest revelation.

Why now? Why here? He groaned inwardly. He'd almost kissed her last night before remembering where he was. It was safe to say that Eliza was unaware of his feelings. And Alex would ensure that she remained unaware until he'd had an opportunity to process them, or alternatively, knock some sense into himself. Maybe he just needed a strong drink.

At this moment, Eliza and her partner, visiting professional Philip Dickson, were the centre of twelve hundred pairs of eyes; it was a busy night at Birmingham's. They were negotiating their way through an intricate step pattern of walks, spins and turns in the middle of the floor. Alex doubted Eliza was aware of the spectators, of the lights illuminating the pearls gracing the ladies' décolletages, or the crystals and spangles decorating their dresses. Or the keen interest from the men.

'Close your eyes,' he wanted to yell at them. Eliza wasn't beautiful by society's standards. And while he knew she thought herself plain, having overheard a conversation with Bec one evening, Alex couldn't agree. Well, not now. Maybe he once had, but it was difficult to remember back to before. Her bobbed, treacle-brown hair hung in a sleek ear-length cut, when it was behaving itself, but more likely curled in every other possible direction, as if free-styled by one of Melbourne's blustery south-westerlies. Her eyes could be as calm and quiet as the centre of a deep forest, or flashing fire like finely cut emeralds. A straight nose, graced with a few freckles, not too long or short. What was there to say about a nose? It fitted perfectly above a set of lips that he wanted to kiss until they were plump and swollen.

These are not the standard steps of the Baltimore, Alex realised, as Eliza's sea-green skirts wrapped snuggly around her long legs as she negotiated a quick change of direction, then rippled outwards to give those watching a glimpse of taut calves and slim ankles, before seeming to float and settle around her hips. Alex imagined Eliza twined around him in the same way as her skirts.

He mentally shook himself. Where had that thought come from? He was in trouble. Unexpectedly, images of Eliza ran like a movie reel – at the breakfast table where he'd idly watched her spar with her brother while he devoured a plate of toast and mounds of scrambled eggs; across the *Pegity* board as she manoeuvred her, usually blue, pegs to form a row of colour; debating the role of modern women and baiting her with the importance of their role in the kitchen. He sometimes thought he'd spent more time at the Sinclairs' house over the years than he had his own. Often arriving unannounced for a meal or just to hang out. And now this! His awareness of her had become tangible – at least to him.

Alex shook himself again, this time physically. Was he *smitten*? His feelings were certainly accelerating in that direction, but he wasn't ready to admit to being more than *affected* – although the word, once conjured, refused to leave him.

Alex managed to regain his composure as the music ended and loud applause drowned out any other thought or sound. He joined in automatically.

Philip Dickson was lapping up the attention, cheekily saluting the crowd. Capturing Eliza's hand, he pulled her into a hug and whispered something into her ear that caused colour to race up her cheekbones. She dipped her head and shared a shy smile with her flamboyant partner, before spinning out to accept the applause with a graceful curtsy.

Alex felt himself take a step forward, his intention to interrupt the intimacy emanating from the couple, before being stopped by a hand on his shoulder.

'What about that drink?' Alex turned to find Daniel studying him inquiringly. 'Little sisters can only demand

and sustain attention for so long. I think it's your shout.'

Alex grasped Daniel's invitation gratefully. He was starting to think Eliza could sustain his attention for considerable periods of time – he felt like a moth battling to resist the attraction of a flame. A drink, yes, and some winter air to clear his head. He knew how to navigate a bar. He was less confident about Eliza at this moment. He gestured for his friend to lead the way.

Zigzagging their way towards the entrance, reminders of dance commitments and a few subtle smiles with invitations for other entertainments settled his equilibrium further – although they failed to spark his interest as before. This was the world he'd become most familiar with. Both he and Daniel were popular with the ladies, and Alex would be lying if he denied that he enjoyed the attention. *Had* enjoyed the attention, he realised.

He left the ballroom, his thoughts and emotions in disarray.

CHAPTER 11

Later

Boughs of bush wattle entwined with the Roman-style pillars provided the perfect vantage point for observation and a respite for Eliza's poor feet. Not the smartest decision to break in new shoes tonight. *Frailty my name is woman.*

'Hiding?' murmured Alex's voice close to her ear, tickling the tiny hairs on her nape – she hoped they weren't visibly standing to attention.

'Truth be known, I was watching Philip cut a swathe,' Eliza returned and inclined her head in the direction of the floor where Philip was leading his partner into a dip, one hand wrapped around the lady's waist, the other cradling her neck. The lady in question recovered and pirouetted down the line of dance.

'I don't know who is enjoying the attention more, Philip or Queenie,' continued Eliza archly.

But Alex refused to entertain any conversation about his current girlfriend, merely raising an eyebrow. His discretion was well known – even in her circles. While whispers circulated about his prowess in keeping a woman satisfied, no detail had ever emerged in the years she'd known him. And until recently, she'd never been curious. To her, he was Daniel's annoying friend who tried to steal her toast – instead of making his own.

'Ah yes, Philip. A flawless demonstration. Quite the showman. Of course, you made it easy for him to look good,' he drawled.

'Why, Alex, was that a compliment?' Eliza teased, noting the slight flush that had risen to his cheeks with amusement. But any delight she may have felt was quashed with his next comment.

'A statement of fact. Our waltz, I believe.'

Eliza arched her brow at his aloof tone but allowed Alex to turn her into his arms and sweep her onto the floor, expertly joining the circulating anticlockwise throng of dresses in every conceivable colour and texture.

As partners went, Alex was her favourite. Not that she'd ever tell *him*. His ego did not need further nurturing. True, he sometimes held her a little close, and his hand did seem to slide a little further down her spine than convention dictated – *like now* – but he was a superb dancer. And one look at his face showed that he was unaware of breaching any etiquette, especially with her. After all, Alex probably considered himself like a brother to her. He was often found at family lunches, dinners and breakfasts – although never on the same day – or lying on the couch in front of the fire or on the grass in their backyard in the warmer months. No doubt he'd be appalled at the direction her thoughts were leading her.

Eliza forced herself to relax and enjoy the feeling of ease of movement with a partner who showed no sign of exaggeration or stiffness. Alex was a smidgen over six feet, the perfect height for her in her dancing heels. Nor did she need to worry about navigating a spherical belly sported by a few of the older set; Alex's was flat. And while she hadn't eyeballed it personally, she pictured it as toned as his muscular legs – which she did sight every summer. But his best feature? A *tight arse*. Eliza smirked. Well, he wasn't her brother, and if God had blessed him with an impressive behind, then who was she not to notice.

Whenever they danced, she was aware of approving and speculative glances from other females. He rarely lacked female attention, and genuinely seemed to enjoy their company, which he demonstrated with an ease often lacked by his contemporaries. Embarrassingly, even her *own mother* blushed when he greeted her with a peck on the cheek.

'Earth to Eliza.'

Snatched from her reverie, she looked up to find smile lines radiating from the corners of his eyes and mouth.

'You didn't hear a word I said, did you?'

Was that a rhetorical question? she wondered. Her brother rarely waited for her answer to such questions.

'A penny for them.'

But Alex was not Daniel. Quickly, her mind searched around for a topic – any topic other than the one she'd been occupied with. It was then that she realised she detected a hint of alcohol on his breath. 'You've been drinking,' she blurted out.

'Nothing serious, I can assure you. A celebration of your performance.' He negotiated a smooth change of direction and gave her a self-satisfied smile. 'No ill effects, as you can see.'

Her attempt at deflection had missed its mark – that always worked on Daniel, too. Alex lifted an eyebrow, awaiting her response.

'I was thinking about Bec's and my plans over the next fortnight,' she improvised. It couldn't be flattering to suggest she'd been distracted with the arrival of thousands of American naval men while dancing with Alex, but in for a penny, in for a pound.

Alex's hold tightened. Attributing it to the need for a quick manoeuvre to avoid two conversing couples in the middle of the floor – awfully bad ton – Eliza found herself tucked against his chest, breathing in the spicy notes of bergamot, lemon, nutmeg and something else she couldn't put her finger on. Whatever it was, it was distinctly Alex.

'In the middle of our dance?' he asked. Eliza thought he sounded hoarse.

'You're right, of course. Where are my manners? But you must admit to a certain energy about the city that is ... diverting.'

Alex executed a series of steps in quick succession that made talking impossible. Eliza glanced up at him and noted that his face had a distracted air. What was wrong now? She'd apologised – sort of.

'Do you have many plans for the fleet fortnight?' he asked finally.

'A few.'

'Mmm. I'll have to review my schedule so I can accompany you.'

'What? No, I don't think that's what Mum intended. I'm sure you have your own affairs to take care of.'

As the music reached its inevitable conclusion, Alex

danced them to a halt, and placed a finger beneath her chin until her eyes met his. 'You are my affair, Eliza. And I take my commitments very seriously.'

Eliza swallowed and managed a smile before she tucked her hand into the crook of his elbow. Consternation surged through her, together with a charge of something else. Awareness? He sounded almost ... possessive. A quick glance at his profile suggested she had to be mistaken. He wasn't even looking at her. *Of course, I don't need to advertise my full itinerary.*

When he next spoke, Alex's tone had returned to the usual teasing one he used with her. 'Thank you for the dance, Eliza. Is there anywhere you'd like me to escort you?'

'Bec is just over there. I'll join her, thank you.'

Standing beside her friend as she chatted to another of their set, Eliza watched Alex's broad shoulders disappear towards the lounge. She wasn't feeling overly 'sisterly' at this moment. She kept recalling the feeling of Alex's fingers trailing patterns at the base of her spine. She didn't think he'd been aware of it himself and she'd pretended not to notice, but she had. It had set off thoughts that she'd never previously considered ... until now. How had admiration for a tight arse turned into an awareness of the whole man? And worse, a desire to sweep her hands over the firm globes. Disastrous! She and Alex were too often in the same company, at home and at various entertainments. She couldn't harbour such a notion. No doubt he'd be embarrassed if she developed 'feelings' for him. He'd either pat her on the head like a favourite puppy or recoil and organise a strategic retreat.

Hormones. That must be it. Not that Eliza knew much about hormones, but she had heard her mother complain –

in confidences with friends over tea – of the effect. Wasn't she a little young for hormones? After all, her mother was fifty. Half a century!

Eliza resolved to put it out of her mind. At least for tonight. And during the next fortnight, she'd ensure she was hard-pressed to find time to give Alex more than a passing consideration.

CHAPTER 12

Thursday 23 July 1925

The Arrival

Amid a break in the misty south-westerly squalls, their party of four squeezed onto a carriage at North Williamstown station despite the occupants insisting there was no room. It seemed Williamstown's shorelines were a popular vantage point from which to witness the arrival of the American armada. Alex charmed his way onto a seat beside a particularly vocal woman and pulled Eliza onto his lap, securing her with a broad forearm. The woman smiled indulgently. *Not every female is immune to me*, he thought. *Only one*.

Eliza appeared to be striving to minimise contact between them. He caught an amused expression on Bec's face as she stood, supported by Daniel against the carriage's rocking motion. *So, I'm not imagining it.*

'Relax. I don't bite ... much,' he murmured.

Eliza pretended she hadn't heard him, a moot point since he leaned forward and pressed his chest against her back, allowing his breath to skim her nape.

As the train pulled into the station at the end of the line, Williamstown Pier, Eliza went to jump to her feet, but Alex stubbornly refused to remove his arm from her waist. 'What's the rush?' he asked.

Eliza ground her bottom into his lap in apparent retribution. He hissed and propelled her quickly to her feet, almost toppling the man in front of her. A hurried and embarrassed apology was made before Eliza turned an exasperated look upon him. Alex shrugged and tapped the end of her nose.

Stepping down from the carriage, he braced himself in the wind. While the Point Gellibrand headland provided an excellent view of the bay across the shipping channel to Port Melbourne and St Kilda, *jeez* it was cold.

Eliza linked arms with Bec and they pushed their way through the jostling crowd. Alex watched them burrow further into their coats – if that was possible – and arrange their felt cloches snugly over their heads and ears.

Daniel was gazing over the canopy of densely packed umbrellas. 'Some of these people must have been here since first light to snare the best spots,' he grumbled. 'Look, some have even brought picnic baskets.'

Alex pointed to a spot further along the foreshore, where wartime wheat stacks had once stood. They picked their way across mud and embedded rock – the surrounds resembling the consistency of pea soup.

Shouts of 'There they are!' from those seated on the roofs of the railway sheds signalled the first sightings. News spread through the crowd, and a lively cheer erupted. Alex doubted whether most people could see anything. He wasn't sure if the shadowy-grey line on the horizon was a ship or a rain cloud.

'Here they come!' shouted Bec over the noise.

Eliza was bouncing on her toes. 'Soon it'll be raining men.'

Alex pursed his lips. He for one was not looking forward to the demands of the next fortnight. Demands of *keeping* his temper, *keeping* track of Eliza, and *keeping* those damn Yanks in their place.

His discovery, just over a week ago, that he was harbouring more than 'brotherly' feelings for his best mate's sister, had rocked him. He'd become uncertain as to how to approach her, how to behave around her, which was laughable given his reputation. She affected his equilibrium. Daniel had remarked on his temper earlier this week when Alex had all but snapped his head off when he'd jokingly referred to Queenie's dalliance with Derek, suggesting Alex had lost his touch. He recalled Eliza's reaction – or lack of – the previous evening. She'd appeared oblivious of the tendrils of awareness he'd felt weaving between them as they'd danced. So oblivious that she could daydream about the opportunities to socialise with other men!

Standing this close to her, he felt the bottom of her skirts wrap against his trouser leg, her hip bumping his as the crowd shifted and surged. Who knew that crowds could be used to such advantage? Her gloved hand carelessly bumped a part of his anatomy which was already under siege. Had she noticed? Unlikely. For all Eliza's independent views, she was an innocent ... or maybe not so innocent ... He did his best to ignore the furtive glance in his direction. Inexperienced but not innocent. Noteworthy! The thought made him harder. He shifted his weight from one leg to the other and thought about mathematics. That had always worked in the past.

The sound of engines transported his attention back to

the sight of six jets from the Royal Australian Airforce. They had been charged with escorting the fleet to their moorings. Circling in formation, they showed off, high above the turrets of forty-four vessels, which then manoeuvred in wagon formation, each with identical copies of the Star-Spangled Banner dancing crazily in the wind. The leaden sky fractured, beaten by glorious sunshine which illuminated the spectacle. More cheers. He wondered at the precision of the officers and seamen in charge of orchestrating the placement of so many ships in such a confined area. Some of the larger ships were en route to Port Melbourne, four, maybe five. It was difficult to tell exactly.

The wind was relentless. *Dredged up from the Antarctic*, thought Alex as he stomped first one foot and then the other. He should have worn thicker socks. And ominous clouds suggested the sunshine would be short-lived. Daniel was the only one who looked as if he was enjoying the conditions. He'd always been like that, even at university. Never complaining of cold locker-room showers or site days inspecting the infrastructure projects they'd been assigned.

An explosion of movement to his left revealed a group of exuberant schoolboys testing their skills and everyone else's patience playing a game of tag. A small boy, the designated 'It', was darting through the crowd in pursuit of six or eight others who were either all oblivious to shouts from the men and squeals from the women or encouraged by the noise.

'It' tagged another, turned without looking and barrelled into Eliza, knocking her and in turn Bec to the ground. They landed with a thump, Bec cushioning Eliza from the full force. The boy's eyes turned as big as a threepence, then mumbling, 'I'm sorry,' he tore out of the hold of a man who held him by his collar scruff and bolted.

Alex swore as he knelt to attend Eliza. 'Are you hurt?'

She shook her head, gasping, 'No ... air ...'

Alex swore again. 'Try to relax.'

Eliza shot him a disbelieving look, wheezing.

'Yes, I know it isn't easy, but if you do, your lungs will reflexively drag in oxygen.'

Alex massaged her back and listened as, after some minutes, her breathing returned to normal. He could see Daniel attending to Bec out of the corner of his eye and ordering people to give him room.

Taking one of Eliza's feet in his hands, Alex flexed it gently one way, then the other, finally drawing a circle with it clockwise and then anticlockwise, vigilant to any sign of pain crossing her face. He repeated the action with her other foot. Satisfied there was no break or apparent sprain, he ran an exploratory hand from her ankle to her knee on both legs. Her knee-high socks seemed to be intact.

'What are you doing?' she hissed.

'I'm examining you for injuries. You had quite a knock.'

'Your hand is halfway up my leg!' she fumed.

'No need to thank me. I don't think you'll be walking far, though.'

Clearly vexed, Eliza scrambled to her feet. Her accomplishment was spoiled as she wobbled to the left before leaning against Alex. 'Blast!'

Alex grinned. 'I told you. Your heel has snapped off.'

Eliza looked down. 'Damn. I've had these less than a month.'

'Everything all right?' asked Daniel.

'No obvious breaks or sprains,' he reported, 'apart from a

broken shoe. How's Bec?'

'A gash on the palm of her hand, a little shaken, but she'll be all right.'

Alex watched Eliza hobble over and embrace Bec, nearly sending them both tumbling into the dirt again, before she planted a kiss on her cheek. She proceeded to inspect Bec's coat, giving it a firm couple of brushes to remove road ash and other grime.

'Let's get out of here,' said Daniel. 'You manage Eliza and I'll support Bec. We'll catch the train back.'

Alex nodded. *Best to employ an element of surprise*, he thought, reaching for Eliza.

'Steady,' he murmured, as he scooped her up and held her close to his chest. Anticipating a struggle, he instructed, 'Just until we clear the crowd and reach the station, Eliza. Be a good girl and pretend you're a lady, not a warrior princess. That's right, now loop your arms around my neck and relax.'

Alex wondered if Eliza could hear the drubbing of his heart. Maybe he was winded. Cold beads of sweat painted his brow as he walked on undeterred by the curious glances they attracted, murmuring the odd apology or request to assist by moving out of the way.

Eliza seemed surprised when he returned her to solid ground, as if awakening from a daydream. He hoped it was of him and not those damned Americans. 'We'll rest here and wait for Daniel and Bec; they're a little way behind. How are you feeling?'

'A bit stiff, but I'll be all right. Bec came off worse; she cushioned my fall.'

As the crowd parted, Daniel and Bec appeared, arm in arm, and the ragged rent through which the sun had pervaded closed and the rain returned.

'Not far now,' encouraged Daniel as he opened his umbrella.

Before Alex could object, Eliza declared, 'I'll be fine to walk. I'll try not to be too sluggish.'

He stood and watched her irregular gait for a moment, before he strode forward and offered her his arm and the protection of his umbrella. Under his breath, he caught himself quietly humming, 'What shall we do with a drunken sailor.' What to do indeed? Eliza was an intriguing package. Was he up for the challenge she presented? What would it take to change her view of their relationship? To touch her heart? The only thing he knew for certain was that it was going to be a long fortnight.

CHAPTER 13

Friday 24 July 1925

Buoyed by the behaviour of the women and girls surrounding her, Eliza had grabbed Bec and elbowed her way to the front of the crowd at the corner of Exhibition and Collins Street. Following Bec's lead, she'd taken off her hat and waved it high above her head at the approaching sound of music and marching feet.

Twisting her head left and right, she saw flushed and animated female faces, on verandahs, leaning out of windows and sitting on balconies. Everywhere, people were filled with joie de vivre, undeterred by heights or threatening rain.

Those representing the USS *Oklahoma* approached, heralded by a gold-fringed banner stretched between staffs on which golden eagles were mounted, as if overseeing their charges. As they marched past, two of the sailors made eye contact and gave Eliza and Bec winks and flirty smiles, holding their gazes until they could turn their heads no more. Bec convulsed into laughter. Recovering from her initial disbelief, Eliza joined her.

'We are going to have so much fun,' yelled Bec into Eliza's

ear as she waved brazenly at another sailor, this time from the USS *Nevada*, who mouthed, 'I love you' as he passed. After the sixth such episode, Eliza wondered how many girls had received *the glad eye*. There seemed to be a liberal dose administered to the female population. Perhaps her mother had the right of it. These Americans did seem to have a way about them.

Eliza watched in amazement as a girl, supporting one half of a large canvas sign proclaiming 'WELCOME', dashed into the path of one sailor and pressed a slip of paper into his hand.

'I bet she's giving him her address,' pronounced Bec with a scowl. 'I wish I'd thought of that.'

Eliza gasped at her audacity. Emboldened, she waved her Australian flag and offered the red, blue and white balloons she'd had thrust into her hand to a passing sailor. To her amazement, he tied them to his belt and saluted her, without barely breaking step. Then and there, she fell in love with the sailors' neat-fitting jackets, cute neckerchiefs and pork-pie hats.

As the last sailor turned the corner, Eliza followed Bec as she tunnelled her way out in the direction they'd come. Heading down Collins Street, they turned into Russell Street and up the steps to the YWCA headquarters. After grabbing bags and umbrellas from the staff room, they met Jenny at the door. She'd returned from overseeing the serving of refreshments to some of the men at the Men's Christian Association's cafeteria.

'They were delightful,' Jenny gushed. 'Yes ma'am, no ma'am, thank you ma'am. And so forward. "What's a pretty gal like you doin' here?" one asked. I had no answer. And then he kissed me.' She giggled.

Eliza and Bec shared their experiences from the march. Jenny shook her head in astonishment.

'They seem very forward,' said Eliza.

'And exciting!' said Bec.

'So, where are you off to?' asked Jenny.

'To the American Football Exhibition match at Richmond with Daniel and Alex,' said Eliza with a wave of her hand in goodbye as she pushed Bec ahead of her down the corridor. 'See you tomorrow.'

Eliza's eyes swivelled back and forth. She found the game very confusing. Which perhaps was not surprising as she didn't understand the rules of Victoria's own football league code, either. She and Bec sat between Alex and Daniel, who seemed intent on insulating them from the crowd, at least the American parts of it. Bec was having none of it and was at this moment getting acquainted with a sailor behind her. Eliza giggled when she heard her friend suggest the fitted leather head gear that extended past the player's ears, tied on with a chin strap, made them look extraterrestrial.

Touchdown. The crowd roared. The USS *Pennsylvania* had scored the first points of the game.

'But that was a forward pass,' umpired Daniel.

'Caught on a dead run and thrown, what, fifteen or twenty yards?' Alex shook his head, clearly impressed.

Eliza looked her fill at the physiques hinted at beneath leather jerkins and khaki knee breeches. Those shoulders were clearly padded – but they did look powerful. They reminded her of Alex's – he yielded a cricket bat as if it were a toothpick. She shook her head in surprise — where had that come from? To quell the thought, she turned around to ask Bec's new friend a question and found herself looking into the cheekiest eyes she'd ever seen.

'Howdy, ma'am,' an equally cheeky mouth greeted her. 'Wondered when such a pretty girl would notice little ol' me.'

In that moment, Eliza made a snap decision to enjoy herself and forget Alex and his toned physique. It was time to practise being less reserved. 'Where are you from?' she asked, returning his gaze frankly.

'If you mean directly, then I'm off the USS *Pennsylvania*. Seaman Leroy Bainbridge at your service,' he said, resting his forearms on his thighs and leaning closer.

'Eliza Sinclair. And this is Alex, my best friend, Bec, and Daniel down the end there.'

'Mighty glad to meet y'all,' said Leroy, receiving a brief nod of acknowledgement from both men. 'And this here charmin' your attractive friend, is my bo, Seaman Franklin Cushing off the USS *Trenton*.'

Touchdown. The team from the USS *Trenton* had evened the game.

'What brings you both here?' asked Leroy.

'We had a free afternoon and were curious,' replied Bec. 'It's very physical. Is the sport popular at home?'

'Yes, ma'am. Eighteen teams competed for the championship last year across the country.'

Eliza, Bec, Leroy and Franklin fell into easy conversation. The men explained a little about the game, its origins from soccer and rugby, and the rules. The girls were avid students. Alex and Daniel gave the appearance of being engrossed in the game, but Eliza could tell they were listening from the angle of their heads.

With five minutes of play remaining, the team from the USS *Pennsylvania* were in the lead, but Franklin refused to write off his buddies.

'They've got time. They're comin' back.'

Leroy slapped him on the shoulder and laughed. 'Not a chance.'

When the final siren sounded, *Pennsylvania* had indeed held onto their lead to win by two points. There was a lot of backslapping, elbowing and even a headlock. Eliza watched their antics with amusement. It would seem men were much the same wherever they were from. Although, it had been some time since she'd seen Daniel or Alex wrestling each other in the backyard. Perhaps they were too mature for that now or had replaced it with wrestling of another kind. Her mind flashed to an image of Queenie, her head restrained within the crook of Alex's elbow, and giggled.

'What's so funny?' asked Bec.

Eliza giggled again and waved away the question. 'You had to be there.'

'Any chance you pretty ladies might be thirsty?' asked Leroy.

'Parched,' said Bec before either Daniel or Alex could jump in.

'You gents, too, of course,' amended Franklin politely.

'What's your pleasure? Our ... what do you call it ... buy?' asked Leroy.

The girls giggled at the turn of phrase.

'Shout. Your shout. It means, you're paying,' said Bec.

Both were unanimous in their choice – Hotel Federal. 'You'll find it on the corner of King and Collins Street, in the city. We'll meet you there.'

Determined to ignore the annoyance emanating from both Alex and Daniel, Eliza followed Bec's lead and rose to her feet, signalling her desire to be on their way. She cast Alex a quick glance, his expression reminding her of the Greek God Zeus. Importance, authority and disapproval were written all over him. She looked around, expecting a thunderbolt, while secretly congratulating herself on the way she'd engaged the new arrivals. Their easygoing charm and gentle flirtation had already boosted her self-confidence, and the fleet had arrived just over twenty-four hours ago.

Wedged in an armchair, sipping her second cocktail, Eliza's eyes idled over the faces of their party. Bec was animated, face, arm and hand gestures becoming more exaggerated as she relaxed, her voice excited. Alex and Daniel's frowns had disappeared, no match against the Americans' hospitality. The men and Bec were engaged in a lively discussion of vocabulary, comparing words and phrases between the two cultures. Eliza had never laughed so much. For all they spoke English, the Australian and American versions contained a number of originalities.

At a low whistle of appreciation, Eliza watched the wide-eyed reaction of the male members of their party to two women poised at the top of the marble staircase which connected the hotel's ground floor and first floor. Queenie and Evelyn. Eliza and Bec sighed in unison. The blonde turned and smiled in their direction, before she collected the brunette and sashayed across to the corner the group had made their own. Behind them, six blue jackets dashed up the stairs, taking the last two together. Sighting their quarry, they made a beeline and arrived at the small party shoulder to shoulder with the two women.

Like the Pied Pipers of Hamelin, but with sailors rather than children or rats in their wake, thought Eliza. Alex and Daniel both had risen politely, Daniel stepping forward to make the introductions, which were a little delayed by the raucous cries as the six sailors caught sight of Leroy. From what Eliza could make of the conversation, they were ship mates from the USS *Pennsylvania* and had been walking down Collins Street when they'd seen *two angels* enter the hotel. They'd set off in hot pursuit, and were none too happy to find Leroy and his buddy already here. They'd seen them first, seemed to be the loudest complaint. Leroy and Franklin drew the sailors a few feet away and directed them back the way they'd come. Reluctantly, they withdrew.

As additional chairs were filched, drinks ordered, and Queenie and Evelyn drawn into the conversation, Eliza wondered whether their appearance was a coincidence or part of a plan. Alex lived in a small suite at the hotel since his parents had rented out their home and accepted an embassy posting to London for twelve months. He seemed to enjoy the freedom it afforded. Perhaps Queenie came here every Friday after work? And maybe not just Fridays – and not just for a drink. Eliza's stomach tightened at the thought and she bit her bottom lip in consternation.

'I've never been on a boat before,' gushed Evelyn, fidgeting with the strands of her necklace. Eliza wondered uncharitably if she was trying to draw attention to her décolletage.

'Beggin' your pardon, ma'am, but it's called a ship. And there are tours planned every weekend of our stay,' said Franklin.

THE BATTLE FOR ELIZA

'But better to come aboard a real ship, like mine, rather than the light cruiser Franklin here is from,' said Leroy.

As expected, this didn't go unchallenged and a short but vigorous debate followed on the superiority of battleships versus light cruisers. From the corner of her eye, Eliza watched Queenie place a hand high on Alex's thigh. Involuntarily, her breath caught. Her eyes locked with his, before she quickly averted them and immersed herself in the conversation to her left. Her sixth sense registered his discreet return of Queenie's hand to the arm of her own chair, and Queenie's fleeting pout.

'I'd welcome an opportunity if you're offering to show us around,' said Daniel, his boyish features energised. 'Alex and I both work in engineering – trains and trams. But a warship, that'd be something else.'

'And would you gals like to come too?' asked Leroy, giving Eliza a questioning look.

A chorus of yeses erupted, and Eliza nodded. 'That would be great.'

'This weekend suit you folks?'

'No.' Eliza and Bec spoke at once.

'Um ...we have to be in at the YWCA,' stumbled Eliza, giving her friend a pointed look. She used to play this game with Daniel when they were children, trying to avoid parental punishment. One would start a story and the other would finish it with the hope that the two cobbled-together parts would be believable. *She hoped Bec was better at it than she had been.*

'I don't remember you mentioning —' Daniel interjected.

Bec nodded, dismissing his interruption. 'Happens every year at this time. Planning meetings for our annual

83

fundraising program.'

Leroy shrugged. 'A week from Sunday, then, thirteen hundred hours.'

'That's one o'clock in the afternoon for you civilians,' Franklin clarified.

'And I'll act as your personal guide,' offered Leroy with a wink at Eliza.

Eliza sensed Alex's regard. His stillness more than anything communicated he was irritated by the sailor's forwardness. Eliza bristled. Well, it wasn't as if Leroy had placed his hand on *her* thigh. She smiled at the American as he leaned forward, one elbow resting on his knee. 'We're looking forward to it, aren't we girls?'

CHAPTER 14

Saturday 25 July 1925

A Very Charming Sailor

At half past two, Eliza checked her wrist watch in the sunlight reflecting off the ornamental pond which lay beyond the patio doors. She glanced around the lounge of Birmingham's Danse Palais at the women and their fashionable attire; there were fifty of them, herself included. This had to be the most audacious thing she'd ever done. She was grateful for Bec's intervention with her wardrobe – *biscuit* would have looked out of place among the eye-catching outfits that surrounded her. But where was Bec? She'd promised to be here for moral support.

A commotion behind the dark-crimson velour curtain separating the lounge from the dance floor had all heads turning. Was it them? The sailors at last?

'Argh ... damn ...'

If it was, they didn't seem too enthusiastic, thought Eliza, before Bec exploded through the curtains, emerging battle worn but triumphant. She made her way between chaises and settees, subsiding onto the seat beside Eliza. 'Bloody curtain,' she whispered.

Eliza grinned and gave Bec's arm a squeeze. 'Did you see them?'

'Aha. They're in the foyer. Mr and Mrs B look like they're reading them the riot act.'

As Bec hadn't lowered her voice, news spread quickly and echoes of 'they're here' could be heard around the room. Short, sharp staccato taps preceded Mrs B's appearance. In contrast, her navigation of the curtain was without incident.

She inspected the assembly, her gaze resting on Eliza briefly, before she continued in a business-like tone. 'Ready, girls? Now, to ease introductions, each young man has been given the name of their partner and their corresponding number on a slip of paper.'

A chorus of *Oohs* erupted. Some girls grabbed hold of each other in an effort to contain their excitement. Eliza twisted her hands in her lap, before Bec untangled one and gave it a squeeze.

Mrs B continued. 'They will find you and introduce themselves. Please remember to behave with decorum. No silliness.'

The group quietened and rose to their feet as one. Eliza fussed with the corsage-like adornment pinned to her dress. Since it displayed her number, she wanted to make sure it could be clearly read.

With a flourish, Mrs B parted the curtains to reveal fifty identical blue service uniforms, distinguishable only by varying heights and hair colour and a mix of expressions. Whether by instruction or training, all fifty stood at ease, hands behind their backs.

In a raised voice, Mr B greeted the assembled, 'A very warm welcome to our visitors and to you young ladies. I'll outline the competition a little later, as I can see you're all eager to make introductions.' As one young sailor, whom Eliza imagined to be no more than twenty, broke rank, Mr B glared at him, stopping him in his tracks. '*In a gentleman-like manner*, please make yourself known to your assigned lady.'

The vaulted ceiling intensified the cacophony of sound that broke out as sailors rushed forward. Eliza was number fifty. And while she understood it had been arbitrarily assigned on arrival, she couldn't prevent memories of school sport selections crowding her thoughts. Pleating and unpleating her skirt unconsciously, she relived the waiting. Knowing she was found wanting but had to be chosen as the teams needed to make up numbers.

Eliza forced a smile onto her face, remembering to keep her lips slightly apart to negate their thinness. Her mother claimed they gave her a severe look when closed. Funny how some comments were never far from her mind.

She observed the scene playing out before her. *A little like a football scrum, if she was honest.* Jenny Butler to her left had surrendered to a bear of a man. *Smart of her*, thought Eliza. Escape would have required executing an unladylike manoeuvre. The man oozed testosterone, which Eliza attributed to the prominent scar running the length of his left cheek. A perfect specimen for a no-strings-attached fling. Others were also quickly claimed, yet here she stood. No sailor in sight. Perhaps he'd taken one look at her and asked to swap.

Eliza turned back towards Bec, looking for some support. But Bec was busy watching events unfold, her eyes darting back and forth, seated on the edge of her chair, a huge smile on her face. Eliza wouldn't be surprised if she whipped out a pen and started making notes.

'I knew I'd get the prettiest girl in the room,' drawled a voice behind her. Eliza swung around and found herself confronted by a broad jaw and bedroom eyes, although the sleepy appearance was at odds with a mischievous glint, of which she was the recipient.

Taking advantage of her immediate confusion, he disentangled one of her hands from her skirt and tucked it into the crook of his arm. 'I'm Wil, and you would be ... Eliza, right?'

'Yes, Eliza,' she parroted, startled by his forwardness.

'Pleased to meet you. Let's take a stroll over yonder and get acquainted, shall we?'

Eliza didn't feel she was in any position to argue since he was in firm possession of her arm. She glanced back towards where Bec sat and got a cheeky thumbs up. Ducking her head, she took a furtive look at Wil to find him chuckling.

'Friend of yours?'

'Um ... sometimes.'

'So, Miss Eliza, tell me a little about yourself.'

Haltingly at first, and then more confidently in response to Wil's obvious interest, she talked readily for a full ten minutes. By this time, they'd reached the far end of the floor and now stood facing the bandstand where the orchestra, Art Bobbie and the Birmingham Syncopators, presided every evening that the Danse Palais was open.

Eliza glanced nervously over her shoulder, surprised at the distance between themselves and the other couples. 'Your turn,' she blurted out.

Wil smiled. An easy, self-assured action that carried all the way to his eyes – caramel with creases at the corners as if he'd been squinting into the sun or laughing a lot. He was enjoying himself, and she was ... flustered!

'Well, Miss Eliza, I'm twenty-six years of age and this is my first time to your fine capital. I'm from America's south, born in a little town in 'bama. I mean Alabama.'

That smile again.

'I've been in the navy comin' on five years now, all of it on the fine battleship USS *Oklahoma*, moored at your Princes Pier,' he said, gesturing with a jerk of his head in the direction of the doors. His coal-black hair, ordered in a relaxed regulation cut, suited him, she decided.

'I've been dancin' since I was in nappies. Or so my mama says. And I've never received any complaints from the ladies on that score.'

Eliza couldn't imagine him receiving any complaints on any score, but kept that thought to herself. He was particularly good-looking, she resolved in that moment. The navy-blue woollen jumper and trousers emphasised athletic proportions.

'Everyone, gather round now,' boomed Mr B, using the ballroom's acoustics to command attention over the hum of conversation. 'I'm going to run through the competition rules and dates, so listen up.'

Wil escorted her back up the floor. He seemed in no hurry, something that did not escape Mrs B's attention and earned him one of her most majestic frowns. Wil sent her an appeasing smile and Eliza felt herself being secured closer to his side.

'It's a three-four tempo,' Mr B reminded them. 'So, style,

rhythm and neat footwork will be the focus. No rapid spins, trick steps, stunts, elaborate arm movements or theatrical gestures.' He paused for effect and glared at those couples closest to him as if expecting dissent. Apart from the scuffing of toes, there was silence.

'The heats are scheduled for Saturday, August first. Ten couples per heat. The final will be on Wednesday, August fifth. Any questions?'

'Respectfully, sir,' drawled a voice from Eliza's right – she was loving the lazy, prolonged rhythm of the southern accent. 'We sail on the sixth and usually got to be back on board twenty-four hours before.'

'Quite right. Good point,' replied Mr B. 'We have received permission for those who make the finals to return late.'

'An' spectators?' the voice persisted.

'Yes, yes. And your mates.'

Eliza suppressed a giggle. She wondered if anyone else had noticed Mr B's crossed fingers. He wasn't the sort to let a little thing like ship rules interfere with his business model.

'Now, we are very privileged to have an old mate of mine visiting from England, Philip Dickson, who has agreed to adjudicate. Some of you will recognise the name. He is a leading waltz advocate and judge.' He again paused and looked out over his audience, only to be met with silence. If anyone had heard of Philip Dickson, they weren't volunteering it.

'And formal attire is the go. For any fella who doesn't have the right garb, come and see me after this. I know a bloke or two who I can recommend.'

'Girls, that goes for you, too,' interjected Mrs B. 'I can provide guidance on your gown choice, if required.'

THE BATTLE FOR ELIZA

'All right, if there are no other questions, we'll end it there. Don't forget that Birmingham's is open every night over the next fortnight. Each night will be a different theme and we're looking forward to making your visit a memorable one. Check the noticeboard for details and tell your mates.'

They were dismissed.

'Well that's that, then,' said Wil. 'I'm guessin' we'll need some practice to get used to one another. When were you reckonin'?'

'Tomorrow. Can you make three o'clock? Here?'

'Yes, ma'am. I can be anywhere, anytime you want me to be.' This was said with an exaggerated wink.

Eliza blushed anew. Wil had a remarkable way about him. She wondered if all American seamen were like this.

'Now, if you'll excuse me, I'll just collect my buddy Johnnie and we'll talk to Mr Birmingham about that formal garb. Can't have me letting you down in the looks department. See you tomorrow.'

Eliza nodded and watched as he turned and strode over to Jenny and her *Bear*, as Eliza had labelled him, or Johnnie as she now knew him. He seemed reluctant to disengage, but after some hearty backslapping, Wil and Johnnie farewelled Jenny and headed in Mr B's direction.

Eliza turned to find Bec standing behind her, almost bouncing up and down on tippy-toes. 'Well, how did it go?' she asked.

'He'll do,' Eliza hedged, and at Bec's disbelieving look, added, 'He is a bit scrumptious, isn't he?'

'Uh-uh. He's perfect for our purposes.'

Eliza narrowed her eyes at her friend, but Bec either chose to ignore her expression or missed it, continuing conspiratorially, 'Did you hear? Queenie's nomination for the competition wasn't accepted.'

Eliza nodded. 'I overheard her the night of the YMCA Ball fundraiser. Sorry, I must have forgotten to mention it.'

'Word has it she acted up so bad that Mr and Mrs B appeased her by asking her to scrutineer for Philip Dickson, the adjudicator on the night. Let's hope she doesn't sour your chances or his impartiality.'

'She wouldn't,' said Eliza automatically. Then more cautiously, 'Would she?'

'No. Reputations would be ruined, especially given the prize money. Forget I said anything.'

Eliza crossed her arms. It was easy for Bec to say – after she'd voiced it. If only Alex hadn't asked her to the Lord Mayor's Ball. Perhaps she could withdraw her acceptance, providing an opportunity for Alex to ask Queenie. But even as the thought entered her mind, she rejected it. She wanted to go on a date with Alex. Even if it wasn't *that* sort of date.

CHAPTER 15

Sunday 26 July 1925

'So, how did it go? What was he like?' asked Bec, tucking her hand into the crook of Eliza's elbow.

They were ambling along The Strand, pretending interest in the grand houses that bordered it. To their right lay the channel of water separating Williamstown from Port Melbourne. And anchored as far as the eye could see, were the ships of the American flotilla. They looked as if they were part of a sea garden resplendent with lights. Each participating vessel had been hung from bow to stern, waterline to masthead with what looked like diamonds.

Eliza and Bec had dropped back deliberately from their party of six, so she could satisfy Bec's curiosity about her practice with Wil earlier that afternoon.

Eliza giggled. 'It was fun. A bit awkward at first – I was as nervous as a beginner. But he was so patient.'

'Can he dance?'

'Like a dream. Even Mr B was impressed. He popped in for a bit and offered to help us. What do you make of that?'

'You're like a favourite daughter to him,' Bec said

dismissively. 'Did anything else happen?'

Eliza refused to meet her eyes, fussing with the cuff of her glove.

'What? Tell me!'

'Keep your voice down,' said Eliza, glancing nervously towards her parents a few feet in front of them. 'After Mr B left, we got talking. He asked me if I had a boyfriend. When I said no, he said he was pleased. I was a bit annoyed ... at first ...'

Eliza swallowed, and then because she and Bec kept no secrets, finished with a rush, 'And then he kissed me.'

'Wahoo! On the cheek?' teased Bec. 'No, wait, it was on the lips, wasn't it?'

'I'm not confiding in you if you carry on like that. Yes, on the lips. It was nice.'

'Nice? Pfff. That boy looks like he's got a bit more than nice in him.'

'All right. All right. It was wonderful!' said Eliza, cooling her burning cheeks with her fingers. It had also been short. Too short. She'd worried that her technique was off, but Wil had been so sweet, explaining he didn't want to scare her off. He'd left her impatient, a little like when she was learning a new dance or new steps ... but more restless.

Bec wrinkled her nose. 'Of course it was. When are you seeing him again?'

'He said that he and a few others were planning on watching the searchlight display from Williamstown. So, we might meet him tonight!' said Eliza, hugging Bec's arm in anticipation.

Glancing up, she could see Daniel gesturing irritably for her and Bec to hurry up. He and Alex had been charged with securing the best vantage points for their party. 'We're being summoned, come on.'

Flares heralded the start of the display and all heads turned to the bay. Eliza, Alex, Bec and Daniel stood side by side. Eliza's mum had been offered a seat a short distance away and her father stood politely behind her, discussing council affairs no doubt, with one of his cronies.

Eliza watched as one by one the ships' searchlights flashed out at intervals. Some pierced the heavens, others aimed at comrade ships. Then, as if on command, they crisscrossed in every conceivable direction. She'd read that over one hundred searchlights had been planned for the display. Standing there, she imagined they were involved in some intricate dance – perhaps a courtship dance. She rolled her eyes skyward at her fanciful notions.

Craning her neck, Eliza was surprised to find that they formed the front row of a crowd that stretched from one end of the channel to the other, as far as her eye could see. The night illuminations raked the waters of the bay, back and forth. A shaft of light, levelled low, struck the shore and crept towards where they stood. Eliza experienced an absurd feeling of being pursued, hunted. It captured the foreshore houses and momentarily blinded her. She closed her eyes and then opened them to watch its return arc travel across the water before rising swiftly, stabbing the low-lying clouds on its way to the skies above.

'It looks like it'd reach right up to heaven, Ma,' enthused one young girl holding on tight to her mother's hand beside Eliza. Suggestions of rainbows, dancing curtains and from one studious young lad, Aurora Australis, no doubt triggered by the strange purple tint emanating from the beams circulated around her.

The sound of a trumpet, then two, a burst of ragtime jazz. Eliza heard delighted squeals, clapping and singing.

'Let's take a look,' she enthused, music as always overriding any other distraction.

Bec nodded and Alex and Daniel gestured for her to lead on.

Eliza squeezed between elbows to find herself in the front row of a circle. At one side, three American trumpet players in uniform, and in the middle, a few couples stepping out.

'Eliza,' a voice called, and she found herself face to face with Wil.

'I told you I'd find you,' he bragged, grabbing her around the waist and leading her into an energetic jig.

The tune finished and Wil pulled her into a hug, before tugging her through the circle of partygoers, behind the three-piece ensemble, and into the shadows.

'You're even more beautiful by moonlight,' said Wil, surprising her with a kiss to her mouth before tucking her hand into the crook of his arm.

Eliza became aware that the searchlights with choreographed precision had concluded. An *Ahh* floated from the crowd like an exhalation of breath as darkness again reigned. Looking up, she encountered pools of chocolate heat. *Alex!* His expression was hard to read. Not so Daniel's, who was stationed directly behind him, arms crossed.

Wil seemed to sum up the situation in a heartbeat. 'Why don't you introduce us, Eliza?'

'Yes, Eliza, why don't you introduce us,' mimicked Alex with a sardonic lift of his brow.

'Wil, I'd like you to meet Alex, and behind him, my

brother, Daniel. And this is my best friend, Bec.'

Wil extended his hand. For a moment, Eliza thought Alex and Daniel were going to refuse to shake it, but they recovered their manners and gripped – maybe harder than politeness demanded, from the expression on Wil's face. Taking Bec's hand, Wil turned it over and extended a small bow and a brief kiss.

'Wil is from the USS *Oklahoma*. We met briefly yesterday,' Eliza explained, trying to stay as close to the truth as possible without furnishing too many details. 'And we happened to run into one another, just now.'

'What are the odds?' drawled Alex, putting his hands on his hips. 'All these people, and you just happen to run into one another.'

'Yes, sir, I'm a lucky man I am,' agreed Wil.

'Why don't you meet Eliza's mum and dad while you're here,' said Bec, commandeering his other arm and dragging him and Eliza towards a group of seats.

Under her breath, Eliza instructed, 'Don't mention the competition. My family and Alex know nothing about it. Understand?'

'Yes, ma'am,' Wil said with a grin, clearly enjoying the intrigue.

The sight of an American seaman flanked by their daughter and her best friend, gave Eliza's parents pause.

'Who do we have here, then?' asked Eliza's father.

'Dad, Mum, this is Seaman Wil Sanders from USS *Oklahoma*. We met yesterday at Birmingham's.'

'Mighty happy to meet you both.' Wil shook hands with her father and sketched a quick bow to her mother.

'Wait up.' The smiling face of Wil's mate Johnnie appeared.

'Seaman Johnnie Sherman at your service.' He saluted her parents in smart fashion and another round of introductions followed. Alex and Daniel stepped forward, giving perfunctory handshakes.

'A wonderful display by the fleet, young fellas,' Eliza's father commended.

'Thank you, sir, we'll pass on your compliments,' returned Johnnie.

Eliza's dad looked at him as if he were pulling his leg, but after studying Johnnie's face, accepted his statement with a nod.

The crowd was starting to drift away, and Johnnie gave Wil a nudge.

'If y'all excuse us. Sir. Ma'am. Gents and ladies. We're due back on deck at twenty-two hundred hours. Our commander will have conniptions if we don't appear,' said Wil politely.

He mouthed, 'Tomorrow' to Eliza as he gave her a wink, and adorned her knuckles with a swift kiss before he turned on his heel. Johnnie offered another salute and a jaunty wave before following him.

'What nice boys. So polite and solicitous of their duty,' approved Eliza's mum.

'They're certainly attentive,' agreed Alex. 'Whether to their duty or something ... or someone else, remains to be seen,' he said.

Eliza found her gaze snared, Alex refusing to allow her to look away.

'They're just as I remember,' continued her mum.

'Humph, like wolves in sheep's clothing,' muttered Alex, continuing to hold Eliza's gaze. She frowned at him. Why was he so annoyed?

'A bit of competition never hurt,' chortled her dad. 'I remember the visit of 1908. Only sixteen ships. Just over two and a half thousand of 'em. Only a week, but they sure put the wind up us fellas. I was glad to see the back of them. And I was married at the time. But your mum caught their eye. Yes, you did, no denying it.'

'Oh, William, you talk such nonsense sometimes,' murmured Eliza's mum, waving her hand in front of her face as if swatting a fly.

This was a story Eliza wanted to hear. Giving Alex a brief smile, she motioned to Bec and they took hold of her mother's hands, dragging her to her feet and linking arms.

'Now, start at the beginning, Mum, and don't leave anything out,' instructed Eliza as they turned for home.

'Oh, it was a long time ago ... they certainly made a girl feel special, though. Not that I was interested, mind you, me being married —'

'To such a good-looking man,' Eliza's father interrupted over his shoulder.

'And with two little ones ...' her mum finished with a smile.

'It made us men appreciate our women in the face of all that rampaging testosterone sweeping the city,' her dad said sagely, clapping Alex and Daniel on their shoulders as they walked beside him, hands in pockets. Eliza imagined deep frowns furrowing their brows.

CHAPTER 16

Monday 27 July 1925

'Eliza, a little more hip into that turn, and stay left ... Wil, your lead into that needs to be confident ... it looks a bit like a half-open gate,' boomed Mr B. 'The filly doesn't know whether to go forward or back ... once more and then we'll call it a night.'

They danced into a pivot, each forward step strong and parallel, moving down the floor. Eliza's hip turn with Wil's stronger lead nearly sent them off balance, and Eliza felt light-headed at the pace they generated. They walked back to where Mr B stood, hands on hips.

'Better ... now you just need to learn to control the power you're creating.' He clapped Wil on the back. 'See you tomorrow.'

Wil nodded and shook his hand.

'Thanks, Mr B,' said Eliza with a quick kiss to his leathery cheek.

He batted her away, grousing as he left the main dance hall, 'Now don't be getting any ideas, leave that nonsense for someone who appreciates it.'

'Like me,' chipped in Wil as he extended his cheek in her direction.

Eliza stepped forward boldly to bestow the same to his proffered cheek. She closed her eyes and leaned in, connecting with Wil's ... mouth. Her eyes shot open to find her gaze captured in his honey-brown hue. Breath mingling, warm air spilling across lips fractionally apart.

'I could get used to your thankyous,' said Wil, brushing her cheek with his finger. 'But I draw the line at sharin' them with your Mr B.'

Eliza blushed, looking away to study the floor.

'Don't be goin' all coy on me ... am I bein' too fast?'

'You are rather ... forward. But it's more that I haven't had much practice. And I don't want to disappoint you.'

Wil lifted her chin with his finger and kissed the tip of her nose. 'Do I look like a man who's disappointed?'

Eliza gave the slightest shake of her head, watching the creases at the edge of his mouth lengthen. He leaned forward, capturing her lower lip and gently nuzzling it. She stirred, the caress provoking a feeling of warmth, like being drizzled in syrup. Not that she'd ever tried that, but she imagined this was what it might feel like.

'Open for me,' commanded Wil softly, as he gathered her closer, lipping and sucking persuasively.

Eliza tilted her head, attempting to fit, and bumped her nose. *That's it*, she thought, *show him how incompetent you really are*. But Wil hadn't seemed to take it as a sign of inexperience. If anything, he moved closer. His tongue took a tour of her mouth. His hands scouted her natural features, coming to rest on her hips.

I wonder if he knows he's navigating unexplored territory, Eliza mused. She heard a soft growl and realised that it had come from her. Wil was now teasing the line of her jaw and tickling the sensitive area at the base of her lobe. His hands were patrolling the base of her spine and the top of her bottom. *Like Alex when we were waltzing*, she thought reflexively. It was followed by goosebumps, unconnected to Wil's treatment of her vertebrae.

Sensing a change, Wil looked up. 'What's wrong?'

'I feel like we're being watched.'

As if on cue, the door to the studio swung open. An avenging angel would have appeared friendlier.

'Ah ... hello, Alex,' Eliza greeted him.

'I hope I'm not interrupting anything.'

Eliza wondered how much he'd seen but was under no illusions from his face and tone that it had been enough. *Great! She could have done without an audience for her first foray.*

'You remember Wil from —'

'The searchlight display,' he finished for her. 'Yes, I remember the happy coincidence of our meeting.' His meaning couldn't have been clearer.

'Hello again,' said Wil. 'Eliza and I were just finishing up.'

'Or just getting started.'

Eliza held her breath. Alex's ire was palatable.

Wil smiled, seemingly unperturbed. 'We're headin' out for a quick drink. Care to join us?'

'No.'

'Alex!' Eliza was embarrassed at his rudeness.

'Another time, then. No doubt I'll see you round,' said Wil politely.

'Count on it!'

'Shall we, Eliza?'

THE BATTLE FOR ELIZA

She slipped her hand into Wil's, glaring at Alex.

Alex gave her a 'this is not over' look, but did not delay their departure.

'I'll see you at dinner,' he reminded her.

Eliza chose to ignore him, walking up the stairs to the vestibule doors and out. It wasn't until they stepped onto the Collins Street footpath that she realised she'd been holding her breath.

'Dinner?' Queried Wil.

'Family night in. Mum insists on us eating together one night a week. Daniel and I chose Mondays as they are the least disruptive to our social calendars.'

'And Alex?'

'He, and Bec, are considered part of the family and join us if they're available,' concluded Eliza with a shrug.

'He was mad as all get out,' said Wil. 'You'd tell me if I was steppin' on his patch, wouldn't you?'

'What?'

'You and Alex.'

'There is no me and Alex. He's acting ...'

'Like a man wound up tighter than a winch.'

'... stupid!'

Wil laughed. 'Darlin', more like as if you are a precious possession.'

'Well, he's taking his honorary big-brother act too far.'

Wil squeezed her hand but thankfully said nothing more.

Alex stood there fuming, both at his own lack of collectedness and Eliza's apparent indifference towards him. She'd looked dazed. Had that sailor's kisses affected her that much? She was an innocent, after all.

'Looking for someone, Alex?'

Alex turned sharply towards Dick Birmingham, silhouetted in the doorway.

'Something. I left an umbrella here the other night, thought I'd drop in and collect it,' said Alex, aware that he sounded terse. *But the sight of Wil's hands caressing Eliza's spine made him want to punch something.* He took a deep breath.

'Well, if you're looking for Eliza, she just left,' continued Mr B as if Alex hadn't spoken.

'Just the umbrella thanks, Mr B,' Alex stated firmly.

'Umbrella huh?' said Mr B, scratching his chin. 'Let's see what we can find.'

Alex followed him to a cupboard in the vestibule of the building, where a collection of orphaned umbrellas, scarves, gloves and even a brown homburg sat awaiting an owner.

'Eliza and Wil are a real chance, you know,' said Mr B casually as Alex continued to sort through the umbrellas until he finally selected one. He hoped Mr B wasn't going to ask him how he knew it was his, since it looked indistinguishable from its neighbours.

'I'll bite. What is it they're a chance for?' asked Alex cautiously.

'The waltz competition. We're giving away one hundred pounds.'

'And Eliza has entered? With Wil?' Alex was dumbfounded.

'Yes, my boy. Why do you think they're spending time together?'

I know why they're spending time together and it has nothing to do with dancing, Alex wanted to shout. But he hesitated. 'Why are you telling me this? You must know that Eliza hasn't mentioned a word.'

THE BATTLE FOR ELIZA

'The heats are on Saturday night, from eight o'clock,' Mr B said, shutting the cupboard doors with a firm shove. 'I think they've planned another practice session late tomorrow afternoon ... Expect you might want to keep an eye on things.'

'Remind me never to play poker against you,' said Alex. 'Thanks for the chat.'

As Alex turned to go, Mr B placed a hand on his shoulder, and at his puzzled look handed him the umbrella. 'Don't forget this.'

CHAPTER 17

That Evening

It was late, and Eliza was sitting in a wicker rocker on the front verandah replaying her time with Wil. Her mother had talked the night of the searchlight display about how charming the American men from the last visit had been – and how persuasive. She sighed, her breath materialising in a small cloud. Much like Wil. Curling the fingers of her right hand in front of her mouth, she blew softly, then repeated it with the left. She'd forgotten her gloves in her haste to avoid Alex.

'Yes, I'll tell her to come in before she catches her death. Goodnight,' Alex called over his shoulder. The front door closed, and the screen door banged shut.

As Eliza stood to make her way inside, a firm palm in the small of her back propelled her off the verandah and down the front path. Gaining the shadows afforded by the elm tree that guarded the entrance to her parents' property, Eliza swung around, the momentum causing her to stumble.

Alex reached out to stop her falling. Although she couldn't see his expression clearly, there was no mistaking the anger rolling from him. It was swamping her like an incoming tide.

THE BATTLE FOR ELIZA

'What did you think you were doing?'

Heat swept up Eliza's cheeks. She thought she'd avoided this conversation as Alex had

seemed quiet but relaxed at dinner. Evidently not.

'Earlier this evening, you mean?'

'Yes,' he ground out. 'What did you think you were doing?'

'Having a lesson.'

'What was the subject?'

Eliza wondered why he felt she owed him an explanation. Annoyed at his high-handedness, she returned, 'Surely, you're familiar with kissing? I understand that you're a bit of an expert, if everything I hear can be believed.' *And not just in kissing*, she added silently.

'That wasn't *just* kissing. He was crawling all over you.'

'Don't be ludicrous! We kissed. There was no petting. Your appearance put paid to that.'

'Right. So, if I hadn't come along, how were you going to extricate yourself when things got too hot?'

'Argh! Too many questions. You're making way too much out of this. Wil is a gentleman.'

Alex raked his hands through his hair. 'Oh, sweetheart, aren't we all until ... well, until we're not.'

At the endearment, Eliza felt her eyes widen, and she opened her mouth in surprise. Before she knew what was happening, Alex's arm snaked around her waist and began pulling her closer, step by step, until they were touching. Without her dance heels, she was at a disadvantage. She refused to look up.

Eliza felt the pad of Alex's thumb brush her lower lip. When she refused to either look at him or open her mouth, he ducked his head, replacing his thumb with his lips. The tip of his tongue teased the seam of her lips until they parted and then he painted the inside of her mouth with soft strokes. She was being tasted ... an unusual experience. *Unusual, but very nice.* Withdrawing, he pressed a kiss at each corner of her mouth and raised his head.

Eliza raised her chin. His eyes reminded her of the searchlights from the ships, scanning her face, as if looking for ... a sign. Unintentionally, she pressed her body closer and he lowered his head, returning to her lips and his previous ministrations. The kiss deepened. This time, his tongue was more urgent, tangling with hers – dancing.

A shiver ran down her spine and Alex's palm traced it – unerringly – his fingers trailing fire. Stopping momentarily in the hollow before her bottom, his hand swept down to claim her derrière, wrapping his palm around one taut globe. *Yes. Very, very nice,* she decided.

Goodness, she knew he was no amateur in the seduction stakes, but she was now coming to realise why he was so desired by the female population. He seemed to know just where to touch her and how much pressure to apply. While Wil's kisses had melted her insides, Alex's ignited sparks, as if he were building a fire.

She wondered how her efforts compared with his usual conquests. Clearly, she was innocent ... yes, well, that's why she'd been practising with Wil ... but Alex seemed ... invested in their encounter. *Oh my God!* What was she thinking? Did she realise whom she'd locked lips with? This was her brother's best friend! Although, she didn't feel very sisterly at this very minute, she admitted. What must he think? She started to pull back.

Alex must have sensed the change, as he delivered one

THE BATTLE FOR ELIZA

final kiss before resting his forehead on hers.

'Talk to me.'

Her mind was whirring, trying to make sense of what had just happened. She wasn't sure what he wanted her to say. What did most people talk about after such an onslaught? Eliza straightened and returned his gaze.

'Thank you.' That seemed like a polite way of starting things off. 'You kiss ... differently to Wil ...' she trailed off uncertainly before realising he may need an explanation ... or reassurance. 'When I said *differently*, I meant that you were great – just *different* great.'

She seemed to have robbed him of speech.

Eliza tried again. 'Sorry, I seem to be having trouble with my words.'

Alex made a strangled sound.

'Don't worry, I won't mention this to anyone. No awkward situations or explanations need arise,' she stammered.

Alex closed his eyes.

'Alex. Is something wrong?'

He opened his eyes and Eliza anxiously scanned his face. Maybe he was sick. Difficult to tell in this light, but his features were somewhat contorted. She took a step back; Alex's hands remained on her hips, so she couldn't escape completely.

'You've been experimenting ... with Wil.'

It didn't sound like a question – more like an accusatory sentence. Even to her own ears, she sounded defensive. 'Well, I don't have a lot of skill in this area. It isn't as if I've been besieged with boyfriends. And Bec tells me I'm aloof, so I'm working on being more approachable.'

Eliza heard him take a deep breath. 'Being aloof isn't necessarily a bad thing.'

109

Eliza hooted. 'Not from my experience. Maybe it works for you – women love the strong, silent type.'

'Perhaps I could help.'

'I don't see how.'

'A little *tuition* ...'

Eliza blinked, and then frowned. 'With you?' At his nod of affirmation, she said, 'Don't you think that would be a little awkward? I mean ... How? When? You're very ... that is ...' And then she simply ran out of words.

'Let's not discuss the details now. I'll give it some thought. We can explore the idea further on Wednesday night at the Lord Mayor's Ball.'

Eliza was only too willing to put space between this conversation and their next. Maybe he'd even forget about it altogether.

'In the meantime, experiment only in your head. Please.'

Eliza quickly detangled herself. 'I promise I won't do anything you wouldn't do,' she relented.

His chuckle followed her all the way to her parents' front door and inside.

Sleep evaded Eliza. Barely a week ago, her prospects for a date let alone a kiss were less than zero, even for an optimist, as she liked to think of herself. Tonight, she'd been kissed by a handsome American seaman *and* her brother's hot best friend, whose potency on her senses had been unanticipated. She pinched herself. *Ouch!* No, she wasn't dreaming.

She needed counsel. She needed Bec. But she doubted that having a glut of interested males was enough of a reason to storm over to her house and demand an emergency congress. It could wait until tomorrow. But no longer.

CHAPTER 18

Tuesday 28 July 1925

Eliza was feeling out of sorts. Despite the cold air inside the dance hall, rivulets of moisture trickled between her breasts and inched their way down her spine. It was the same step, time and time again. It went missing, her feet obstinate in their refusal to dance it. Her eyes stung, and she could taste salt on her top lip – in that little indent just below her nose.

Wil had been patient. They'd walked through the routine again and again. At walking pace, everything fitted together like the pieces of a jigsaw. But, danced at pace, she would tense and they would teeter, a hair's breath away from overbalancing. He'd told her she was overthinking it. Eliza knew he was right, but her feet stubbornly kept listening to her head rather than execute what her body wanted to dance.

After two hours, Wil had excused himself to get back to the ship as he was rostered for cleaning duty – curfews were not to be trifled with. She'd stayed to walk over the routine and the troublesome step a few more times before calling it quits.

She paused and recalled his leaving. He'd kissed her

lingeringly and then impatiently – lips, tongue and teeth – a new element, but not unwelcome. *Although, his kisses lacked Alex's volatility.* She shook her head. *This was not a competition.*

Eliza was annoyed that she hadn't been able to speak to Bec. She'd been missing in action from their regular morning train, and any opportunity after the staff meeting had been lost when she'd headed out on factory visits with the Employment and Vocational Secretary, Miss Timms. She hoped they'd be able to catch up this evening. Her mum was hosting Wil and Johnnie for a home-cooked meal and Bec, Jenny and Alex had been invited. It was why Bec hadn't made her usual Monday-night appearance – two consecutive evenings away from her parents' table were frowned upon by her father.

Humming one of her favourite tunes, Eliza refocused on the task at hand and started to waltz. As she danced into the pattern of troubled steps, she admonished herself. *What is so difficult about a forward step, a cross behind, a side step and then a step out to promenade!* Her speed for one. She'd approached it like a freight train, and as she stepped out and then across herself, she'd nearly tripped and fallen.

Eliza was tempted to stamp her foot. So, she did. Twice. One of the benefits of having the building to herself.

A laugh exploded behind her.

She stopped and swung around, blood thundering in her ears. Why hadn't she locked the doors after Wil's departure? And then she saw his silhouette. Alex. She'd know him anywhere. For some reason, that annoyed her, and when he continued to stand there raking his gaze from the top of her head to the tip of her toes and everything in between, her annoyance only increased.

THE BATTLE FOR ELIZA

He seemed in no hurry to say anything. She thought she might burst into flames under his studied gaze, but from annoyance, embarrassment, or something else she couldn't decide.

When Alex had admitted himself to the Danse Palais, he'd tormented himself with thoughts of what he might interrupt and whether he could be accused of stalking. *He didn't care.* Last night he'd travelled home, secretly pleased with his quick thinking. *Tuition* would serve Eliza's purpose in furthering her skills, and his in transforming her image of him from fraternal to romantic. He'd also hoped it would stop her experimenting elsewhere. But her parting remark had stayed with him. Little minx, she must have known it was hardly reassuring. He didn't want others to find her more approachable. He closed his eyes and groaned. How had things turned out so awkwardly? This was not his usual style.

Wrinkling his nose in distaste at the smell of stale air and wattle flower, he'd paused to allow his eyes to adjust to the gloomy interior. He'd heard a soft shoe fall, a drag of heels and then the whisper of suede on timber, before he'd caught sight of her.

She appeared to be alone. Arms suspended in midair as if holding an imaginary partner, face bathed in perspiration and brows knitted in concentration as she navigated a series of what looked like quite complex steps.

Her skirts swished and then flipped out to provide a glimpse of toned thighs, before settling back around her calves so quickly he thought he'd imagined it. Although, his cock told him otherwise. Her linen blouse was plastered to her torso, outlining her svelte form.

And then she stomped her foot, twice. Unintentionally, for he had been enjoying the view, a laugh erupted from his throat.

'Hello, Alex. What a surprise.'

'The surprise is all mine. I'm sure I heard you tell your mother last night that your intended destination this afternoon was the library. Something about collecting a book you'd ordered.'

Eliza smoothed her palms down her skirts and moved to the side of the floor to sit down on one of the chaise lounges, patiently awaiting tomorrow night's crowd.

He moved towards her. 'Are you alone?' He scanned the room, pivoting three hundred and sixty degrees.

She met his gaze squarely. 'I'm here practising. Yes, I'm alone.'

He watched her tuck a strand of hair behind her ear. Alex was a master of equivocation and deception, but Eliza, thank goodness, was not. As her telltale sign revealed.

'So, how long ago did he leave?'

'Who?'

He advanced to stand in front of her. 'Let's not play games. Wil, of course. Not long, I'd guess. It looks to have been a strenuous session. Was it all dancing?'

Eliza gasped at the innuendo. 'How dare you!'

'I dare. So, was it?'

'Yes!' she spluttered, clearly outraged. 'Not that it is any of your business. Not even Daniel would ask such a question.'

'I am *not* your brother, Eliza. I thought last night might've hinted at that fact.'

He watched her eyes and knew the instant she caught his meaning, her pupils darkening to pools of emerald green.

He could drown in her eyes.

Her lips parted into a little 'oh' and he trailed a finger down her cheek and across her lower lip. When her tongue traced his finger's path, Alex took her face in both hands, his intent to rob her of speech with the first touch of his lips. To his surprise, she encircled his wrists with her fingers not to push him away, rather to pull him closer and tangle them into his unruly curls.

Alex dropped to his knees, gathering her to his chest. He felt the dampness of her blouse through the material of his shirt, her nipples on point, pressing into his chest. They were going to drive him mad if he didn't touch them. Moving one hand to her nape to support her head, he skated the other to the apex of her breast. She pressed it emphatically into his cupped palm, and he rolled the areola between thumb and forefinger, until he elicited a muffled sigh. Gliding his mouth down her neck, he replaced his fingers with his mouth, licking then sucking through the fabric of her blouse. First the right nipple, then the left.

Eliza had commenced her own exploration, chasing his hairline to the collar of his coat and then inside. He felt the muscles of his neck relax under her touch and heard her groan in what he interpreted as frustration if her next words were any indication. 'Too many clothes!'

Alex fought to reassemble his wits just as Eliza appeared to be losing hers. *Thank God for hard floors and knobbly knees.* Summoning all his remaining strength, he swept Eliza off the lounge and into his lap, wrapping her close as he settled onto the floor. His cock throbbed and vaulted to attention at the feel of her derrière. *Down, boy, this is not the time*, he commanded.

They rested for some minutes without words. Alex took the opportunity to pacify his erection and formulate a credible explanation for what had just taken place. He had no idea what Eliza was thinking. *She'd better not be comparing him to Wil.* Just the thought aroused him, but not in a good way. In the way of men competing, physically, and inflicting bruises.

'Is this part of my ... tuition?'

Alex's laugh detonated from his chest. But at Eliza's crushed look, he sobered and kissed her lingeringly on the lips. 'You might say that,' he sighed when he pulled away.

'Do you think I'm over-compensating?'

Alex's confusion must have shown on his face, for she continued, 'For my aloofness. Do you think I'm becoming too forward?'

'Why would you say that?' asked Alex in a strangled voice.

'Well, I was quite enthusiastic as I didn't want to appear aloof. But then I didn't want to throw myself at you, either ...' she trailed off, the colour of her cheeks expressing her embarrassment.

'Ah. Yes, it can be a fine balance,' said Alex, trying not to smile.

'Don't you dare laugh at me, Alex Heaton. Remember this was your idea.'

'Let's put it this way. If you were being too forward, I'd be wanting to put distance between us. Do I look like I'm trying to do that?'

'No, but you did stop things just as I was getting my nerve. What did I do wrong?'

'You did everything right, Eliza. But I'm conscious of where we are. Anyone could walk in.'

'Oh my God, you're right,' said Eliza, looking around and scrambling to her feet. Her bottom awakened his cock, which he covered by drawing his knees to his chest and remaining seated on the floor.

'About the library,' said Eliza, looking down at him. 'You won't say anything to Mum or Dad ... or Daniel, will you? Mr B admitted that he may have inadvertently mentioned the competition and Wil's and my participation to you.'

Inadvertently indeed. The old devil couldn't have been more blatant.

'I won't volunteer any information, Eliza, but I won't lie. If I'm asked outright, I'll admit to knowing,' Alex told her.

She gave him an exasperated look. 'Well, just don't put yourself in a position where you're asked anything.'

Eliza flounced away to change her shoes and scramble into her coat. Alex hid a smile. Eliza flouncing. This was new. He imagined the many ways he could employ to tease her out of her flounce. His cock twitched again, and he hugged his knees.

'I've gotta run. Some of us don't have time to sit around. I promised Mum I'd help her with dinner. See you tonight.' And with that she was gone, fastening the buttons and buckle on her coat as she went.

'See you,' replied Alex, watching her departure from his position on the floor. It was only then he realised he was grinning like an idiot.

CHAPTER 19

A Home-cooked Meal

'You shouldn't have ...' exclaimed Eliza's mum, blushing profusely before burying her face in a large bunch of flowers.

Wil and Johnnie had arrived that evening bearing flowers, chocolates and stockings. Eliza, Bec and Jenny had taken quick possession of the stockings, running their fingers reverently across the silk and exclaiming in delight.

'No trouble, ma'am. We're mighty obliged to you and your husband for the invitation,' said Wil. 'Right, Johnnie?'

Johnnie wrenched his gaze from Jenny, who was pretending to ignore him. 'Mighty obliged, ma'am.'

Alex was not accustomed to feeling like an extra in a play. Especially not in mixed company. He and Daniel stood with their hands on their hips. In contrast, Eliza's dad seemed somewhat entertained by his wife's girlish exclamations.

'Bloody hell!' said Alex in an undertone to Daniel, as he watched pleasure flood Eliza's face.

'They're smooth, I'll give 'em that,' agreed Daniel with a glare at everyone and anyone who would make eye contact.

But no one was looking at Daniel ... or Alex.

118

'And silk stockings ... that's a bit much, isn't it?'

'Yes, I'm surprised Mum hasn't stepped in to confiscate them.'

'Ahem. We're delighted to welcome you to our home,' said Mr Sinclair, taking control of the situation. *He must have sensed bloodshed wasn't out of the question if this had continued for much longer*, mused Alex, his jaw clenching as he watched Wil wink at Eliza.

'Yes, welcome. Please make yourselves comfortable. We're dining informally tonight, so grab any spot,' said Mrs Sinclair. She flapped her hands in the direction of the kitchen table, which was groaning under the weight of plates, cutlery and crockery that was artfully arranged across a tablecloth bordered by pale-green koalas, paws clasping gumtree branches.

Out of deference to their hosts, the chairs at the head and tail of the table were left vacant, but everything in between was up for grabs. Wil held out Eliza's chair, positioned to the right of her father, and saw her seated. As he turned to take the seat beside her, Alex slid into it and patted the one beside him.

'Take a seat, Wil. It's the quick or the dead around here.'

Wil flashed him a polite smile, ignored the proffered seat and secured the one opposite Eliza. Johnnie seated Jenny between Wil and himself.

'Move up a bit, would you,' said Bec to Alex, attempting to wedge a chair into the gap between him and Daniel. Alex moved up obligingly, abutting his chair and left leg with Eliza's. She ignored him.

'A bit of a squeeze, sorry, the table only seats eight,' said Eliza's mum.

'No need to apologise, ma'am,' said Wil. 'Any table that's not rockin' and rollin' is fine with us. Hey, Johnnie?'

'You've never been in a naval mess if you think this is a squeeze,' agreed Johnnie. 'And the company is far less attractive.' This he directed towards Jenny.

Both men rose as Mrs Sinclair slid the roast from the oven, and insisted on carrying it, the vegetables and accompaniments to the table. Flustered, Mrs Sinclair pretended to wave them away, although she handed over the platter without hesitation, observed Alex.

'No need to get up,' Eliza murmured to Alex out of the corner of her mouth.

Bec and Jenny giggled.

'There's always the dishes.'

More giggles.

Alex glared across the table at where Wil would have been seated if he weren't playing knight errant. Bloody Yank sailors, they just didn't play fair!

Eliza's father ceremoniously carved the lamb, the meat blushing pink, juice soiling the white damask and causing Eliza's mother to tut-tut in annoyance. Plates were passed around the table until everyone's was filled to their satisfaction. A short prayer of thankfulness led by Wil completed dinner preparations.

The visitors ate heartily, enthusiastic in their praise and unreserved in manner and conversation. Wil had a library worth of tales which he was only too willing to entertain the table with, and Eliza and Bec bombarded him with endless questions about life on board and the numerous ports he'd visited. Johnnie's quieter interjections and observations were well timed and appreciated, especially by one young lady

THE BATTLE FOR ELIZA

seated to his right, Alex noted.

He was pleased to see tiny telltale signs that Eliza was flustered by his leg pressed intimately against hers – pink cheeks and more animation than was typical of her. A couple of times, she'd moved her leg to escape and he'd subtly flexed his thigh, chasing and regaining connection. It held the promise of a game to be explored without an audience – especially this audience.

By the time a steaming apple pie and custard were delivered to the table, conversation was more subdued and being tossed between those sitting directly across or beside the other.

Eliza was still studiously ignoring Alex and the warmth of his thigh.

Halfway through dessert, Eliza giggled, although she attempted to cover it with a cough. Alex watched Mrs Sinclair glance at her curiously. So, he hadn't imagined it. Eliza seemed puzzled and roused, her eyes darting between her plate and Wil.

Alex recognised the tactic and the signs. Eliza was on her way to becoming aroused. No doubt the effect of some exploratory touches under the table. He debated his next move, hypercritical to call out the sailor for something he'd employed with great effect himself on occasion. But this was Eliza. And Wil was trespassing. Whether he knew it or not, Eliza was *his*. The certitude of the pronouncement surprised him, both its speed and surety.

He needed a diversion. Looking around the table, he surveyed the empty dessert bowls.

'Dishes,' he heard himself say to the table at large. 'We'll clear the table and do the dishes. It's the least we can do after

121

such a fantastic meal.'

'There's no rush, Alex,' protested Mrs Sinclair.

But Alex would not be deterred. He realised Wil wasn't fooled by the way he cocked his head and lifted a brow – but he refrained from comment. *What else could he do under the circumstances?* Alex thought.

A lively debate ensued over who the collective 'we' included. In the end, he and Jenny manned the sink, Daniel and Bec took up tea towels and Eliza made sure everything was put away so that it could be found again. The naval contingent's offer of assistance was waved away democratically, and they were left to exert their charm over the host and hostess. Mrs Sinclair moved to the seat vacated by Eliza and the opportunity for further amorous advances was lost. Alex quietly congratulated himself.

The suggestion of coffee and tea with Anzac biscuits and vanilla slices was welcomed, and Eliza and Bec demurred any overtures of help as they set about arranging cups, saucers and plates.

Alex was pleased that the new seating arrangements placed Eliza at the opposite end of the table to Wil. He took the empty seat between Bec and Mrs Sinclair. By the end of the evening, he was surprised at how much he'd enjoyed the high-sea tales by the Americans, and their reactions, on discovering how often they'd been the brunt of Australian humour.

The Sinclair hospitality did not extend to a bed, for which Alex offered up a prayer of thanks. He hadn't come prepared for a scenario where Wil spent a night under the Sinclairs' roof, in close proximity to Eliza. Feeling magnanimous, he volunteered to escort Wil and Johnnie safely back to Flinders

Street. From there, regularly patrolled trains would ferry the men to their vessel docked at Princes Pier, Port Melbourne.

Their departure threatened to be as effusive as their arrival, but Alex was having none of it. Being threatened with more than an hour's wait should they miss the train departing in ten minutes, Wil and Johnnie bid reluctant farewells before striding away with Alex towards North Williamstown station.

Secure in the knowledge that Daniel would escort Jenny the two blocks to her home, Eliza and Bec retreated to Eliza's bedroom. Bec was spending the night.

'That was fun,' said Bec, toeing off her shoes and falling backwards onto Eliza's chenille bedspread. 'I think we can expect some news from Jenny any day.'

'What?'

'No matter, I can see you're preoccupied ... what's with Wil and Alex?'

Eliza grabbed a cushion and hugged it to her chest as she told Bec about the developing familiarity between herself, the handsome American seaman and Alex. It didn't seem right any longer to refer to him as her brother's best friend. She even told Bec about the under-table shenanigans from this evening.

Bec listened without comment, idly stroking the tufted lattice design beneath her fingers with a smile.

'What should I do?' asked Eliza.

'About what?'

Eliza levelled an exasperated look Bec's way and then threw the cushion at her friend for good measure.

Bec caught it and tucked it beneath her head. 'Let me get

this straight. You complained you couldn't attract a man. Sobbing on my shoulder about the fact you'd never been properly kissed and how you were lucky not to have been despatched to some imaginary great-aunt.'

Eliza groaned and closed her eyes.

'Now you have two men vying for your attention, raining kisses —'

'One man. Alex is helping with my education.'

'Right!' said Bec, rolling her eyes. 'So altruistic of him.'

Eliza grinned. 'All right, I'm not that naïve, but Queenie is still firmly in the picture and I can't compete with her.'

'I fail to see the problem. Treat it for what it is – an education in savoir faire. And there's no need to give away everything. If you get my meaning.'

Eliza smiled ruefully. 'I do. I'm finding it's what makes dalliances so difficult. At heart, I'm a keeper kind of girl.'

'And given the choice, who would you keep?' Bec asked, all trace of humour gone.

Eliza bit her lip. *Did she dare give voice to her heart? To act on hopes recently kindled?* She gave Bec a guilty smile. 'Alex. My appetite for private tuition is surprising even me.'

CHAPTER 20

Wednesday 29 July 1925

The supper bell sounded, and for the first time in more than a fortnight Alex felt he'd been given a reprieve from the tightrope of emotions he'd been walking with Eliza. Wil's absence accounted for much of his relaxed disposition, he admitted, but Eliza too seemed different. Alex thought back to the session with the mayoress's charity cases. He'd seen a side of Eliza he hadn't experienced – confident, candid and more than a match for five headstrong young women. This was the Eliza that was in evidence tonight.

Tucking her hand into the crook of his arm, they negotiated their way through a glade of Japanese bamboo and palms, beneath which baskets of poinsettias had been studded in a mossy bank. The exhibition building had been transformed from its draughty, cavernous environs to an oasis of greenery littered with blue, red-and-white flowers, lights and stars. Eliza's head darted left and right, looking like a spectator at a tennis match.

Alex placed a hand in the small of her back as they negotiated the dining area, marvelling at the tissue-paper effect of her gown. He'd entertained thoughts of unwrapping her all night. In certain light, the jade colour appeared shot with silver and he'd imagined he could glimpse the contours of her body – the indent of her waist, the curve of her hip.

'Have I told you how lovely you look tonight?' Alex murmured, leaning towards her as he seated her at their designated table.

'I don't think so,' she replied honestly, fingering the material. 'But I agree, Christine has outdone herself. It's a beautiful gown.'

Eliza's assurance didn't appear to extend to her own attractiveness, he mused. 'Not just the gown, Eliza —'

They were interrupted by the arrival of Daniel and Evelyn and the moment passed, although Alex took note of the puzzled expression that crossed Eliza's face. He looked forward to helping her untangle her thoughts later.

Evelyn was complaining about the loss of her flask, confiscated by one of the societal matriarchs who'd caught her imbibing in the ladies' room. 'She promised I could collect it from her before I leave – though how I'll find her in this crush, I'll never know.'

Bec and her date for the evening, resplendent in his blue-and-gold dress uniform, arrived arm in arm.

'Everyone, this is Warrant Officer Jim Johnson. Jim, this is ... well, everyone,' Bec said with a laugh. Alex guessed Bec had imbibed from her own flask before joining them. He wondered if Eliza had one hidden in her garter but quickly dismissed the thought, remembering the way the material of her dress caressed her hips and thighs.

'Mighty glad to meet y'all,' said Jim, offering a general salute before seating Bec beside Daniel and assuming the chair next to Eliza.

'Did anyone see Queenie?' Evelyn asked the table in general. 'She arrived with Derek. Apparently, he secured a last-minute invitation and since she was at a loose end ...' She trailed off as if realising where her reflections were headed, and glanced nervously at Alex, Eliza and then Daniel.

Alex's mouth tightened. Social arrangements like the sort he shared with Queenie were fun ... until they weren't, and then they became tedious. Extricating himself would be tricky, especially when Queenie showed all the signs of still being invested in their dalliance. Tonight loomed as ... awkward.

Bec broke the silence after unwrapping the gift adorning her place setting. 'Now this, Jim, is an ancient Australian hunting tool.' Bec flexed her wrist experimentally in a way that made Alex think she might send it skimming over the heads of the supper guests. 'Have you heard of a boomerang?'

'Yes, ma'am. Do them things really fly? And return?' Jim asked, examining his with renewed interest.

'Oh yes. We use them to round up small children when they won't come home when they're called.'

'Really? You serious?'

'No, Jim, she's pulling your leg,' Daniel said, shaking his head. 'You know, fooling with you, joking,' he clarified after seeing the confused expression on Jim's face.

Bec patted Jim's forearm. 'Don't mind me. Just having a bit of fun.'

'What about those drop bears that you were telling me about, Miss? Are they real?'

'Well, not exactly,' Bec admitted. 'Sometimes the koalas do drop from trees. If they're dizzy or not holding on tight.

But not routinely.'

Eliza let out a choked laugh. 'Not the drop bears! Bec, how could you?'

'Well, he was asking …' Bec trailed off.

'Anything else we need to clear up for you, Jim?' asked Daniel, trying to maintain a solemn expression.

'I hope we haven't missed anything important?' asked a low voice behind Alex's left shoulder. He didn't need to turn around to recognise Queenie's smoky tones.

'Darling. So glad you made it. I'd just told everyone the good news,' said Evelyn, patting the seat beside her in invitation.

Alex and the other men had risen to their feet automatically. Alex introduced the newcomers to Jim before returning to his seat. He was gratified when Derek slid into the seat beside him, having settled Queenie near Evelyn. He ignored her reproachful moue.

Derek, heedless to any undercurrents, launched into the story behind his last-minute invitation, his luck in securing Queenie as his date, and his confusion as to what protocol to observe when introduced to the admiral and his wife.

'I bowed, like I did when I met the Prince of Wales that time. The admiral tried to shake hands. We ended up exchanging nods.'

The term 'dolt' is much too generous, thought Alex, amused despite himself. He wondered if the admiral had shared his opinion.

'He probably thought you were checkin' the shine on his shoes.' Jim laughed.

The strains of Australia's national anthem brought everyone to their feet. In undertones, Jim pointed out the members of the admiral's party as the orchestra followed with the Star-Spangled Banner.

Supper turned out to be a lively affair. The conversation flowed easily, aided by everyone's determination to enjoy themselves and each other's company. Despite this, Alex felt the weight of Queenie's gaze across the table at numerous intervals. Determined to protect Eliza from any barbed innuendo, he used a lull in the conversation to invite her to dance.

Rising, Alex explained to the table in general, 'Excuse us. I hear a waltz, and it has our names on it.' He watched Eliza bow her head at the implication and tuck her hair behind her ears as she accepted his escort. *Finally, some hope*, he thought. *She isn't unaffected.*

'Why did you say that?' she asked as he propelled her towards the dance floor beneath an archway of flowering yellow wattle.

'Well, there's a waltz playing, can't you hear it?'

'I mean, why did you say it like that? *I hear a waltz and it has our names on it*,' she persisted. 'Was it for Queenie's benefit? Are the two of you arguing? I saw the looks she was giving you.'

'Eliza, I love waltzing with you. And for the record, Queenie and I are not arguing.' Alex groaned inwardly at how dry and matter-of-fact he sounded.

'I see ...'

I doubt it, he thought. *And I don't know how to explain my thinking at the moment without making a mess of things.*

'I mean, I don't want to waste our time together talking about Queenie. Let's just dance.'

She nodded and he pulled her into his arms, so close

that the tops of her thighs brushed his. He wondered if the friction would dissolve her dress. Then they'd have to leave ...

'But —'

'Shhhh.'

He stroked the heel of his palm up and down her spine, feeling her relax, vertebrae by vertebrae. Careless to any impropriety, he then rested it in the small hollow at the top of her derrière, surreptitiously drawing tiny circles at the base. He tucked the hand he was holding close to his chest.

'Did you just sniff me?' he asked.

When Eliza directed a discreet glance at his face, he locked eyes with her.

'I thought you told me to *shhhh*. That would be preferable right now.'

'Preferable, but not half as much fun. Explain yourself, madam.'

Eliza sighed. 'I wondered whether you'd been drinking.'

'And why would you think that?' he asked.

'Because of how you're acting,' she mumbled, before burying her face in his shirtfront.

'How am I acting?'

'Like we're on a date ... or something.'

'We are on a date,' Alex whispered, dropping his voice an octave and pressing his mouth to her ear.

She lapsed into silence.

Alex wished he could tell what she was thinking. Should he say something? Take a risk and declare his feelings? Was it too soon? After all, just over two weeks ago, they were arguing over a basket of scones.

CHAPTER 21

Later

'Mind if we cut in?' asked Derek's irritating voice.

Alex's face must have expressed the savage feelings that the question invoked as Derek drew back a fraction and positioned Queenie slightly behind him as if for protection.

Alex warred with himself. Good manners required him to accede to Derek's request, but his instinctive reaction was to refuse and abscond with Eliza to someplace where no one could interrupt them. Of course, that would cause a scene and untold embarrassment.

Reluctantly he relinquished her, holding her hand a fraction longer than was necessary to try to communicate that their parting was not his preference. He was happy to see that Eliza looked like she'd just woken from a dream, a befuddled expression in her eyes, her lips parted as if in surprise.

Thankfully, the music tempo changed to that of a jazz foxtrot requiring a little more distance between partners than the waltz encouraged. As Derek danced Eliza down the floor, Alex heard him start up a ready stream of conversation.

He looked down into Queenie's face and forced himself

to smile. 'You look lovely tonight, my dear.' As opening gambits went, he thought it a good one.

Queenie inclined her head in acknowledgement and gave a shimmer, the satin weave enveloping and accentuating her curves, the fiery red hue reflected in the crystal-bead fringe. 'Yet not enough for you to abandon *her*,' she accused.

Alex raised an eyebrow at her tone. He didn't think he'd ever heard quite that note of pique in Queenie's voice before. It wouldn't be gentlemanly to remind her that they weren't exclusive or that he'd never intimated his heart was engaged in their liaison. If memory served him, she'd done most of the chasing.

The eyebrow had done the trick. Her tone moderated. 'I do hope we weren't interrupting anything important. Eliza looked a little ... agitated. Is everything all right?'

'Did she? Nothing for you to concern yourself about,' he said.

'I'd hate for Eliza to get hurt,' she persisted, unperturbed by his subtle warning.

'Why would she get hurt?' asked Alex and then wished he hadn't as he caught a triumphant gleam in Queenie's eye. He ensured his features were schooled into their usual urbane countenance.

'As you say, it's not for me to concern myself with ... but she's such a little romantic, and you're so ... practised. It would be easy for a girl to get the wrong idea,' she purred.

'Well, lucky there isn't any likelihood for misunderstanding,' he said.

'And then there's the little matter of Wil ... he's besotted. You must have noticed how Eliza lights up whenever he's around. You wouldn't want to spoil her chances, would you?'

Yes, I would! thought Alex fiercely. *In a heartbeat!* He'd need to have a word with Wil. Poaching carried serious consequences this side of the Pacific. Maybe he'd suggest to him to save his efforts for his next port – New Zealand.

'As astute as ever, my dear,' Alex said aloud, before leading Queenie into a pirouette as the last strains of the music died away.

'Oops, sorry,' apologised Derek for the third time in the last few minutes. 'I seem to have two left feet this evening.'

'And how lucky that you saved them both for me,' returned Eliza, wriggling her toes in her shoes to make sure they still were in good working order.

Looking up, she caught Derek's surprised expression and immediately felt guilty. It wasn't his fault she was out of sorts, but he could help that his dancing bore a close resemblance to that of a praying mantis – all arms and legs. She added a polite smile as a small concession to her terse words.

'Maybe move your feet back a little quicker,' he suggested.

Really! So now it was her fault? Eliza gazed up at the forest archways above the dance floor and counted to ten ... and then kept counting until she could summon her sense of humour, picturing Derek, mantis-like, with a triangular head and bulging eyes ...

'Enjoying the evening so far?' she asked cheekily.

'It's been grand. The bow thing was a little awkward, but the admiral and his wife were such good sports. The mayor was a little taken aback. But Queenie helped smooth everything over. Had them eating out of her hand.'

Eliza could imagine. *The admiral and mayor had probably been salivating*, she thought unkindly.

'You know there's nothing going on between Queenie and me ... we aren't serious, or anything. Just a bit of harmless fun.'

Oh my God, thought Eliza, *please don't suggest that we get back together!*

She remained non-committal in the hope of deterring the suggestion, but it seemed that Derek would not be discouraged.

'We could pick up where we left off,' he said affably, as if suggesting they share a meal. 'Make our own fun, you and I.'

Eliza had read that the female mantis would often cannibalise its partner. Even before consummation. Little wonder if its prospective mate was as inept as Derek.

'Um ... I don't think so,' said Eliza. 'Best we remain friends. Platonic friends.'

'No need to be hasty. Have a think about it. Oops, sorry, those toes of yours again.'

Eliza had never abandoned a partner in the middle of a dance before, but Derek came close to becoming her first. Thankfully, as the music ended, Alex appeared with Queenie in tow. He masterfully reunited Queenie and Derek, took hold of Eliza's hand and bid the other couple goodbye.

'And good riddance,' Eliza muttered under her breath.

'Did I just hear you wish Derek good riddance?' asked Alex in mock horror.

Eliza sighed. 'Just me being churlish. Derek stepped all over my feet, then blamed me and my lack of dancing skills. He then cheerfully suggested we start dating again.'

'What? You're not considering it, are you?' asked Alex. '*Are you?*'

'Yes,' replied Eliza, her humour returning. 'I'm sure that

under Queenie's tutorage, he's much improved. If I can have her work on his dancing ... he'll be a prize catch.'

Eliza slanted a look at Alex from the corner of her eyes. His jaw was clenched and his smile, if you could call it that, looked grim. Alex compelled her in the direction of the balcony stairs, reminding her of a determined tug boat. They passed a bed of 'red-hot poker flowers' standing sentinel – she could have used one of those on Derek, she mused.

Leading her to the farthermost corner, Alex saw them seated and then turned to her. 'Tell me you're not serious.'

'Well, I did suggest it wasn't such a good idea ... but he encouraged me not to be too hasty.'

Eliza smiled into Alex's disbelieving face. She wondered how long she could string this out for. Maybe she'd ask his opinion. Or suggest they list the pros and cons before taking a vote. She suppressed a giggle. She'd never known Alex's sense of humour to go missing before.

'So, I've given it some thought.' She paused.

'And?'

'I'm going to decline,' she said, bumping him with her shoulder. 'How stupid do you think I am?'

'Do you want me to take care of him?'

'What?' Eliza asked. Alex sounded like some protagonist knight.

'I mean, would you like me to have a word with him? Warn him off?'

'Thank you, but I can take care of myself.'

Alex nodded, although he didn't look convinced.

Silence followed.

'You and Queenie looked very cosy,' Eliza ventured at last.

'Eliza, let's not discuss my relationship with Queenie.'

Why was he terse with her? Eliza's humour evaporated. 'Right. So, you can pass judgement on my non-relationship with Derek, but I'm not allowed to comment on yours with Queenie.'

'My arrangement with Queenie has nothing to do with us.'

Eliza sucked in a breath. 'You're absolutely right, Alex. There is no *us*, so what possible bearing could your arrangement have.'

'Eliza, that's not what I meant ...'

'I'm not going to quarrel with you, Alex. I overstepped the mark. Call it ... sisterly concern. I'm sorry. It won't happen again.'

'You are *not* my sister.'

'That's true. I'm not your sister ... and finding it difficult to be your friend. You know, I miss our old rapport.'

'I can explain ...'

Eliza rose to her feet. 'No need. Look, there's Bec and she's waving us to come and join her and Jim. Shall we?' Not waiting for an answer, Eliza turned and navigated her path along the balcony, back the way they'd come.

Relationships, she decided, were so much easier when your heart wasn't involved.

CHAPTER 22

Thursday 30 July 1925
It Had to Be You

'Ain't this the cat's meow? We don't have anything like this back home.'

'It's pretty special,' agreed Eliza, smiling as she watched Wil contort his neck to take in the theatre's interior, keeping one hand on his hat and the other tangled with hers. 'The Princess is my favourite theatre in all of Melbourne.'

Wil had managed, she didn't know how given its popularity, to acquire two tickets to the musical comedy *No, No, Nanette*. She clutched the rolled art souvenir they'd been handed on arrival to her chest – she was going to frame it.

'Lovin' those little pictures on the walls. And those sculptures.'

'Rumour has it that they're figures of some of the city's waitresses.'

Wil peered closer. 'Well I'll be.'

Eliza grinned, leading him up the marble staircase. 'Come on, let's have that drink you promised me.'

Hesitating at the entrance to the first-floor lounge bar, Eliza marvelled, as she always did, at the bank of floor-to-ceiling stained glass windows that formed one wall. The effect was better from the street side, where the internal illumination rained a kaleidoscope of colour over the pavement.

'Yoo-hoo ... Eliza ...'

'Ain't that Alex's friend?' murmured Wil, calling Eliza's attention to Queenie, who was waving her arm like a giant palm frond in the far corner. An impassive Alex stood beside her.

Eliza felt her enthusiasm for the evening wane. 'Yes.'

'We don't have to join them.'

Eliza sighed. 'It would look rude. It's only one drink.'

Wil navigated their way as quickly as the crowd would allow.

'Hello, Eliza.' Queenie kissed the air to the side of Eliza's face in greeting and gave Wil a considered inspection before offering him her hand. 'I'm Queenie. I don't think we've been introduced.'

Alex seemed to come to life, manufacturing a smile and completing introductions.

Wil caught the attention of a circulating waiter. 'A drink anyone? Eliza, champagne? Two ... make that four, will you?'

The waiter proceeded to pour four glasses from his tray, stuffed the note Wil offered into his pocket and melted back into the crowd.

'Thanks, and cheers.' Alex raised his glass.

'Cheers,' returned Wil.

'Enjoying your time in Melbourne, Wil?' Alex asked politely.

'It's been the bee's knees. Everyone's been so welcoming. And Eliza here has made things extra special,' replied Wil as he wrapped an arm around her waist and kissed the side of her temple.

Eliza felt her eyes widen in surprise, but conscious of Alex's gaze, pretended that this was a common occurrence, even managing a benign smile. She didn't know what Alex wanted of her. Their quarrel – if you could call it that – had thrown her off balance.

Sipping her champagne, she listened to the conversation, glad she wasn't called on to do more than nod and smile. Queenie was at her most gregarious – she loved an audience.

'Time to take our seats,' said Queenie as the melodic chimes sounded. 'Where are you both sitting?'

'Dress circle,' said Eliza, examining the tickets Wil handed her.

'Us too. How fabulous. Row H, down the back, away from prying eyes. You?'

'Um, towards the front, row A.'

'Maybe see you at the interval ... or afterwards,' cooed Queenie before ushers led them in opposite directions.

Not if I have anything to do with it, Eliza vowed. She was here to enjoy herself. Wil, she was discovering, was attentive and seemed to like touching her – a brush of a hand on her arm, gentle pressure on her back. And then there was that kiss in the bar – he'd caught her off guard. She wasn't used to being on the receiving end of such open shows of affection.

The hum of conversation quietened as act one opened – heralded by the parting of the majestic rose-and-gold-brocaded curtain. Wil didn't wrestle her for the armrest as Alex had done on their previous outing. Instead, he gathered her hand in his, holding it in his lap. Eliza could imagine Alex raising an eyebrow, but it wasn't as if they were engaging in activity that would shock polite society. Later, she could feel Wil's thumb shaping circles on her wrist. She felt fluttery and reminded herself to breathe. Was she supposed to notice or to return Wil's action, Eliza wondered? She was such a novice in these things, it was so frustrating.

During the interval, Eliza declined the experience of circulating. The thought of her nose pressed against suit coats or attending to a spilled drink ruining her silk-velvet dress, while conducting a conversation over the noise of a thousand others, was not appealing.

Instead, she and Wil stood, hip to hip, gazing out over the balcony to the stalls below, and the pit beneath the stage where the orchestra were planted.

They discussed the décor. Wil wasn't fussed with the *rose du barri* colour scheme for the furnishings, declaring it too feminine. 'Couldn't see this lasting long in our quarters,' he quipped. 'Maybe more that colour on that yonder wall.'

Eliza conceded the Wedgewood blue might be more appropriate.

Conversation turned to the performance. They agreed the storyline took a little concentration, but that the pitfalls and complications acted out were fun, the dancing energetic and the songs memorable.

'Does Alex have any prior claim to you, Eliza?' Wil asked suddenly.

'Um … Why do you ask?'

'He watches you.'

Hope ignited, but Eliza quashed it – the memory of Alex's brusque refusal to discuss Queenie's status in his life, fresh

THE BATTLE FOR ELIZA

in her mind. Still, they'd gone beyond a familial relationship and she owed it to Wil to be honest ... well, more honest. 'We're ... friends,' Eliza prevaricated.

'The eyes are an index of a man, Eliza, and his are bold, possessive and unwaverin' where you're concerned.'

This time the flame refused to be extinguished, despite Eliza reminding herself that outside of a couple of kisses she had no evidence that Alex's attention had gone beyond friendship. And those kisses could be part of his tutoring. How gauche would she feel if she read more into things than was intended? 'Perhaps he's being protective. You sailors have a reputation, you know ... dangerous and dashing.'

'Is that what they say?'

'Among other things,' teased Eliza with a tilt of her head and what she hoped was a coy look.

'Would you be interested in some dangerous dancin' and a dashin' supper after this?' asked Wil with a wriggle of his eyebrows.

'Maybe I could be persuaded,' Eliza agreed with a smile, happy that the conversation had steered away from Alex. If only she could control her thoughts as easily. Wil's observations had sent an electric charge through her – bold, possessive and unwavering, he'd said. Was it possible Alex had started to see her as something more than a friend? And what did that mean? He seemed as involved with Queenie as ever. And what about Wil? Did she have feelings for him? She didn't think her heart was involved. But she enjoyed his company ... and kisses ... It was all too confusing!

As the lights dimmed, they resumed their seats.

Eliza and Wil didn't encounter Alex and Queenie as they made their way out of the theatre. They'd hurried out in the first wave of exits to avoid the crush and were soon tripping along Collins Street on their way to Birmingham's.

'Thank you, Wil. That was so much fun.'

'Anythin' for my best girl,' said Wil, swinging their joined hands back and forth in an exaggerated manner. 'Now it'll be my pleasure to feed you ... and then we'll dance the night away. I don't have to be back on ship until three, so plenty of time to see you home afterwards.'

Birmingham's was crowded with sailors and girls. Wil paid the entry fee, Eliza shrugged out of her coat and left it in the care of the attendant, and they paused at the entrance to observe the scene.

Eliza noted that the Birmingham Syncopators were in fine form. Hundreds of couples were circling the floor to the jazz melody 'Yes Sir That's My Baby'. Some walking, the essential of the foxtrot, others doing variations, with side steps, turning and reversing, but all had their partners firmly in an embrace.

Wil whispered the word 'supper', took hold of her hand and they plunged into an ocean of blue jackets and diaphanous dresses, emerging at the entrance to the lounge where a fare of sumptuous proportions had been laid out.

An enthusiastic shout sounded and Eliza found herself escorted to a small table where Johnnie and Jenny Butler sat.

'Join us. We just sat down,' Johnnie said, clapping Wil on the shoulder.

Eliza gave Johnnie a shy smile, Jenny a quick hug and sank into the chair beside her.

'We've just been to see *No, No, Nanette* at the Princess. Have you seen it?' At the shake of Jenny's head, Eliza enthused, 'It was very funny. You must go.'

THE BATTLE FOR ELIZA

'Baby, do you want to go?' asked Johnnie, laying his arm along the back of Jenny's chair and looking at her much like a puppy at an ice-cream.

'If we have time ...' said Jenny cryptically with a matching smile.

Eliza's antennae bristled. The energy between Johnnie and Jenny was electric. Something was going on. What was it Bec had intimated? She wished she'd paid attention.

'Didn't you promise me supper?' asked Eliza of Wil, eager to have Jenny to herself.

'These Australian girls, always thinkin' of their stomachs,' teased Wil with a wink at her.

'Come on, Johnnie, our girls need sustenance.'

As they left for the supper table, Eliza turned to Jenny. 'Anything you want to tell me?'

Jenny hesitated.

'Don't even think about suggesting there is nothing going on.'

From the neck of her dress, Jenny withdrew a chain with a silver ring set with diamonds dangling from the end. On closer examination, it was a white gold band encircling a central stone. It was the biggest diamond Eliza had ever seen. Her eyes widened at the implication.

'This means, you're ...'

'Engaged,' finished Jenny. 'Johnnie asked me earlier tonight. You're the first person I've told ... I am super excited.'

Eliza looked at the young woman, her boss and friend for the last eighteen months, and pulled her in for a hug.

'Oh my ... you sly thing ... I am so happy for you ... but are you sure? It's only been a week!'

'I know ... things have moved quickly. Johnnie's going

143

to ask for a licence and permission to waive the three-day notice period so we can be wed before he leaves for New Zealand.'

'And what about you? What are you going to do when he sails?'

'He wants me to travel to Alabama to meet his parents and be there when his ship arrives in a few months. He's going to wire them to expect me.'

'Jenny —'

'How am I going to tell my mum?' she wailed.

Before she could respond, she heard a muttered oath from Johnnie, who had returned and was pulling his intended into his arms. Wil also returned, juggling a plate of food.

'Now who's upset my girl?' Johnnie said, directing a glare Eliza's way.

She was both intimidated and touched by Johnnie's protectiveness. His scar stood out something fierce when he was mad, making him look gladiatorial.

'I was just telling Eliza our news ... and then I remembered I still have to tell Mum. I feel sick at the thought.'

'You leave everythin' to me, darlin',' he said, kissing her forehead. 'I reckon she'll be as pleased as punch.'

Evidently, Johnnie hadn't met Mrs Butler, a thought Eliza kept sensibly to herself.

'Let me add my congratulations, Jenny,' said Wil. 'Johnnie's been sweatin' like a sinner in church these last few days. I'd hate to have sailed with him if you'd turned him down.'

'Don't you be listenin' to him, darlin', he's just messin'.'

Wil grinned.

'This really calls for champagne ... but we'll have to make

do with lemonade and cake. Here's to Jenny and Johnnie,' toasted Eliza.

After supper, Wil led Eliza onto the floor and wrapped his right arm around her waist, securing her right hand and holding it close to his chest. Eliza was surprised but not perturbed. She tucked her face into his shoulder and surrendered to the sweet jazz, the slow tempo perfect for her mood. *It Had to Be You* – maybe it was a sign.

CHAPTER 23

An Hour Later

Alex arrived at Birmingham's feeling out of sorts. He'd spent half his time at the theatre evading Queenie's flirtatious invitations and curbing her wandering right hand as it had inched its way up his thigh. The other half had been split between trying to follow an increasingly complicated plot and wondering what Eliza saw in Wil. At one stage, he'd heard a growl and realised when Queenie sent him a concerned look that it had emanated from him. *What did the seaman have that he didn't? He wasn't conceited, but he did own a mirror and women didn't flee at the sight of him. Quite the opposite!*

Alex's temper was not improved at the sight of Eliza enveloped by Wil on the dance floor. His mouth tightened and it was all he could do to return Queenie's commentary civilly. She excused herself to freshen up and Alex took a deep breath.

Someone clapped a hand on his shoulder and Alex swung round with a thunderous look in his eyes. Daniel's face swam into his vision, the lights from the chandelier giving his skin a bronzed hue.

'Mate? What's up?'

'Remind me how long these *Jack Tars* are in town?' Alex emphasised his question with a jerk of his head in the direction of the dance floor.

Daniel paused, a little bewildered by the question. 'Day eight. Another six days. Why?'

'Damn fine brother you are. You're supposed to be chaperoning your sister.' This last statement he said with a glare in Daniel's direction.

'And here I am. You're not making any sense,' said Daniel, shaking his head.

'That marine has been romancing Eliza all night ... getting up close and personal ... first at the theatre and now here ... hey ... where are they off to?'

Alex stepped in the direction of the couple as they weaved their way towards the entrance.

Instantly, Daniel's hands were around Alex's shoulders, holding him in place. 'I don't think that's a good idea in your state. Where do you think you're going?'

'Where do you think they're going? Aren't you concerned?'

'Wil is escorting Eliza home. He spoke with me earlier,' Daniel dismissed Alex's question. 'What's wrong with you?'

'Well, I don't like the way he looks at her. And I don't like the way she's looking at him. She shouldn't be encouraging him. Who knows what'll happen?'

'I think it's time we had a chat,' Daniel returned firmly, arresting Alex's attention and halting his tirade. 'If my best mate is going to start acting like an idiot over my little sister, then I better understand your intentions,' he continued in the same tone.

Alex shrugged Daniel off and took a step back.

'Tomorrow. I'm not in the mood to explain myself tonight.'

'Make it breakfast. At the Federal. And make sure you are in the right mood as I have a few questions, and you better have some answers. In the meantime, don't do anything stupid. In fact, it might be best to take yourself home.' And with that Daniel strode off.

'Everything all right, sweetie?' Queenie asked as she boldly attached herself to his left arm – he could feel the warmth of her right breast pressed to his bicep.

'I'm not good company at the moment,' he said, giving her a wry smile to soften the rejection. In previous months, Queenie would have jollied him out of any mood. She was playful, sure of her own attractiveness, and as provocative as hell in that racy, seductive way that many of his set tried to emulate. The world was changing, and he wasn't complaining. But her hair colour was all wrong – no treacle tresses – her mouth a little too wide and glossy, and he doubted she could blush to save herself. Unlike someone else he knew.

Queenie pouted.

'Sorry, but I have some homework to do for a meeting tomorrow.'

'I could help you.'

'Not tonight. But thanks, anyway. Would you like me to see you home?'

'I think I'll stay a while. When will I see you?'

'Saturday. I plan to watch the competition heat. You're acting as Philip's escort, aren't you?'

She smiled in response. 'I'll save you a dance ... if I remember.' And with that she melted into the throng of

THE BATTLE FOR ELIZA

dancers milling around the edge of the floor. He wondered how long Queenie would disregard his growing indifference and what she'd do about it.

He sighed. A fabulous end to a night when he'd been increasingly frustrated and derailed by Eliza ... and now he had a best mate to placate.

CHAPTER 24

Friday 31 July 1925

'Never could handle a confrontation on an empty stomach,' said Daniel, wiping his fingers on a serviette. 'And I've never had to call anyone to account over Eliza before. Certainly didn't think it'd be you, mate. What's the go?'

Over a piece of buttered toast, Alex eyed his best mate. He'd expected after Daniel's remarks the previous evening to be met with heated words, questions and denouncements. Instead, they'd discussed the tram electrification project Alex was working on, exchanged gossip from the Lord Mayor's Ball and made plans for the weekend. All the while working their way through the offerings from the Federal's breakfast buffet.

Alex was glad that Daniel looked as uncomfortable as he felt. He called for more coffee and took a gulp from the replenished cup. 'I've developed feelings for Eliza ... I think I'm in love with her.'

'You mean in lust.'

'I'm going to forget you said that.'

'I mean, with her new hair, clothes and attitude, I'm not

surprised. She seems more confident and attractive. And then there's the attention she's receiving from that navy bloke.'

'I will not be held responsible for my actions if you continue, best mate or not,' growled Alex.

'What about Queenie? If you're serious —'

'I am serious.'

'Then you can't continue your arrangement with her.'

'I have no intention of doing so. But it's complicated,' said Alex, rubbing his eyes. 'I think she already suspects. I've been making excuses for a week or so now as to why I can't spend the night.'

'You, celibate! That explains your temper of late.'

'No. My temper is the responsibility of your sister. Her refusal to see me as anything more than an adopted big brother. The amount of time she devotes to Wil. The attention she's drawing with her new looks and attitude. She just doesn't make it easy.'

'Goodness, you do have it bad,' said Daniel, shaking his head. 'And all that ...' he waved his hand around, unable to find the word, '... for my little sister! It's hard to imagine. No, don't hit me. I feel relieved that you've left out any messy emotional stuff. There's only so much a best mate can deal with, even on a full stomach.'

'I assume we're not drawing pistols at dawn, then?' Alex joked.

Daniel shook his head.

'Then you've no objections to me pursuing her?'

'As if Eliza would thank me for interfering,' said Daniel.

'Any advice?'

'I don't feel comfortable giving you advice on romancing

my sister. Only that if you're serious, you must break with Queenie. For good. I won't stand by and allow Eliza to be hurt.'

'I have no intention of hurting her. In fact, I seem to be the only one suffering at this point in time.'

Daniel rubbed his chin. 'I can't see your usual stratagems working on Eliza.'

'No. I've tried ...' Alex paused to reconsider the wisdom of sharing with Daniel any details of his actions to date. He settled for, 'A couple of approaches, but she ends up laughing or giving me a friendly punch on the shoulder. She's impossible to get close to.' *Not entirely true*, he reflected, *he had had some success.*

'Argh, I've got to go. You've got that distracted air about you,' said Daniel, pushing back his chair and rising. 'One piece of inside information I can offer. Apparently, Eliza has entered some waltz competition with that sailor fellow.'

Alex nodded.

'Complicit, are you?'

'No, but I have my sources.'

'Well, *Table Talk* delivered the news to our house yesterday. And let's just say it wasn't well received. There were even tears,' said Daniel, rolling his eyes. 'I stepped in and assured my parents that you and I would be in attendance ... heats are tomorrow night.'

'I'll be there.'

'Good. As will I, despite having had other plans for tomorrow night. Thank goodness Evelyn is understanding. Although it'll cost me,' Daniel said, sharing a wry grin with his friend. 'Thanks for breakfast. See you tomorrow.'

Alex ordered another coffee. He was glad he and Daniel

had cleared the air. He didn't want to lose his best mate. They'd learn how to navigate those topics that would now be off limits, which would require some getting used to. His more immediate problem was charting a course in pursuit of Eliza. Like an alpine bog, one wrong step ...

They had seemed to be getting on so well at the Lord Mayor's Ball until the conversation had turned to Queenie. Eliza's words came back to haunt him. *'There is no us.'* He probably had bruises from the number of times he'd kicked himself after his handling of things that night.

Daniel was right. He couldn't make progress with Eliza, until he'd ended things with Queenie. Nor could he warn off Wil. He'd come close the night he'd escorted him and his mate Johnnie back to the city after dinner at the Sinclairs' home, but that Johnnie was as big as an ox, and that scar ...

Then again, maybe he didn't need to warn off Wil. After all, he was only in town for another six days. It was unlikely that anything too serious could develop in that time. Maybe he could take things slow, take opportunities as they presented themselves and court Eliza in earnest once the Yanks had sailed. That would also give him a week to end things cordially with Queenie. Not for him, the frenzied merry-go-round permissiveness heralded by others – old-fashioned manners were part of his personal code of behaviour.

Alex smiled. He loved a good plan.

CHAPTER 25

That Evening

'Bec, I hardly recognise myself,' exclaimed Eliza as she studied her face by the overhead light and the wall mirror in the staff room at Birmingham's. It wasn't large – Eliza had seen bigger closets – but it was private. Her eyes were the first thing she noticed. Bec had accentuated her eyelids with coppery gold and highlighted the inner and outer corners with silver sheen. Combined with the eyelash beautifier, her green eyes seemed to blaze from her face. She held the ballgown for this evening's competition heat in front of her and examined the effect.

'Stunning. Even if I do say so myself,' remarked Bec from behind her shoulder.

When Eliza turned around to give her friend a hug, Bec cried, 'No! You'll smudge all my good work.' So, she satisfied herself with a noisy air kiss to both Bec's cheeks.

'Reward me by reporting the progress of your romances,' Bec instructed, pulling up a chair.

Eliza made a face and returned the gown to a peg on the wall. '*Haphazard* would be the word I'd use,' she confessed.

'Wil's great fun. We've been to the movies and the theatre. Our practice sessions – even the lessons with drill sergeant Mr B – are enjoyable. Wil's kisses make me feel like I've been wrapped in a warm blanket.'

'And Alex?'

Eliza hugged herself. 'The opposite. He makes me feel as if I'm about to self-combust. And if I take the initiative, he calls a halt to things … Wil says Alex watches me. I don't know, Bec. And Queenie is still in the frame,' she finished glumly.

'I'm not so sure. Queenie hasn't had her usual sparkle of late. And Alex seems … distracted. I'd go as far as saying, uninterested.'

'I don't know about that. They were at the theatre the other night – back row – probably engaged in their own petting party.'

'We could give them a test. See how much of the story line they remember,' Bec joked. 'Now, let's get you dressed for this rehearsal.'

Eliza stripped and shimmied into her gown. She presented her back to Bec to attend to the tiny buttons while she twitched the layers of sea-green chiffon to make sure they draped correctly over the asymmetrical hem. It was a daring dress, a hint of calf and knee and an opening at the front to allow for greater movement. Iridescent round and tear-shaped sequins were sewn into the topmost overlay and sprinkled across the bodice.

'You look like a princess,' said Bec as Eliza turned to face her.

Eliza crossed her arms. 'It's beautiful, but I feel so exposed. Maybe if it had sleeves or a higher neckline.'

'You look good enough to eat. Alex will go berserk when

he sees you in this.'

'Do you think so?'

'Oh, I'll bet money on it. Although, he'll probably disguise it under his usual social mask.'

There was a tap on the door. 'We're starting in ten minutes, girls,' called Mrs B before they heard her stiletto clicks fade away.

Eliza took a deep breath, smoothed her hands over her skirts and assumed the poise of a freshly tutored debutante as she opened the door.

'How's Jenny? I haven't seen much of her lately,' asked Bec.

'It's a wonder she remembers to turn up to work some days. She forgot two meetings this week, and the YMCA head she was meeting with was not impressed,' said Eliza.

'What about the wedding planning?'

'She said that Johnnie smoothed everything over with her mum, who has resigned herself to a small wedding and is making plans to travel to the States with Jenny to meet the in-laws.'

'That's exciting. I expect she's nervous, though. Has anyone organised a present and drinks?'

'That was supposed to be me! Thanks for the reminder. And all before next Tuesday!' exclaimed Eliza. 'I'm going to need help.'

'Lucky you have a best friend who is a planning extraordinaire.'

Arriving on the edge of the floor, they waved to Wil, who sauntered over. 'Hello, beautiful ladies.' He leaned in for a welcoming kiss, but Eliza fended him away.

'Bec here will skewer you if her hard work is smudged,' she said, waving to her face.

Winking, he took her hand and made a show of raining kisses from her fingers to the top of her shoulder. 'I hope that's acceptable?'

Eliza batted him away, laughing.

He grazed the back of Bec's hand with a quick kiss before stepping back.

Wil's reaction bolstered her confidence, but the menacing look Mr B sent in their direction reminded her that wolf whistles played no part in ballroom etiquette.

She chided him softly, 'Shhhh. You'll get us kicked out of the competition.'

'Well, you should have thought of that before you dressed so darn pretty. We could always skip the dancing.'

'Wil!'

'Hush, I'm only jokin'.' He clasped her hand and gave it a squeeze.

Divided into sets of ten, Eliza and Wil were in the group that would take the floor last. The atmosphere was electric with nervous energy, and even the band seemed to be affected as their first few notes of a practice song were off-key.

Eliza glanced around the assemblage. Tuxedos were the uniform of choice for the men. In contrast, the plumage of their partners was a kaleidoscope of colours and styles. Jenny, beautiful in pink, was snuggled close to Johnnie, standing towards the back of their group, waiting for their turn. Eliza caught her eye and mouthed, *Good luck*.

A flash of silver announced the presence of Queenie, who'd arrived at the edge of the floor with Philip Dickson, the adjudicator. A murmur of appreciation and a couple of modulated whistles whispered through those assembled. Eliza wished she had a quarter of the woman's confidence and pizazz. A demure smile, at odds with the thigh-length slit in her gown and the wink she directed at one of the sailors closest to her, graced a face lightly powdered and rouged.

Mr B managed proceedings with military precision. He introduced his wife, resplendent in a gown covered with gold sequins, then Philip and finally Queenie, whose job was to manage Philip's hurriedly scribbled notes and scorings on the night. The rules were announced, and each partnership would be introduced before taking the floor. Each group was given one song to warm up to, before competing.

Eliza's nerves increased as the rehearsal continued. Every insect imaginable was fluttering, buzzing or jumping around inside her stomach. Butterflies, bees, grasshoppers, sandflies ... a veritable menagerie.

'Can I have the final group to the side of the floor, please?' boomed Mr B.

'That's us, babe. Relax. It's only rehearsal,' said Wil, giving her hand a reassuring squeeze.

Eliza smiled and took a deep, calming breath.

'Miss Eliza Sinclair and Seaman Wil Sanders,' announced Mr B, before Wil spun her onto the floor and tucked her hand into his elbow. He walked across the floor to position them nearest to where Bec sat.

'Good luck, you two,' Bec called encouragingly as the music began.

Eliza felt stiff and uncoordinated. She missed a lock step and stumbled through a series of fallaway steps before recovering her poise and managing to complete their warm-up.

'Well, if that's the worst you're going to throw at me, I think we'll be fine,' said Wil in a matter-of-fact tone.

THE BATTLE FOR ELIZA

'What? I'm dancing like someone with two left feet.'

'Or someone who cares too much. Is it the money?'

'No. I don't care about the money.'

'Then let's just concentrate on having some fun, huh? Getting out and enjoying ourselves,' said Wil, his tone turning serious. 'It's not every day I get to dress up and dance with a princess.'

'Flattery will get you everywhere,' said Eliza with a smile.

Finishing the warm-up, Wil guided Eliza to the far corner of the floor, devoid of other couples who had congregated closer to the band. As the music started, Eliza focused on Mr B's instructions during their lesson earlier in the week. *Take one step at a time, dance into your knees and centre yourself on your partner*, he'd said. She found herself relaxing and started when Wil spun her into a curtsy. It was over. She couldn't have told anyone what they'd danced, but Wil was smiling, so she must have done well.

'Wow! That felt great. Dance like that tomorrow night and I'll be in heaven,' Wil enthused.

'I can't remember much after the opening bars,' admitted Eliza, still feeling a little dazed, as if she'd misplaced time.

'Gather around, everyone,' boomed Mr B, waiting until they'd all shuffled forward before continuing. 'Tomorrow night, you'll return to your seats until the scores are tallied and the ten couples to move forward to the final are announced. After that, the floor will be opened to social dancing. Any questions?'

Someone asked what time they could access the building and whether the floor would be available for practice beforehand.

'Five-thirty and yes, until seven-thirty,' responded Mr B.

'Anything else? No? Good luck. And don't forget dancing tonight starts in an hour, buffet supper until midnight.'

Murmurs of appreciation followed the announcement. A buffet supper meant no formal interruption to dancing and attendees could graze when and as often as they liked. Eliza was a big fan as her idea of food was purely to fuel the body for more dancing.

Promising to meet back in the lobby in half an hour, Eliza and Bec took their leave of Wil so that Eliza could change.

Raised voices assailed them as they walked down the corridor. Through a doorway on the left, they glimpsed Queenie, hands on her hips, and Philip Dickson, arms crossed over his chest, in discussion. At the same time, an unseen hand closed the door from within with a firm click, hiding the confrontation from curious eyes.

'I wonder what that's about?' mused Eliza, opening the door to the staff room.

'I'm not sure, but something happened while you were on the floor,' said Bec, spinning her around to deal with her buttons. 'There were a few terse words, before Philip distanced himself from her, choosing to watch the heats with Mr B.'

'I didn't notice anything. I was too busy enjoying myself,' said Eliza with a roll of her eyes as she peeled the gown down her body. 'Who knew that having fun was so akin to hard work.'

As they walked back towards the ballroom, having wrapped and stowed Eliza's gown in readiness for tomorrow evening, Queenie drifted towards them. Her face mirrored none of the turmoil of her discussion, although she wore a distracted air.

'Hi, Queenie,' said Bec. 'Beautiful dress.'

'What? ... Oh, thank you. A present from my aunt.'

'Will we see you later tonight?' Bec asked over her shoulder as she continued down the corridor.

'I expect so, unless I get a better offer.'

Eliza directed a smile Queenie's way, stepping sideways to allow the woman to pass, before moving to follow Bec.

'An exquisite ballroom dress you wore earlier, Eliza. A real man catcher. Fishing for anyone in particular?'

Eliza laughed. 'I don't know what you mean.'

'Don't you? You'll need more than a dress to satisfy Alex's appetite.'

Eliza directed another smile Queenie's way before escaping. She took a deep breath to slow the pounding of her heart as she caught up with her friend.

'What was that about?' demanded Bec.

'A compliment. Of sorts. Backhanded, straight down the line.'

'And what was that about Alex? Was she warning you off?'

'You would put a bat to shame,' said Eliza, shaking her head. 'Yes. Not that Queenie has anything to worry about from me.'

Bec's enigmatic smile lingered in Eliza's mind for the rest of the night, invading her thoughts at the most inappropriate times. Promoting possibilities and opportunities she'd never entertained seriously before. It was amazing what a dress could do for one's confidence.

CHAPTER 26

Saturday 1 August 1925

'How are you feeling?' asked Bec, twining her arm with Eliza's as they stood watching the couples on the dance floor glide past.

'Nervous. I'm glad Mum and Dad decided not to make the trip in tonight. Daniel assured them that both he and Alex would be in attendance. Dad's reaction to this dress would have been to add a coat, for warmth.'

'What was Alex's reaction?'

'He didn't say anything. But he keeps watching me, as if I'm some sort of puzzle.'

Bec smiled.

'Stop that. Your smile cost me sleep last night.' And not just Bec's cryptic smile, she admitted. Increasingly, she'd been dreaming of Alex, his attentions – mirroring Wil's words of the other evening – growing bolder, more possessive and unwavering each time she closed her eyes.

Bec chuckled. 'Here's Wil, looking very debonair. He should add some spice to the evening.'

'Hello, darlin' girl,' said Wil. A broad smile accompanied

a kiss to the top of her shoulder. 'See, I remembered not to muss up your beautiful face. And hello to you, too, pretty lady,' he directed to Bec.

It wasn't until Eliza's eyes collided with Alex's, a few feet away, that she realised she'd automatically sought out his response to Wil's greeting. His eyes blazed, contradicting a face schooled to blandness.

Wil turned his head to discover the cause of Eliza's distraction, offering Alex a tight smile and a brisk salute. Eliza heard him chuckle as he turned back to face her. 'He looks like a pirate, without the eye patch.'

'And the parrot,' Bec added, flapping her arms.

Eliza giggled.

'That's better,' approved Wil. 'Let's go and warm up. Excuse us, Bec.'

Alex gritted his teeth as he watched Wil lead Eliza onto the dance floor, and Bec turn and walk towards him. She was formidable and took her role as best friend seriously.

'Good evening, Bec.'

'It shows promise.'

At his raised brows, she smiled pertly and turned to stand beside him to better view the floor. 'What do you think of Eliza's dress?'

'The colour suits her,' he replied. He could have added he found the design tantalised and tormented him. He was still devising the best way to get Eliza out of it. But that thought couldn't be shared in company, certainly not present company.

'Is that the best you can do, Alex? She looks like a dream.'

'Remind me when you and I started sharing confidences?'

asked Alex, folding his arms.

'Since you started to pay attention to my best friend,' said Bec, attending to an invisible speck of something on the bodice of her black dress before spearing him with a look.

Alex wasn't a chess player, but he played a mean game of draughts and he would not be lured to affirm or deny the truth of Bec's comment.

Alex smiled. 'Daniel's frequent dereliction of duty means Eliza's wellbeing falls to me. It pays to be attentive.'

Bec's hoot of laughter had heads turning.

'What's so funny?' asked Daniel, appearing beside them.

'Alex and I were playing truth or dare, but I fear he's broken the rules and so must pay a forfeit.'

'Pay her no attention,' said Alex. 'She's high on the night's excitement.'

'I hope so for your sake. I still wear the scars from previous penalties,' teased Daniel.

A fierce ally and a dangerous enemy, thought Alex. He needed to maintain Bec's support.

At eight o'clock, a drum roll cleared the dance floor, and Mr and Mrs B took centrestage to welcome everyone and thank them for coming.

They must have made a striking couple when they'd competed, Alex mused. Mr B liked to boast that they'd never been beaten in waltz at any competition level – local, state or national. On the odd occasion that they were coaxed into a demonstration, they were spellbinding. Mr B always finished these dances by patting his wife on her bottom and telling her that she was improving and to keep practising. It always got a laugh.

Philip Dickson, the flamboyant dance master, spun onto

the floor and finished with a bell kick to the left and then to the right to great applause when introduced. He in turn gestured for Queenie to join him as Mr B explained her role and the rules of the competition.

Alex watched her sashay onto the floor amidst whistles and cheers. She blew kisses to the crowd before aiming one directly towards him. Amused, he caught it and pretended to pocket it, as Queenie returned to the sidelines.

'Not well done of you,' hissed Bec. 'What are you playing at?'

Alex raised a single eyebrow, choosing to ignore her.

Bec scowled, giving him her back to speak to Daniel.

Alex swallowed. Bec's barb had hit its mark. *Such a stupid thing to do. He'd been acting ... reacting to Queenie's blatant show ... of possession.* He berated himself, realising the display of proprietary had been targeted at both Eliza and him. To demonstrate Queenie's supposed importance in Alex's affections. And he'd played into her hands. *What must Eliza be thinking? God, he was such an idiot!* His eyes sought Eliza. He watched her fuss with Wil's collar points and sighed. *They looked like an old married couple.*

Eliza admired how the light from the chandeliers reflected in the silver sequins that covered Queenie's dress – she resembled a flame.

But she was unprepared for the kiss and her reaction.

'That girl knows what she wants,' remarked Wil in Eliza's ear.

'And how to get it,' said Eliza, annoyed that Alex had play-acted catching it and secreting it in his pocket, earning him a scorching look from the sultry blonde. She wondered *what else they were still sharing ... and how often.*

The Syncopators played the opening chords of the waltz 'Kiss Me Goodnight', and the first group of dancers were introduced to the crowd amidst loud cheers.

As if sensing she was upset, Wil complained in her ear, 'Help, I've got two sabres threatening my throat.'

Eliza looked up to find him pushing and pulling at the points of his wing-tip collar.

'They're there to make sure you keep your head up,' she teased, patting his cheek and taking over.

As the second group were introduced, Eliza tamed Wil's collar points. If it had been a ruse to return her good humour and relax her, it had worked. Alex was all but forgotten and only a few butterflies remained.

Eliza turned her attention to the floor and was soon caught up in the music, the performances and the atmosphere. The crowd felt like a warm hug. The shipmates of the sailors were boisterous, their cheering on occasion drowning out the band. Laughter, cries of *don't give up your day job*, and suggestions that the men's technique resembled *swabbing the deck* were interspersed with applause and calls of *well done*.

By the time Eliza and Wil were called to the floor, she was feeling calm. During the warm-up, they'd almost collided with Johnnie and Jenny; contact was avoided by a swiftly executed spin turn.

'That was a bit of excitement,' said Eliza, her eyes darting left and right, anticipating another collision.

'Navigation never was Johnnie's strong point,' said Wil with a scowl at his friend over the top of Eliza's head. 'We'll start at the opposite end of the floor from him for the heat.'

The music ended. The couples repositioned themselves

around the floor, Wil keeping Johnnie starboard, much to Eliza's amusement. To the sounds of 'I'm Forever Blowing Bubbles', Eliza tuned into the music and Wil's cues. She heard the crowd as from a distance – she'd have had to have been deaf not to hear anything. Briefly, she registered Alex's face as they danced past – but it was gone before she could gauge his reaction.

As the orchestra concluded the melody, Wil spun Eliza towards the side of the floor, where she pirouetted and sank into a curtsey in front of her best friend, brother and Alex. As she rose, she spared Alex a furtive glance but kept her eyes deliberately focused on Bec and the smile she found there. She was still upset by his public display of intimacy with Queenie.

Calls of 'Well done' followed her and Wil across the floor to join the other couples to await the results.

'Trouble's brewing,' murmured Wil, nodding to where Queenie sat, adorning a tiny table surrounded by scoresheets. She covered a small yawn as she watched the efforts of Mrs B to organise and tally the scores. In contrast, the Palais matriarch's lips were pursed, cheeks drawn. Mrs B waved Queenie's hand away from a pile of papers she'd been intending to pick up. 'But here comes the cavalry,' he quipped as Mr B and Philip Dickson arrived on the scene. In a matter of minutes, Philip had replaced Queenie, who was escorted by Mr B to the lounge.

Eliza held her breath as the band's drum roll introduced Mr B and Philip Dickson to the floor to read out the ten finalists.

'In no particular order …' announced Mr B loudly.

After couple number five, Eliza still retained hope for

Wil and her. By couple number seven, her shoulders had slumped, and after couple number nine was read out she turned to Wil with disappointment written across her face.

'And last, but certainly not least, Miss Eliza Sinclair and Seaman Wil Sanders.'

'Come on, honey, that's us,' said Wil, grabbing Eliza's hand and pushing through those couples who'd missed out, including Johnnie and Jenny.

Eliza couldn't stop smiling, her happiness bubbling up inside her and flowing across her face. Her joy seemed limitless. She hugged Wil's arm so tightly that he jokingly complained he'd have bruises.

'Join us for the finals on Wednesday August fifth, at eight o'clock to see who will be crowned Birmingham's Fleet Waltz Champions,' Mr B reminded everyone. 'And following the competition, we'll have a demonstration of the Charleston by some of the folks from the USS *Pennsylvania*.'

That news was met with applause, after which he continued, 'A huge thankyou to Philip Dickson, his assistant, our very own Queenie Nolan, and of course my own dear heart, Nola.' More applause. 'Social dancing until midnight. I leave you in the melodic hands of Art Bobbie and the Birmingham Syncopators. Take it away, Art.'

Eliza turned to make way for the dancers flooding the floor and was crushed in Bec's arms before being spun in a circle.

'Congratulations! You must be so excited,' gushed Bec. 'This calls for a new dress.'

'What? No, this one will be fine.' Eliza laughed at her friend's enthusiasm.

'You have no say in it. Christine and I have it all worked out.'

'Congratulations, little sister, you did great ... you, too, mate,' said Daniel, planting a kiss on Eliza's cheek and clapping Wil on the shoulder.

'I'm glad all the years of bruised feet weren't in vain. Well done,' drawled Alex.

'Mine or yours?'

'Mine, of course,' said Alex, smiling. 'Good job, Wil,' he added.

'Let's move to the side before we get run over,' said Eliza, becoming aware of the irritated looks their small group was receiving camped in the middle of the floor.

'Well done, Eliza,' called Derek as he danced past. 'Save me a dance.'

'Me too,' said Colin, dancing closely behind Derek. 'You looked great.'

Eliza beamed.

'Sounds like a fella better get in early.' Securing her hand in a firm clasp and with a brief 'Excuse us,' to the group, Alex pulled Eliza back onto the floor. The melody transitioned from a jazz foxtrot to a waltz.

'That's better,' murmured Alex as he gathered her closer.

'Alex!'

'Shhhh. Just let me hold you,' Alex crooned in a low voice, as if soothing a child.

'Wouldn't you rather be returning Queenie's kiss?' she asked, placing a hand on his chest in an attempt to put some distance between them. 'It must be burning a hole in your pocket.'

'I don't blame you for being upset. Queenie was ... well, being Queenie. And I was ... being thoughtless and stupid.'

CHAPTER 27

Eliza relaxed her hand on his chest; he seemed sincere, but she was still suspicious.

'Tell me what I can say or do to make you believe that I was just acting a part.'

'Read minds, do you?' asked Eliza.

'Only yours, and not very well.'

Looking up, she spied her nemesis as she'd begun to think of Queenie, dancing towards them in the arms of Derek.

'What are you thinking?' asked Alex.

'That we're about to be cut in on.'

In a move that surprised Eliza for its speed and successfulness, Alex danced them into a series of turns and through the curtain to the side of the band. Eliza stopped short, faced with an enormous figure of an American eagle and Australian kangaroo – it must have been three times her height and about the same width. The kangaroo looked like it had its arm around the eagle. Covered in gold glitter, they sparkled eerily in the half-light.

Alex grabbed her hand, pulled her into the space behind

the stage prop and placed a finger across her lips, just as a shaft of light appeared from the direction of the ballroom. Someone had followed them.

'What are you doing, Derek? I'm not in the mood for a dalliance,' warned Queenie's distinctive voice.

'I was sure I saw Alex come in here.'

'Well, he's not here now,' she snapped. 'Come on. That kangaroo's eyes are giving me the heebie-jeebies.'

Eliza stifled a giggle. The thought of Queenie being given the eye by the marsupial was hilarious – another male conquest to add to her list.

Eliza listened intently. A moment later, Alex motioned for her to follow him and led her deeper backstage. Her breath hitched when she realised that their destination was the same bench on which she'd sobbed her heart out to Bec after discovering Derek with Queenie.

'What's wrong?' asked Alex.

Eliza shrugged. 'Memories of a failed rendezvous, a few tears ...' she confessed.

'Derek.'

'Uh-uh.'

'Are you having regrets?'

'God no. Wil has done more for my confidence than Derek ever could,' admitted Eliza, before ducking her head and taking a seat. *Fantastic! I censure Alex for his behaviour with Queenie but boast of my own with Wil.* Another awkward conversation with Alex. She felt like a gauche teenager. 'Can I ask you something?'

'Shoot.'

Eliza hesitated. She couldn't believe she was about to be so bold. But she could think of no other way – outside of pretending she had a friend who was interested – in knowing how attraction worked from the male side. 'How do I tell if ... Wil is interested in me ... you know, in an *intimate* way?'

Alex cleared his throat. 'In a physically intimate way?'

'Yes,' whispered Eliza.

'Are you interested in him, in that way?'

'Maybe ...' she replied cautiously.

'Because of how he makes you feel?'

'Kind of ...'

'Does anyone else make you feel *that way*?'

Eliza swallowed. *Why did she always seem to be the one making admissions?* 'You do ... during my tuition,' she whispered, before covering her cheeks with her palms.

'Does that upset you?'

'It confuses me,' Eliza blurted, turning towards him. 'Because ... well, because it's just supposed to be practice.'

'Sometimes, what starts out as practice can evolve,' said Alex.

'Has that been your experience? With Queenie ...'

'Eliza, I've never taken on another ... student before you. Although, sometimes I wonder who's teaching whom.'

'But I'm so inexperienced,' said Eliza, speaking to the underside of his chin.

'Only in the mechanics. You're a quick study. We do have to remedy one thing, though.'

'What's that?'

'You talk a lot.'

Eliza opened her mouth to utter a retort, and Alex swooped, covering her lips with his own, the tip of his tongue boldly exploring her mouth. God, he tasted delicious. Was that peppermint? And there were those flames again, dancing Medusa-like at her core, causing her to forget why she was so upset with him.

Sensing their time was short, Eliza slipped the buttons of Alex's waistcoat and ran her palms over his chest. She could feel heat through the thin material of his cotton shirt ... and nipples. Her thumbs went to work only to be stilled by a hand that flattened her palm. She suppressed a groan of frustration.

'Is it my technique?' Eliza asked, her eyes glued to his chest.

'What?'

'The reason you're stopping me ... I thought you'd like it ... I did last time,' she ended on a whisper.

'I do, sweetheart ...'

She quirked an eyebrow. Alex's actions were not those of a man who was enamoured with her technique.

'But I thought you wanted an answer to your question.'

'I'm listening.'

'So, do you ever find Wil staring at you? Following your body with his eyes?'

'This is so embarrassing. How would I know? Forget I asked.'

'Because when a man is attracted to you, he'll watch you. His eyes will be drawn to certain parts of you.'

Alex's gaze drifted downwards, resting on her breasts, her hips and then her legs. Eliza moved restlessly on the bench. Wil's words came back to her – *He watches you.*

'He'll want to get closer.' And matching his actions to his words, Alex lifted her onto his lap.

Eliza approved the improvement of his accessibility and immediately cupped his jaw. Her tongue flirted with the pulse drubbing at the base of his throat before it trailed butterfly kisses up his neck. He smelt reassuringly of warmed spices – like a rich fruitcake fresh from the oven. She loved fruitcake.

'To touch you,' Alex continued in a warm baritone.

She felt him run his palm up one calf, over a knee and onto her thigh, and realised he'd taken advantage of the carefully disguised slit in her overskirt. She tilted her hips forward, hoping he'd touch her ... there.

'God, Eliza, slow down.'

'Am I doing it wrong again?'

'No! But if you continue, I'm going to spend in my trousers like a pimply youth on my first carnal foray.'

'Now who's talking ... too ... much,' whispered Eliza, punctuating her words with kisses along his jaw.

Alex placed his hands on either side of her face and kissed her gently before wrapping his arms around her and hugging her to his chest.

'Hush,' he soothed her. 'You were perfect. But we've been gone a while, and this is not how I'd like us to be discovered.'

At Eliza's look of disbelief, Alex repositioned her on his lap and took her hand and placed it on the front of his trousers. They were tented like a flagpole at full mast. She proceeded to trail her fingers along the length of the tripod of material, and then stroke it, back and forth. She giggled when Alex's cock displayed the agility and coordination of a gymnast.

'Easy,' moaned Alex, reclaiming her hand in his. 'He likes you. Very much. And he doesn't need more encouragement.'

'Does he have a name?'

'Yes, but formal introductions will have to wait for another time.' He grinned. He seemed to be enjoying her playfulness, at least.

A footfall sounded. Alex mimed to Eliza to be quiet, helped her gain her feet and brush her skirts into place.

A voice hissed through the semi-darkness, 'Eliza, are you here?'

'Bec! What are you —?'

'Saving your butt,' she announced cheerfully as she came into view. 'You've been gone now for two, maybe three songs. And your American beau is getting restless.'

Eliza watched Alex scowl.

'And your brother's doing a poor job of pretending he's not concerned as to your whereabouts. Are you all right?'

'Yes, fine. Alex and I were —'

'No time for details. We need to get you both back, but to different parts of the ballroom.'

'We?' Alex asked.

'Did you find them?' came an exaggerated stage whisper.

'Yes. Over here. Oh, don't look like that, Alex, Mr B was worried when Eliza disappeared. And I needed help.'

'Why didn't you erect a sign?' Alex groused.

'Don't you bedevil young Bec here. She's trying to do the right thing,' rebuked Mr B, giving Alex a cuff on the shoulder.

Alex fell silent and shot Eliza a rueful smile as he squeezed her hand.

'What's your plan,' asked Eliza, sounding more composed than she felt. Her best friend and Birmingham's patriarch had almost discovered her wrapped in Alex's arms. She'd been in no condition to think of consequences. Thankfully, someone had.

'You and I will exit through the side door over there and

continue onto the ladies' room, so that you can change into your evening dress. We'll say you had a small tear and we were delayed making some repairs.'

Eliza nodded, 'All right.'

'Alex will emerge beside the band with Mr B. You've been inspecting the stage props for next Wednesday's competition final. Mr B needed an engineering opinion on ... something. You'll work it out,' Bec said, throwing her hands in the air. 'I can't think of everything.'

In the end, Eliza doubted their story was fully believed, but Alex, Daniel and Bec joined forces to impart enough gravitas to avoid anyone disputing it. Even Mr B played his part. Wil played along, but it was clear from his expression as he commandeered Eliza for the next dance, that battle lines had been drawn.

CHAPTER 28

Sunday 2 August 1925

'I'll stop all you folks coming aboard if you don't form a line,' shouted the young officer armed with a megaphone, straddling the USS *Oklahoma*'s gangplank.

Wil and Johnnie grinned as the crowd jumped to attention, jostling one another, before they fell into an orderly train. 'Take no notice of Abe, his bark is worse than his bite,' said Johnnie. 'Wants to head west when he's discharged and become one of those movie people.'

Eliza nodded, distracted by the activity on the opposite side of Princes Pier on the USS *Seattle*. 'Coaling,' explained Wil. 'The coal comes from a barge moored on the other side. Dirty work. So glad we're not coal-fired. I don't miss that. Nearly ruined my good looks, it did.'

Eliza nodded, tipping her head to one side as if assessing the validity of his words. 'I see what you mean. Such a shame.' Wil retaliated by grabbing her around the waist and tickling her, his face an expression of mock outrage. Despite her howls of protest, he wouldn't let up until she told him she was sorry.

'Look, they're imitating the brass band,' exclaimed Jenny as she clapped her hands in excitement. Sailors with coal-smudged faces were improvising with shovels, brooms and mops, playing them as if they were instruments – strutting up and down the ship. Young women gathered below, dancing and flirting with the men above. The members of the Salvation Army Headquarters band also hammed it up, entertaining audiences both on and off the ship.

Eliza and Wil had spent the morning practising at Birmingham's under Dick Birmingham's shrewd eye. At lunchtime, they'd collected Jenny from the YWCA headquarters and travelled by train from the city to meet Johnnie at the pier. Bec was still to arrive. She was travelling from Williamstown with Daniel.

When Wil had heard they had arranged to tour another battleship, he'd immediately insisted that he and Johnnie host a private tour of the USS *Oklahoma* and invite Jenny along. Alex, Daniel, Queenie and Evelyn would tour the *Pennsylvania* with Seaman Leroy Bainbridge, whom they'd met at the football match, as arranged.

Eliza was surprised at the carnival-type atmosphere that consumed the pier and the waterfront. The air pulsated with the sights, scents and sounds from booths, marquees, bands, food vendors and roving entertainers. Pedlars, selling everything from miniature flags to wattle blossom and boomerangs, wove their way through the throng of people.

Eliza glanced at her watch. One o'clock. Where was Bec? Every minute brought more and more Melburnians, pouring out of train carriages, motor buses and cars. But no Bec.

It seemed ship tours were popular. The mounted police

had been brought in to shape the throngs into groups and queues. Although, at best they were managing to stop people from being trampled or run over.

'We're here. At last,' said Bec as she shouldered her way over to Eliza and gave her a hug. 'Who knew your brother had no sense of direction. Hello, everyone.'

Daniel, following in her wake, rolled his eyes. 'Don't ask,' he told Eliza at her puzzled expression. 'Afternoon, all. Have you seen Alex or any of the others?'

Eliza shook her head. 'Where did you arrange to meet?' she asked.

'At the pier,' said Daniel. 'Who knew it would be such a madhouse. It was only that Bec spotted your bright-blue hat that we found you.'

'What about the fella from the *Pennsylvania*? Where was he meetin' you?' asked Wil.

'Well, we didn't fix on an actual spot,' admitted Daniel.

'Details aren't Daniel's forte, he's more of a big-picture man,' quipped Bec, smiling into his scowling face.

Eliza watched the exchange with interest. There was a new tension between her brother and best friend she'd never observed before.

'Wait here. I'll survey the pier from the gangplank. See if I can spot 'em,' offered Wil.

'Who doesn't adore a decisive man,' said Bec with a dramatic sigh as Wil tunnelled his way through the crowd. Daniel deliberately turned his back on her and started a conversation with Johnnie.

'What's going on?' whispered Eliza.

'Your brother can be so irritating at times.'

Eliza frowned. 'Go on.'

'From Williamstown to Flinders Street, I listened to him espouse the ideas and projects he had for the city's tram network. But he couldn't answer a single practical question about what that meant for "Joe" commuter. And then, from Flinders Street to here, he went into detail about his troubles with Evelyn. Detail I didn't need to hear. Thank goodness it's a short trip.'

Eliza stared at her, not quite sure what to say.

'And then, to cap it all off, he asked for advice. What do I look like? An agony aunt?'

Eliza giggled. 'What did you say?'

'I told him she sounded like a lot of trouble and to dump her.'

Eliza gasped. 'You didn't!'

'Yes, I did.'

'What did he say?'

'That if I didn't want to help, just to say so. Argh! Men!'

Eliza laughed. It was no secret that she and Bec found Evelyn tiresome. Always bleating about something and hanging off her brother like a barnacle.

'Found them. They were over yonder, wandering around like sheep,' called out Wil, as he marshalled Alex, Queenie and Evelyn before him.

Face to face with Alex, Eliza was unsure how to act. Here was the man whose penis she had petted last night. Was there a protocol for such meetings? He seemed unaffected, smiling and laughing at something Daniel was saying. As she watched, Queenie wrapped herself securely around his arm.

Eliza forced herself to look Alex in the eye, acknowledging his greeting with a casual smile. She was conscious of both Queenie's and Wil's regard.

'Shall we board before the ship gets too crowded?' Wil asked, recapturing her attention.

She nodded and he took hold of her hand, motioning to Johnnie to collect Jenny and Bec and follow him to the gangway. To Daniel and Alex, he spared a nod towards the USS *Pennsylvania* and tipped his cap. 'That's your ship over there, I'm sure you're hankerin' to get aboard. We'll be off.'

'Holler if you need anything, we're only next door,' joked Johnnie, as he followed in Wil's wake.

Alex watched the small party snake their way towards the *Oklahoma*. He lost sight of them momentarily before spotting Eliza as she walked up the gangplank and stood beside Wil as he spoke with the megaphone-wielding seaman. He saw Wil tuck one side of Eliza's hair behind an ear, and whisper something that caused her face to light up. His gaze bored holes in her back, where Wil kept a protective hand, but unaware, she jumped onto the deck of the ship and disappeared from view.

'Now that we've seen them safely on board, shall we?' asked Queenie with an arched brow and a tug on Alex's forearm.

Curving his lips into an automatic smile, he nodded absently and led the way behind the Salvation Army Band, which was taking a well-earned break, skirted a small crowd that was applauding the efforts of a juggler with a dozen china plates in the air, before joining the queue for the *Pennsylvania*.

'Can you see that bloke we met at the football?' asked Daniel, craning his neck. 'What was his name? Leo? Roy?'

'Leroy,' supplied Alex while he scanned the pier. 'And no

… hang on a minute, I think that's him. The one signing that girl's handkerchief. Wait here.'

At Alex's approach, Seaman Leroy Bainbridge stuffed the piece of cloth back into the hands of a young woman looking at him imploringly and kissed all ten fingers, before he turned towards Alex.

'Another conquest?'

'They're all so pretty. Hard for a fella to say no. There just aren't enough hours in the day.' Leroy grinned.

The old Alex could sympathise. The new Alex thought about the wasted hours and days in pursuit of chance encounters, casual sex and petting parties. He clapped Leroy on the shoulder in the international sign of male understanding and steered him towards where the others waited.

'Welcome aboard the oldest battleship in active service in the American Navy.' Wil spread his arms in welcome.

Eliza looked around, fascinated by the near-gleaming brass, smudged at intervals by little and large fingers alike, and the bleached white decks. 'Everything is on such a huge scale – those funnel things, guns, fittings, lights – how big is it?' she asked.

'Five hundred and eighty-three feet – nearly the length of nine of your cricket pitches end to end,' said Johnnie. 'We're carrying one thousand, two hundred and seventy-four men and our armoury consists of ten fourteen-inch, twenty-one five-inch and two three-inch guns and a couple of torpedo tubes —'

'And a seaplane. I read all about it in Saturday's paper. It's shot into the air from the deck like a boy tossing a pigeon,' interrupted Bec. Can we see that?' she asked, jumping up and down.

As if on cue, the roar of an engine from the direction of the bow of the ship stopped Johnnie's reply.

'This way,' said Wil, who began to politely shoulder his way towards a small crowd which had surrounded the aircraft. It was perched in its catapult, two men occupying the front seats, in earnest conversation, ignorant of the attention they were attracting.

Eliza gazed in amazement.

The engine was suddenly cut, and the two men dismounted and walked off, still deep in discussion.

'This thing actually flies?' asked Bec.

'Yes, ma'am. Both Johnnie and I have been aboard. You think the take-off looks hairy, you should see the recovery. There's always a medical officer on stand-by in case of an accident.'

'A pity they don't offer civilian passenger flights,' rued Bec, gazing longingly at the aircraft.

'No non-combatants, ma'am,' confirmed Wil, then began shepherding them in the opposite direction.

They wandered on. The vessel was a cross between a small city and a large country station. There was a foundry and blacksmith shop, a barber shop, printing office as well as a bakery and butcher shop hung with large carcasses of meat. A tub of peeled potatoes sat outside the potato-peeler room, containing two remarkable machines that made short work of a bag of spuds. Eliza was disappointed to learn that neither Wil nor Johnnie could explain the workings.

'Never thought much about it,' said Wil with a careless shrug. 'As long as they keep turnin' up on my dinner plate.'

A glimpse of two sailors playing cards on the floor behind a roped-off area adorned with a printed sign that said, *Visitors Not Allowed*, reminded Eliza that this was a home away from home for those aboard, albeit a lonely one at times.

'We're goin' to look in on our chaplain about Tuesday's ceremony,' said Johnnie as they assembled at the bottom of the stairs that would lead them up and out onto the upper deck. 'Meet up at the top of the gangplank. Give us half an hour, bo.'

The strains of a ukulele met them as they emerged. Drawn to the railing by a crowd – some dancing, others singing – Eliza could see, suspended on a swing off the side, an African-American sailor sitting with his back against the ship's grey hulk, instrument in hand, crooning, 'It Ain't Gonna Rain No Mo'. He appeared unaware or indifferent to the growing crowd. Balanced on another hanging seat to his left, sat a young man, paint brush in hand. Below him two more men, slapping on the same grey paint, were perched in a punt which bobbed precariously on the wind-whipped water.

'This is about as exciting as it gets in the day of the life of a sailor,' Wil said with a grin. 'Painting, polishing and scrubbing. One end to the other. And then we start all over again.'

'I could think of worse ways to see the world,' said Bec, leaning far over the rail to attract the workers' attention. She had competition from the small gaily beflagged boats ferrying sightseers for a close-up of the vessels berthed at the pier.

'Unfair advantage,' grumbled Bec, as one enterprising woman from a launch bridged herself across to the punt, legs in one craft and arms in the other. She was hauled back to safety amidst wild cheers and no doubt relief from the two sailors in the punt who thought they would be capsized into the freezing waters.

'Come on,' ordered Wil.

They found Jenny placating an unhappy Johnnie.

'What's up, bo?' asked Wil.

'The wedding's been moved to early afternoon. Preacher Griffin must officiate at the handover of our new mascot. And that's more important, apparently.'

At Wil's confused look, he said, 'We're gettin' our very own kangaroo – Okie.'

'Wow!' exclaimed Eliza. 'A kangaroo!'

'Yes, ma'am. And while I'm mighty pleased and all, it does rather put a spanner in our plans.'

'Nothin' we can't sort out,' Wil said, clapping his buddy on the shoulder. 'But I'd rather do it over some grub and a hot drink than here, freezing my behind off. Excuse my language, ladies.'

'Lead on,' the women chorused.

'Hey, where are you five going in such a hurry?' Daniel's question stopped the excited chatter mid-sentence.

Alex had spotted Eliza disembarking from the *Oklahoma* as they'd walked past on their way to the Port Melbourne railway station. He and Daniel would have liked to have spent longer with Leroy, but Queenie and Evelyn had shown a growing lack of interest with boilers, guns and anything remotely mechanical.

Quick as a wink Bec wrapped one hand through the crook of Eliza's arm, the other through Wil's and declared, 'Can't stop. We have a wedding to plan. Ta-ta.'

'Wedding? Whose wedding?' demanded Daniel.

'No time. Chat later,' sang Bec as she drove a path through the crowd of onlookers.

'Cheeky,' drawled Queenie. 'Is your father at home, Daniel?'

'What? Why? You don't think she meant Eliza? Do you?'

'Well, Jenny's wedding is old news ... and it's planned ... I would guess.'

'Oh, Daniel, how exciting,' gushed Evelyn.

Daniel looked at her as if she'd grown another head. 'I have to get home,' he said abruptly.

'I'll come with you,' said Alex. 'We'll take a taxi, my shout. It'll be quicker.'

'You're deserting us?' wailed Evelyn.

'No, no of course not,' said Daniel. 'We'll drop you in town on the way.'

'Don't bother,' replied Queenie, securing Evelyn to her side. 'There is still so much to see here.'

Alex followed her gaze to a couple of naval officers standing a few feet away whose interest had been piqued by Evelyn's lament of desertion.

'Shoo. Both of you. Go home and sort things out,' said Queenie. 'We'll be fine.'

Alex could see that Daniel's distress over Eliza's plans was warring with his manners and concern about leaving Evelyn.

'It's no trouble to drop you in the city.' Daniel grabbed both of Evelyn's hands.

'No need,' said Evelyn, untangling herself. 'We'll be fine.'

'All right,' said Daniel resignedly. 'I'll see you tomorrow night.'

Queenie dismissed Alex with a kiss before sauntering towards the two officers.

'Why can't your sister stick to the plan?' asked Alex as they travelled towards Williamstown.

'What plan?'

'My plan, of course!' said Alex. 'Things would be a lot simpler.'

CHAPTER 29

Monday 3 August 1925

The band's tempo transformed the energetic dance steps of those assembled to a subdued shuffle, allowing for the entwining of limbs and whispered confidences.

'I might start purring if you persist,' said Wil.

At the change of pace, Wil had taken the opportunity to dance Eliza into a small space near the railing, from which the faint lights of Williamstown could be seen across the channel. Hands clasped loosely in the centre of her back, he guided her in a slow circle. His coal-black hair, unencumbered by his normal white cap, gleamed in the soft light. Eliza had wondered what it would feel like and lifted a hand to act out her thoughts. Soft and silky, like an oriental rug she'd felt once, although a little spikey.

'I also enjoy a good massage if you're so inclined.'

'I'm not really dressed for that,' Eliza replied cheekily.

'I can take care of that.'

Eliza chuckled. 'I'm sure you can. But remember, I've seen the size of your bunk. A strong deterrent to amorous adventures.'

'Is that the only hurdle?' asked Wil, his face a study of seriousness.

She watched the shadow and the light, thrown by the coloured globes decorating the awning overhead, flitting across his expression. She didn't pretend that she didn't know what he was referring to. 'It's ...'

'Complicated?'

Eliza nodded.

'It doesn't have to be.'

Eliza snorted.

'The way I see it, you've been under Alex's nose for years and he's now woken up and developed a hankerin' for you. And I'm in his way.'

'You have a knack for boiling things down to the bare bones, don't you,' said Eliza, feeling the heat rise in her cheeks. *Could it be that simple?* she wondered. *Had she awakened Alex?* A tingle ran from her head to her toes.

'Reckon I do. The real question, sweetheart, is what ... and who do you want?'

'I started off wanting to have some fun. And to be kissed properly. And now ...'

'You're getting all that action and more,' he stated matter-of-factly.

'Goodness, you make me sound like a flirt! No. I'm saying that until recently, I'd never thought of Alex in that way. He offered to tutor me in the fine art of engaging men and now I've started wanting something more.'

Wil hooted. 'He what?'

'Keep your voice down. I'm a little aloof when it comes to men and he offered to help me overcome it.'

'My darlin' girl, there are only two reasons a man like Alex would offer to help you, and since Queenie has probably made herself available to provide all the bedroom action he needs – not sayin' he's partakin' – that leaves only one. He's interested in you. More than interested – enamoured.'

Eliza frowned. She hated thinking about Alex with Queenie ... in that way. And how would he ever be satisfied with her, a novice, when he was used to ... to ... She couldn't even find the words. Her newly acquired confidence did not extend to the bedroom.

She took a deep breath. 'I'm afraid he's just playing around. After all, I'm nothing like his usual conquests.'

'I'd lay money that he's playing for keeps. Alex is no fool ... But where does that leave us?'

'You know I really like you – we have a lot of fun. You were responsible for my first real kiss and because of you I no longer think of myself as *dull*. But I'm just another girl in a different port.'

'You wound me!' protested Wil, releasing a hand from the small of her back to press it over his heart.

Eliza gave his nose a tweak and applied a quick kiss to his mouth, which was gaping in surprise. 'Not deeply. And I've heard the New Zealand girls are just as lovely. You'll forget me like that,' she said, clicking her fingers for effect.

'You are so harsh.' Wil waggled his brows. 'My heart's not a chalk board, you know, easily erased and written over.'

Eliza gave him a mock-consoling look. 'Do you use that line with all the girls?'

He dropped a kiss onto her forehead. 'You're brutal.'

They continued their slow shuffle to the music in silence. Despite Wil's protest, Eliza didn't feel as if she'd wounded him too deeply. His next words confirmed it.

'Have you given any thought as to how to get Alex to declare himself?'

'I don't think I can. Not even Queenie's managed that.'

'As they say back home, *cain't never could*. We need a plan. Bec's announcement about the wedding planning clearly rattled him ... and your brother. For different reasons, though, I'm guessin', he said with a laugh. 'The look on their faces. Priceless!'

'You weren't around for the interrogation from Daniel when I got home. Alex didn't say a word, just watched and listened. That's hardly the reaction of a man who's enamoured, is it?'

'Darlin', he's just playing his cards close to his chest. Probably waitin' until I'm out of the picture ... And just for the record, I'm not departing the field, so he can expect some competition.'

Eliza felt a tingle of excitement. She didn't need hordes of men. Just one. *Although, it didn't hurt to have another in reserve*, she thought wickedly, *especially one as good-looking as Wil*. Hadn't the girl guides taught her to *be prepared*? ... And to keep her strength up – she was ravenous.

'Is there anything to eat onboard?'

'Always thinkin' about your stomach. Let's go find us the buffet. I think they've set up on the gun deck. Cake, ice-cream and punch.'

As he tucked her hand into the crook of his arm, she leaned over and gave his cheek a loud smack of a kiss and mouthed, 'Thank you.'

Eliza and Wil looked cosy, too cosy, veiled by a potted palm, shuffling in a token response to the band's outpouring. Who knew the same steps could be adapted to so many tempos? As they turned, arm in arm, Alex watched a tender expression play across Wil's face as they passed beneath the light of a Chinese lantern.

Three more nights until Wil departed the city. Alex was losing confidence in his plan to wait things out. After all, Jenny Butler was marrying that mate of Wil's. She'd met him through the same dancing competition as Eliza had met Wil. What if Eliza got caught up in the excitement and fancied herself in love with the American? And what if it wasn't just a fancy … that faux wedding announcement of Bec's yesterday had winded his confidence.

He watched Queenie float past in the arms of one of the officers, playing with the buttons that secured his jacket. He couldn't drum up any enthusiasm to assess whether this was another Derek, designed to make him jealous, or whether she'd already moved on and he hadn't been paying attention. It reminded him that he still hadn't taken any steps to formally end things with her.

'Enjoying yourself?' asked a voice he was coming to dread.

'Not really,' he replied distractedly. 'Come to cheer me up?'

'I'm not really your type. Have you seen Eliza?'

A loaded question if he'd ever heard one. 'No, Bec. Not for an hour or so,' he lied. And from the expression on her face, she knew it, too. She'd probably watched him mooning over her like a boy.

'What are your intentions?'

'Ah, I'd forgotten we're now close confidants.'

'You're running out of time, Alex. Behind that Alabama charm lies a man of strong desires and intentions. I read that the courts are waiving the necessary three-day notice for nuptials.'

It wasn't until Alex had control of his temper and had turned around to speak with her that he realised Bec had slipped away as stealthily as she'd appeared. *Damn!* He'd end things with Queenie tonight and then be free to pursue Eliza in earnest. No more waiting.

Sated by an abundance of food, the melodies of saxophone and trombone and the attentions of some of America's finest sailors, Eliza was enjoying herself immensely, with Wil never too far away. She'd caught a couple of glimpses of Alex, once on the dance floor, and then sharing witticisms with a group of men who were leaning against the rail. And she'd felt him watching her. Nothing obvious, but whenever she'd glanced his way, their eyes had connected. She was always the first to avert hers. He'd winked once. Wil had caught the exchange, scowled and whisked her on a tour of the aft deck.

At midnight, the ship turned into a pumpkin and all guests were escorted off to the sounds of 'Waltzing Matilda'. Curfew did not deter Wil and Johnnie from declaring their intention to escort Eliza, Bec and Jenny back to Williamstown. That was until their warrant officer appeared and scuttled any plans, despite their assurances that they'd return within a couple of hours.

Jenny soothed Johnnie, reminding him that their wedding was only twelve hours away. Wil made much of his farewell from Eliza. Wrapping her in his arms, he rained kisses in between compliments on her dress, her hair, her face. With a giggle, Eliza whispered he was destined for the stage, before she pushed him towards the gangplank with a reminder that they had a wedding to attend later today, and he needed his beauty sleep. As she turned back to the group, she saw Alex helping Queenie into a cab, the yellow paint making a vivid picture against the drab background of the pier and the grey bulk of the battleships.

Conscious of his duty, Daniel waved aside the girls' assurances that they could navigate their way home, declaring he would accompany them. Evelyn shrugged resignedly at the abrupt end to her evening.

'It's freezing, let's get moving,' Bec said as she stomped her feet and rubbed her hands together for effect, before she strode off towards the train waiting patiently for the revellers.

'Naughty of Alex to whisk Queenie away like that,' mused Evelyn. 'I didn't even get to say good night. He sure seemed like he was in a hurry.' This last comment was made with a sly look at Eliza.

Thankfully, Daniel was disinclined to encourage Evelyn's observations further. He gave her an enigmatic look, murmured something that ended in 'darling', and bundled her up the steps and into the carriage.

For Eliza, the magic had disappeared from the evening. As she seated herself beside Bec, she felt as energetic as a punctured balloon. Alex had made his choice clear this evening. She was a diversion, nothing more. It was the Queenies of the world that captured and held his attention ... and whom he went home with at the end of an evening.

Alex hoped his actions wouldn't be misinterpreted, but he could think of no other way to proceed. Not since Bec had planted her seed about time running out. Damn her. And he could hardly announce that he and Queenie were leaving so that he could break up with her. She was seated beside him, thankfully not snuggled against his arm as usual. Her provocative fragrance cloaked the interior like a blanket. He wondered why he'd never noticed how overpowering it was before. He sighed. They pulled up at Hotel Federal and the driver jumped out to open the door, almost invisible in the dark in his smart brown uniform.

Queenie yawned and stretched like a disgruntled feline, before fixing her almond-shaped eyes on Alex's face, an unspoken question burning from her blue eyes.

'I thought we could have a quiet drink,' explained Alex. 'We need to talk.'

She nodded before elegantly exiting the taxi, showing just enough leg to attract whistles from a small group of sailors weaving down King Street.

Seated in the lounge, she extracted a cigarette and inserted it into a Bakelite holder decorated with the image of a young woman dressed in a green Charleston dress, then she lit it. Two perfect smoke rings sailed towards the ceiling before she spoke.

'We've had some fun.' Another smoke ring joined the first two.

'Yes, we have.' Alex took a sip of his whisky, the taste of spices and boiled sweets tantalising his tongue. 'But we —'

'Don't let's be tiresome. We've become predictable, you and me. And you've set your sights on another.'

'Yes, I have, and it's serious ... at least it is for me.'

'Ah, you're not sounding so sure of yourself. This must be new ground for you.'

'Queenie, I'm not going to discuss my feelings with you.

As you said, we've had some fun. A lot of fun. You're a woman that *knows her oil*, and I've been the lucky recipient. But this is the end for us.'

Queenie drew deeply on her cigarette, observing him over the tip. 'And you're wanting me to bow out gracefully?'

'Your dalliance with Derek would suggest you're tired of me and looking to move on.'

'Not tired ... just hoping for some attention.'

Alex scoffed gently. 'You're never short of attention.'

Queenie smiled.

'Don't make this any harder than it needs to be.'

Leaning towards him, she levelled him with a sultry look, which he couldn't fail to interpret given the hand inching its way up his thigh. 'Are you sure?'

'Yes, I'm sure,' he said, stopping her hand before it reached his crotch.

'I hope she's worth it.'

'She is.'

Queenie stubbed out her cigarette in the ashtray beside her.

'I'll see you home,' Alex offered.

'Don't concern yourself. I can take care of myself.' Summoning a waiter, Queenie ordered a taxi cab. 'Preferably driven by a woman,' she added. 'I'll wait downstairs.'

Alex stood politely. 'Goodnight.'

Queenie's eyes were steely when they met his. 'You're a wicked man, Alex. You'll need to come on bended knee to get back in my bed should you change your mind.'

'I won't change my mind. Goodbye, Queenie.'

Throwing her coat over her shoulder, Queenie strode towards the staircase, where the steward was waiting to escort her to the waiting taxi cab. She aimed a seductive smile to the poor man, who was clearly unused to being on the receiving end of such attention. He reminded Alex of a puppy brought to heel. She didn't look back. Alex subsided into his chair and indicated his desire for another whisky.

What was his next move? Queenie was right, he was on new ground – in unknown territory. He hated to admit it, but he needed help. Tipping back his whisky, he decided to call it a night. As he rose to his feet, he noticed Queenie's white fur-cuffed gloves discarded on the arm of a chair. She must have forgotten them in her haste to leave. Picking them up, he contemplated leaving them at reception in case she returned, before he decided that was unlikely and took them with him to his suite.

CHAPTER 30

Tuesday 4 August 1925
Jenny Says 'I do'

'Demure ...' breathed Bec, her hands clasped like a nun to her breast. 'Not a collarbone in sight.'

Eliza gasped. 'Did you run out of material?'

'This is the height of Paris fashion,' Christine Tailleuse remonstrated as she brushed the black velvet gown with her hand.

Eliza was unconvinced. She felt exposed and self-conscious. She was once again standing plumb on the dais, while Christine circumnavigated her. Really, the Spanish had taken less time to circle the globe. Twisting her head to try to see what was happening, Eliza was sharply ordered to remain facing forward. When she sighed, she was told to stand up tall.

'Bec!' appealed Eliza. 'It's missing bits ... lots of bits.'

'It's bold and sexy and ... perfect!' argued Christine.

'Trust me, trust us ... please! The final nail in Alex's coffin. I can't wait to see his face,' pleaded Bec.

Christine, satisfied with her adjustments, positioned a full-length mirror to allow Eliza to examine her appearance.

Eliza could admit to loving the cut. The long, unembellished lines accentuated her height, the folds allowing maximum freedom of movement, which she approved after a couple of exploratory dance kicks.

She twisted around to study the back – the missing section. Lattice-type straps served to secure the bodice, *secure* being a matter for debate. She focused on the skirt, emblazoned with starbursts of pearl, emerald and sapphire strass, connected by strings of rhinestones to a large brooch that rested at the base of her spine. This she approved of. The effect in motion would be stunning – whirlpools of eddying colour.

'Of course, *ma chérie*, you will require black silk lingerie. Not those sensible cotton undergarments that you insist on,' said Christine emphatically.

Eliza smoothed the fabric over her hips.

'Do not be embarrassed. They will feel delicious on your skin and importantly will be indiscernible, no rucks or bulges,' she continued with a shiver of pleasure. 'I have just the thing.'

Eliza grinned. She could do this, she decided.

Eliza and Bec decorously closed the door lettered *Christine T* to the modiste's rooms, checked the spacious corridor for patrons, and finding none, dashed in the direction of the main stairs rather than await one of the three elevators. While one of the features of the modernisation of the Capitol Building, Eliza had a fear of confined spaces and preferred to control any descent from heights at her own pace.

Emerging onto the footpath, they turned right towards Flinders Street Railway Station, continuing at a brisk pace. Eliza checked her wristwatch – they had just enough time to catch the train to Bec's place, change and get to the church for Jenny and Johnnie's wedding.

It was to be a quiet affair. Jenny's mother had insisted on the ceremony being held at St Andrew's in Williamstown. Johnnie had insisted on having his chaplain, Lieutenant Theodore Griffin, officiate. And Jenny had negotiated the stalemate in a manner worthy of any admiral. Both her mother's and Johnnie's ministers would preside. Jenny had said that the resident minister, Reverend Stewart Thomas, had been very accommodating. After she'd explained everything, he'd assured her, in his broad Glaswegian accent, not to worry her *wee* self or upset her *maw* any further. He and the chaplain would work it out between 'em, if she could organise a *wee* meetin'.

Johnnie had later said he'd wished he'd been a fly on the wall at the conference, wondering whether the two would be able to understand each other's thick accents.

Deep in conversation, arm in arm, shoulder to shoulder, cloches low shading their eyes, coat collars turned up against the wind and moving at pace, Eliza and Bec were intercepted as they crossed Collins Street.

'Alex!' exclaimed Eliza, just before she and Bec almost demoted him to the dirt of the footpath.

'Alex,' greeted Bec. 'What brings you to the Paris end of town?'

'Recruitment for a special project. And I do my best thinking out walking,' he replied cryptically, removing his hat and fidgeting with the brim with gloved fingers. 'Where are you both off to in such a hurry?'

Eliza determined they had less than ten minutes to catch their train and had herself and Bec in motion before Alex could discern her intentions. 'Can't stop. We're off to Jenny's wedding and have no margin for chit-chat. We'll be back at the Y after four if you want to drop by to toast the happy couple,' she added. Alex hadn't been invited to the wedding; he wasn't a close friend of the family. His acquaintance with Jenny was the consequence of his relationship with Daniel.

Alex scowled, his brows a straight line above eyes that had turned the colour of brown mud. As if remembering where he was, he nodded, clamped his fedora onto his head and waved them on their way.

'I wonder who Alex is recruiting? And why? Maybe it has something to do with his recent promotion to the tram electrification project,' mused Eliza.

'Special project my aunty,' said Bec under her breath as they paused and waited for the traffic policeman to signal safe pedestrian passage across to the station precinct. 'I doubt it has anything to do with the tramways. My guess is that Alex needs help navigating affairs closer to the heart.'

'When has that become a speciality of yours?' asked Eliza.

'Since he started trifling with my best friend,' said Bec fiercely. 'If he's serious about you, then he's got to prove himself. Alex is realising just how precarious his position is.'

Eliza smiled and gave Bec's arm a quick squeeze. 'Remind me never to get on the wrong side of you. Quick, there's our train. Run!'

Wrapping her coat snugly around her to ward off the breeze stealing into the carriage – they were known as ice chests for a reason – Eliza gave Bec an assessing look.

'I know you have the best of intentions, but I can handle Alex.' As Bec opened her mouth to protest, Eliza continued, 'Shhhh, I'm not saying I don't need your help ... or Wil's. But I've finally realised that I'm not *dull*.'

If anything, Bec's expression became fiercer.

'You set the wheels in motion when you bullied me into a new wardrobe and entering the dance competition. A stroke of genius. And Wil, well let's just say his ... attentions have boosted my morale. And Alex's tuition ...' Eliza giggled, 'has fuelled hope ... and honed my skills.'

She watched with surprise as Bec dabbed at her eyes. Bec never got teary. She got angry, she fumed and on occasion she swore, but she never succumbed to tears. Bec squared her shoulders and gave Eliza a half-smile. 'You were never dull. You just lacked confidence.'

'But I'm still not, what were your words ... fascinating, compelling, attractive and intriguing. So, I still need your help. Alex needs to find me irresistible.' She accompanied this last statement with a clap of her hands, before covering her lips like a small child. 'Let's talk to Wil, too. He offered to help the night of the dance onboard the *Oklahoma*.'

'I can't imagine he'd be happy to hand you to Alex on a plate,' said Bec.

'I admitted my preference for Alex. He pretended to be wounded and said he wouldn't withdraw his attentions. But he's not serious about me.'

'You're becoming a regular Mata Hari!'

'Let's hope I don't suffer the same fate; a firing squad seems a tad extreme for a few kisses.'

The wedding was an unassuming affair. A dozen guests

attended, including the best man and maid of honour. But what it lacked in extravagance, it made up for with sentiment.

Mrs Butler's tears began even before the couple took their place at the altar. Eliza's father pressed a supply of handkerchiefs into her fingers at regular intervals on one side and Eliza's mother held her hand on the other.

Bec had tears in her eyes for the second time that day and Eliza joked that she was becoming a regular watering pot. Bec pulled a face and gave her an affectionate punch in the arm.

Wil and Johnnie looked delicious in their uniforms. A fleeting feeling of guilt assailed her. *Should she be ogling other men if she purported to be enamoured with Alex?* Deciding she wasn't a nun, and even if she were, she still had eyes and the Lord would want her to use them, she looked her fill.

'What?' asked Eliza in response to Bec's elbow in her ribs.

'You look like the cat that swallowed the cream, give it up,' said Bec.

'I'm just appreciating the view.'

Bec's laugh was extinguished by an explosion of sound from the organ as the Wedding March announced Jenny's appearance and progress down the short aisle, accompanied by her brother, George.

From the time Jenny appeared, Johnnie had eyes for no one else. He made a grab for her hand long before George was ready to release it and tucked her possessively into his side. The Reverend Stewart Thomas smiled and bade George take his seat to ease any awkwardness. Johnnie went up in Eliza's estimation. Here was a man acting with his heart, not his head – conventions be damned. Would Alex be as ardent with the one he loved? As single-minded? As committed? And could that be her? She hoped so, as every day that passed, she was falling further in love with the man.

Jenny looked beautiful in a simple gown of pale-pink brocaded crepe de chine. A lace veil, *something old*, secured by artfully arranged orange blossoms, had been gathered and carefully draped from her crown, falling gracefully to her shoulders. The effect left her face entirely uncovered, and both Eliza and Bec sighed at the look she bestowed on Johnnie as she recited her vows, which earned them a look of disbelief from Daniel, seated on Bec's right.

For his part, Johnnie had to be called to attention by his lieutenant chaplain before he found his voice and stammered through several 'I do's'. He needed no such prompting at the pronouncement, 'You may now kiss the bride.'

CHAPTER 31

The Reception

'I promise to return her, we're not leaving the premises,' assured Eliza, deftly separating the newly married couple. In truth, Johnnie's devotion combined with his bear-like appearance, had some of Jenny's friends and colleagues intimidated. Eliza explained this to her in hushed tones before releasing her into a huddle of eager well-wishers.

A small reception had been planned at the YWCA office to give family, friends, staff and a few of Johnnie's shipmates an opportunity to celebrate with the couple. Jenny had been relieved when Bec had suggested it as her mother's finances would have been severely stretched to host the gathering and she was too proud to accept Johnnie's offer of money.

The couple's arrival had been greeted by loud cheers and showers of orange blossom, which Eliza and Bec had spent time early that morning preparing.

'Where's my girl scurryin' off to?' complained a familiar drawl, before Wil snaked an arm around Eliza's waist and planted a smacker on her open mouth. She retreated a few inches and levelled him with one of her stern teacher looks.

'Hello, you,' she greeted him. 'Bec and I are hosting, so I was just off to check on the food. Come on, I could use an extra pair of hands.'

'Mine are a little occupied at the minute,' he returned with a sly wink. 'Can't Bec handle things without you?'

'Yes ... no ... I can't find her. So, you're it. Come on.'

Amid general grousing, Wil released her and followed as she swept along the corridor to the kitchens at the back of the building. They found trays of sandwiches and cakes peeking from under netting weighed down by beads sewn into the hem, but no sign of Bec or anyone else.

'Good plan. Lurin' me back here to have your wicked way,' said Wil as he advanced towards where she'd walked to examine the assembled drink jugs.

'Wil,' she squeaked, quickly ascertaining his intentions and placing the island bench between them. 'There's a roomful of guests to feed. We haven't got time to dillydally.'

'One kiss,' he argued, eyeing her.

At the shake of her head, he announced, 'Or I'll dive across this bench and they can eat flattened sandwiches and cakes.'

'You wouldn't!'

'Do you really want to test me?'

Eliza narrowed her eyes and tilted her head, trying to decide how serious he was. Taking a step to her left, she bumped into a crate of drinks stacked on the floor. Wil took advantage of her momentary loss of concentration and captured her with ease.

Laughing, she surrendered. 'All right, one kiss. And then you're helping me cart this food out to the masses. Deal?'

'Deal.'

'Close your eyes,' ordered Eliza.

At his compliance, she leaned in to plant a kiss on his temple. But he was awake to her attempted prank and captured her head in both hands to create the perfect angle for his version of a kiss. Recognising she'd been outmanoeuvred, Eliza decided to enjoy the moment. His expertise in this arena had never been in doubt, although she now realised, he wasn't the one that made her heart tighten with anticipation or her pulse accelerate as if she'd just finished a hundred-yard dash. *It was Alex ... and it was he she'd fallen in love with.*

'Are we interrupting anything?' an angry voice asked.

Wil and Eliza groaned at the same time, before breaking apart and turning to face Alex and Bec.

I can explain, Eliza wanted to shout – but of course she didn't. She doubted, from the set of Alex's jaw and his icy appraisal, that he'd listen, anyway. And she couldn't blame him. In contrast, Bec looked as if she was relishing the fury visible on his face.

'There you are!' exclaimed Eliza to Bec, ignoring the maelstrom of emotions. 'I came looking for you.'

'Well, here I am,' said Bec in a business-like tone, following Eliza's lead. 'And I've brought reinforcements – apart from Daniel who seems to have disappeared. What's the plan?'

'We need to circulate with these trays and jugs and top up the drinks in the ice tubs.'

As was her way, Bec took charge. Placing a tray in each of Alex's hands, she instructed him not to return until both were empty and to find Daniel and ask him to report for kitchen duty. Wil was despatched with two crates of drinks to replenish supplies.

'That should keep them apart and busy for a little while,'

said Bec, dusting her palms together. 'Now, what did we interrupt?'

'Despite how it must have looked, nothing serious. Wil was just fooling around. And I ... went along with it.' Eliza covered her face with her hands.

'Are you sure you haven't changed your mind? Wil looks tasty in his uniform.'

'He does, doesn't he? But no, I haven't changed my mind. Wil is only making mischief.'

Bec appeared to study her, although Eliza could see from the look in her eyes that she was miles away. When Bec's eyes met hers, she nodded slowly and gave her a quick hug, before turning on her heel and heading out the door. Eliza shook her head. Sometimes her friend could be as enigmatic as a sage.

Alex was frustrated. He had not come to play footman, yet here he was smiling and exchanging pleasantries as he negotiated the room by weaving between small groups of excited faces as he dispensed the contents of his trays. Wil had also been conscripted, and from the look on the seaman's face, was as pleased with events as Alex was. The thought brought the first smile to his face since interrupting Eliza with Wil in the kitchen.

Bec's restraining hand had been the only thing that had prevented him from marching over and plucking Eliza from Wil's arms. Kidnapping had topped a list of options that had included maiming Wil or having him arrested and confined to his ship. He'd hoped that his kisses were enough to satisfy her curiosity and her hunger – but obviously not. He was losing his mind. No woman had ever frustrated and beguiled him as Eliza had. And after Bec's behaviour in the kitchen earlier, he wasn't sure he wanted to seek her advice. Her allegiance would always be to Eliza. He'd need to figure out his next move on his own.

'Why the scowl?' Daniel asked as he juggled a tray skyward to avoid tipping it over a group of sailors who'd erupted into a jig.

'This wasn't how I imagined spending time with Eliza,' groused Alex, turning sideways to make room for a woman bustling towards the circle of women around the bride.

'But it illustrates your domestic prowess. It's one way to a girl's heart.'

'That might be your way,' said Alex with a smirk. 'I prefer a more subtle approach.'

'And how's that been working for you?'

Alex glared at him, before turning on his heel, Daniel's laughter dogging his steps.

Alex was glad when the announcement was made that the bride and groom were leaving, as it meant that the celebration was winding up. After navigating the horseshoe of people, Jenny and Johnnie left for a night at an undisclosed location – Johnnie refusing to divulge any information despite the numerous questions as to their plans. Given the snippets of stories he'd heard about pranks played on newlyweds by the seamen in attendance, Alex thought it a prudent decision.

Manning the sink with Daniel, elbow deep in suds as they helped with the clean-up, Alex was still at a loss as to how to convey the news of his and Queenie's split. He didn't want to make a proclamation, but it was important that Eliza knew. And it would be useful for Daniel and Bec to also be in the loop.

Evelyn appeared beside Daniel, brown eyes snapping, top lip curled, ignoring his attempt to kiss her cheek. 'He hasn't told you, has he?' she snarled, jerking her head towards Alex. 'He dumped Queenie. The poor girl is inconsolable.'

Alex and Daniel exchanged looks, perfected through years of friendship, the type that replaced whole sentences and messy emotions. Clearly satisfied with the answer to the question he sought, Daniel discarded his tea towel on the bench and concluded the silent discussion with a manly slap to Alex's shoulder.

'Think you can handle things from here?' Without waiting for an answer, Daniel turned and bundled Evelyn out of the kitchen. He waved an absent goodbye to the rest of the group, who were either pretending absorption in their respective tasks or perfecting the art of avoiding eye contact.

Alex drew on his store of arrogance to shrug off Evelyn's theatrics. It was laughable to imagine Queenie languishing. It was more likely she was suffering vexation that the conclusion was at Alex's initiation and not her own. He dried his hands with Daniel's discarded tea towel and turned to face those remaining in the kitchen. The number had dwindled to a handful. He recognised four of the Y's staff as they backed out of the door, looking anywhere but him, probably off to spread the news. Bec approached him under the guise of tidying the benchtops. Her 'congratulations' was conveyed quietly, but the impact of the one word was made stronger by a smile that reached her eyes. He reserved comment.

One of Wil's ship buddies skidded to a halt at the doorway, saluted and commanded Wil to board the taxi out front. At Wil's hesitation, he urged, '*Now!*'

Alex fought an urge to roll his eyes at the navy man's long-winded departure. The performance was as much a demonstration of his affection for Eliza as a warning to Alex to *leave his gal alone*. His suspicions were confirmed as Wil passed him and murmured, 'This changes nothin'.'

'I'll see you out,' said Bec, hustling him down the corridor.

Alex smiled. And then there were two. Perhaps Bec's allegiances stretched to him, too. He wished he knew Eliza's state of mind, but guessed it was swinging like a pendulum from her wide-eyed stare.

'It was amicable,' said Alex into the silence. 'Although, it wasn't quite how I intended to break the news —'

'Evelyn does have a flair for drama,' conceded Eliza, untying the apron she'd used to protect her dress and folding it.

Silence.

'Well, I'm sorry,' said Eliza, smoothing her skirts with the heat from her palms.

'You are?'

'Well, yes. Even if it was amicable, I'm sure it hurts. But with your reputation, I'm sure you won't want for female consolation.'

Alex nearly choked. What to say? Didn't she realise that his breakup with Queenie was because of her? Did she just think they'd got tired of each other?

'I thought that maybe we could console one another.'

He watched her eyes widen. 'You want me to replace Queenie?'

'No! Yes! But not how you think.' His fingers snaked through his hair in frustration. This was not going well. And if he were not mistaken, he could hear Bec clomping down the corridor towards the kitchen, her heavy tread like the hands of a noisy clock, signalling that time was running out. Galvanised into action, he shut the door and turned the key. As Bec's face appeared in the glass panel contained within the door, he signalled ten minutes with his fingers and pulled down the blind.

Breathing quickly, he turned to face her. 'Now, where were we?'

Eliza, hands on hips, replied, 'You were explaining my role replacing Queenie. And by the way, Bec's got a master key, so don't waste those ten minutes.'

'Of course, I'm not asking you to replace Queenie.'

'I'm not good with fast and loose —' began Eliza.

'For God's sake, Eliza, it's not about the sex. I mean ... your experience,' he amended, watching the pink in her cheeks heighten to a colour usually achieved through manufactured means. Taking advantage of her fascination with tracing the patterns in the linoleum with her eyes, he closed the distance between them until he was standing a hand length away.

Alex took a deep breath. 'Eliza, I broke up with Queenie because I have developed an interest in someone else. That someone is you.' As her eyes lifted to focus on his face, he willed her to believe him. 'An interest that can't be confused with brotherly.'

She continued to study him.

'I'm going to kiss you. I don't usually ask permission, so if you don't want this, you'd better speak up now.' Resisting the desires surging in his trousers, he approached her slowly – communicating in a way that required no words.

Eliza's hands reached for his lapel of her own volition. He closed the gap, backing her against the timber edge of

THE BATTLE FOR ELIZA

the bench. His lips secured hers, his hands skimming up her waist, the sides of her breasts.

He could taste the champagne she'd consumed to toast the happy couple. He wondered, as she snuggled closer, whether it had dampened her inhibitions. She didn't seem perturbed by the hard ridge pressing into her ... down there. When she flexed her hips forward, it nearly took his breath away.

He became aware of someone pounding on the door, followed by a stream of expletives. He watched Eliza's eyes open and saw his aroused state mirrored in her eyes.

'Eliza, are you all right? Damn you, Alex, open this door!'

'One more minute, Bec. I swear she's unhurt,' Alex called, unwilling to break his connection with Eliza.

'One minute. And then I'm coming in. I have a key.'

Alex groaned. 'A regular rottweiler.'

Eliza laughed. 'A friendly one.' At his look of disbelief, she added, 'She's just being protective. You have a reputation.'

'I know it's not the fashion, but I want to court you. Exclusively.'

'Thirty seconds and I'm coming in!' shouted Bec.

'Come to lunch tomorrow and we can talk. Just the two of us. Without any well-intentioned friends.'

Eliza hesitated, before nodding.

Alex had enough time to kiss her quickly, position her in front of him – for his modesty – and loop an arm possessively across her hip before the door was flung open. Bec marched in, looking as if she was ready to avenge any wrong that Alex had committed towards her best friend.

Eliza removed Alex's arm and moved across the floor to wrap her friend in an embrace.

'I'm unhurt,' she joked. 'Two arms, two legs —'

'Heart?'

'Still intact.'

Alex wished he could say the same; his was slightly bent and out of shape. And until Wil's status in Eliza's life was resolved, it would likely remain that way. He consoled himself with the thought that he'd made progress. At least Eliza hadn't rejected his attentions or intentions outright and tomorrow would be another opportunity to advance his cause.

CHAPTER 32

Wednesday 5 August 1925

Eliza rushed up the steps of the Federal before her head reminded her feet that sporting a robust glow was not the most attractive way to greet Alex and she slowed her pace. Deciding that another few minutes could be put to her advantage, she entered the ladies' powder room and flung off her coat, hat and gloves. Approaching the mirror, she grimaced at the sight that met her. Released from imprisonment, her hair had decided to riot, and no amount of patting or persuading could tame it. Thank goodness her face wasn't as red as it felt. Applying a hint of colour to her lips, Eliza tucked her bangs behind her ears, picked up her belongings and walked calmly out and towards the central red-and-white marble staircase that would deliver her to the first floor.

Alex had crossed and uncrossed his legs a dozen times before Eliza appeared at the door of the dining room looking somewhat windswept but composed. He exhaled, realising that he'd feared she wouldn't show. It seemed that nothing in his life had prepared him in his pursuit of this woman. Deciding to put one foot in front of the other and hope for the best, he reached her in a few strides and took her by surprise by swinging her in a circle. As her feet reconnected with the carpeted floor, he took her face in his palms and kissed her.

'Alex!' she admonished. 'People are watching.'

'Let them. I thought you might have changed your mind,' he said. 'I'm glad you didn't.'

'I hummed and hawed. Sandwiches in the park with the birds, sitting in winter's elements or an à la carte at the Federal in comfort with you.' She spread her arms. 'It was a tough decision.'

'I hope my company tipped the scales,' Alex said, holding his breath as he waited for her answer.

'Of course. You're a much better conversationalist,' she replied with a wink.

'Minx!' Capturing her hand, he towed her towards their table, tucked away in a corner shielded from curious eyes. As they made their way, they could see pedestrians harassed by the wind blowing down Collins Street, hunched into their coats, hands buried in pockets or holding tightly to hats. But as soon as they were seated, the busyness of the city faded away, and the waiter's efficient but unhurried service in no way intruded on the intimacy that Alex had taken great pains to create. He was pleased that their chairs had been placed side by side as he'd requested – removing the barrier of the table between them went some way to assuaging Alex's craving to be close.

Searching for a safe topic, he landed on the evening's competition final. 'How are final preparations for tonight coming along?' he asked.

'We're as ready as we'll ever be.'

A shot of what he distilled as jealousy, rocked him. It was her casual yet warm expression '*we*' that had ignited it.

Oblivious to his reaction, Eliza continued, 'Bec and I are staying at the Y tonight and she'll help me get ready. Christine is bringing my gown to Birmingham's – she's refused to let it out of her sight.' She sighed. 'Although I'm not surprised, it's beautiful – despite the lack of material.' She laughed. 'Christine was quite affronted at my suggestion to add bits.'

'What bits?' asked Alex cautiously, his antennae tuned to her answer.

'Mmm. The back, for starters ... and the sides, too.' She paused as if cataloguing the missing parts in her mind.

Alex maintained a calm expression with effort, covering an impulse to object with a sip of water – wishing it were liberally laced with whisky.

'It's not my usual style, but I love it. Wil and I have had one practice, under Christine's and Mr B's critical eyes, and it felt ...' she giggled, 'as if I wasn't wearing anything.'

This was not a safe topic. Thoughts of Eliza in her dishabille, of Wil's hand in contact with her bare back, a lingering touch, a chance caress, so easily explained or dismissed as accidental – he should know – had Alex ordering that whisky. At his raised brow, Eliza declined any alcohol, citing the need to keep her wits about her for tonight's performance.

'Win or lose, we'll celebrate,' said Alex.

'Yes. Wil has colluded with Mr B for the patio and garden to be available for a private party from ten until midnight – he must be on board his ship by the early hours of the morning. We'll celebrate the outcome of the competition and his last night in town.'

Alex's plan had had a much smaller audience in mind, but he could hardly begrudge the American a farewell party – if it would help him on his way. But Alex didn't want to spend any more precious time talking about Wil.

'Um, do you remember our conversation last night?' he asked.

'In the kitchen at the Y?'

'Yes. And my question?'

'I remember.'

'Have you given it any consideration?' Alex asked, covering her hand where it lay on the table.

'I have questions.'

Alex groaned inwardly at her practical tone. This did not bode well for shared confidences. He nodded for her to continue, steeling himself for an interrogation.

'Is it true, you and Queenie have broken up?' At Alex's nod of affirmation, she persisted. 'For good?'

'Yes. Forever. I knew you wouldn't take me seriously until Queenie was out of the picture. In truth, she lost my attention some time back, but the situation was ... convenient.'

Narrowing her gaze, Eliza asked, 'How do I know that I'm not just your next ... convenience?'

'Because it's different.'

At her dubious expression, he continued, 'The way I think about you is different. Whenever another man looks at you, touches you, speaks to you – I want to punch them. I've never felt that possessive about Queenie – about any other woman before you.'

'Hmm, pretty words, but I'm not convinced.' Tucking her

hair behind her ear, Eliza attempted to remove her hand from beneath his.

Alex was having none of it. He scooted his chair closer, pressed his leg against hers beneath the white damask tablecloth and secured her hand. 'Is it because you're in love with Wil, Eliza?'

Eliza turned to face him. 'I have become very fond of Wil. He makes me laugh ... he makes me feel attractive.'

'And I don't?' Alex was puzzled. How could Eliza not know how alluring she was to him? How she made him feel? He adjusted himself under the guise of repositioning the napkin in his lap.

'You ...' Eliza studied their entwined fingers. 'You ... watch me, confuse me with your kisses and tempt me.' As her eyes returned to his face, he saw that confusion was mirrored in their depths. 'And give me butterflies.'

Alex thought that last statement sounded like an accusation. To be sure, he asked, 'That's a good thing, isn't it?'

'I guess. Maybe ...'

'Eliza, just give me a chance.'

Eliza shrugged her shoulders. 'I'm concerned that I'm not your type. That you'll get bored —'

'You're exactly my type,' he interrupted. 'It just took me time to recognise it.'

Eliza pressed her lips together, watching him. 'I want to believe you, Alex.'

'I think I'm in love with you.' Alex searched her face, hoping for a clue to her feelings, but her eyes were fathomless. 'And from what you've just said, you might be a little in love with me, too.'

Who knew Eliza had such a fine poker face? Alex thought. He'd just told her he thought he was in love with her ... he'd never said that to any woman before. Shouldn't she be gushing sentimentalities? Dancing around the table? Rushing to the rooftop? Not Eliza. Apparently, she wasn't finished with her questions.

'What about my tuition?'

He caught the hint of a smile in her tone. Leaning towards her, he whispered, 'I won't lie. I expect we may need to increase your number of hours. A sacrifice that I'm prepared for.' Capturing her chin in his fingers, he kissed her lingeringly. 'I'm ready to start at any time.'

Eliza rolled her eyes and pushed him away with a laugh.

'But I'm not prepared to share your tuition with anyone, Eliza.'

'I don't expect to share you, either,' she responded automatically.

'I can assure you that won't be a problem. Does that mean you agree to me courting you?'

Eliza smiled, turning to the fish the waiter had laid in front of her. 'How do you propose to go about our ... courtship?'

'The usual way. Movies, dinners, long walks, flowers, presents ...'

'And extended bouts of tuition.' Eliza's teasing tone and coquettish glance had Alex heating up. He felt a warm tide drifting into his cheeks. Another first. The thought of enjoying Eliza's uninhibited responses, being the first to introduce her to desire, made him hard.

'Hours ... and hours,' he confirmed, caressing her thigh under the cover of the table.

'Alex!' Eliza wasn't sure if the heat she was experiencing was from the intensity of Alex's tone, his hand on her thigh or the excitement that it invoked in her. Physical relations with Alex would never be considered a chore. Already, tendrils of awareness were travelling from her thigh to the pit of her stomach.

She'd overheard him described as a 'complete package' by members of her set. And Queenie had been both admired for managing to keep his attention and envied for her good luck. Would she, Eliza, be able to sustain his interest? He'd said that he thought he was in love with her. *Thought!* She was no longer in doubt of her feelings, but it seemed his still had a way to go. Her heart was basking in his declaration. Her head was suggesting she proceed with more caution. And could she get used to the admiring and enquiring female glances that he seemed oblivious to? *God, she wanted to think that she could.*

'Why the solemn face?'

Eliza decided she might as well be honest if they were to have any chance. 'Women are drawn to you,' she began, holding up her hand as he opened his mouth to interject. 'Just hear me out. It's not your fault, you're just naturally good-looking ... charismatic. Women won't believe that you're attracted to me exclusively. Especially if Queenie couldn't hold your attention.'

'I will give them my most arrogant expression,' which he proceeded to demonstrate. 'I'll be haughty, detached and indifferent. I'll refuse to dance ... to even speak with anyone but you ... or I have a better idea. Maybe we'll just stay away from people altogether,' he said, waggling his eyebrows.

Eliza shook her head at his antics. 'And what will you do

to disguise your tight, grab-a-handful behind?'

'Eliza, I'm shocked! But very pleased you've noticed.'

'I've often thought it your best feature,' she continued, enjoying their easy banter.

'Do you want to know what I love about you?' asked Alex, moving to place his mouth against her ear to avoid being overheard, as unlikely as that was, cocooned as they were in the corner.

Eliza held her breath.

'Your rioting curls which confound your attempts to suppress them – like now. The deep green pools of colour which I use as my compass to your thoughts and feelings – although not always successfully. The five freckles across your upturned nose.' Between each admission, Alex swirled his tongue around the rim of her ear or flicked it between the back of her lobe and the top of her nape. Eliza heard herself utter a small moan and opened her eyes in astonishment at her own wantonness.

'I love —'

'Am I interrupting anything of importance?' purred a voice that Eliza knew only too well. Queenie!

She watched Alex look up, acknowledge the efforts of the head waiter to protect their privacy, and discharge him with a shake of his head. 'As it happens, you are,' he replied, moving to place an arm around Eliza's shoulders. 'You'll understand if we don't invite you to join us.'

Queenie pouted and her scarlet-tipped fingers covered her heart. 'You wound me. Not so long ago —'

But Alex appeared to be in no mood to afford his ex-lover the stage she was hoping for. 'I don't wish to be rude,' he cut her off, 'but is there a reason you've sought us out?'

'Not Eliza, darling,' said Queenie with a pitying look in her direction. 'I've sought you out so I can collect my things from your suite. It'll only take a few minutes. I'm sure Eliza won't mind.'

Eliza wondered if she were invisible. It was like one of her teenage dreams. Boys asking other girls to join them in a game or to the beach in summer, all the while speaking over and around her.

Eliza recoiled at Alex's tone, glad after all that he wasn't speaking to her. 'What things?'

Queenie didn't look daunted. 'Darling, I'm sure Eliza doesn't want to hear an inventory. Suffice it to say, there are things that a girl needs ... but if you truly don't have time, then maybe just my gloves. I can pick up the other things when it suits you.'

Eliza saw the exact moment when realisation hit Alex. *Queenie's gloves!* She could almost hear him say it. She wondered how much time Queenie had spent in his suite. Were her *things* to be found in the wardrobe and bathroom cabinets? She felt the poached fish turn over in her stomach. She would not be sick – she'd not give Queenie that satisfaction.

Alex was watching her. He looked like he was contemplating his next move. While she didn't want to be left here alone with Queenie, the idea of Alex taking the woman to his suite appealed even less.

'I'll be all right for a few minutes, Alex. You don't want to be responsible for Queenie getting chilblains,' she heard herself say. She was pleased with how steady her voice sounded.

He kissed the top of her shoulder, promising, 'I'll be back

soon,' before hastening towards the lifts.

Queenie pulled out a chair and subsided like a sated feline. 'Mind if I smoke?'

'Actually, I do. Would you like a drink?'

'No, thank you, this is not a social call.'

They sat in silence for a few minutes, which for Eliza was the extent to which she could remain still without fidgeting. In contrast, Queenie looked like a pampered cat, nonchalantly powdering her nose with the help of a gilt-backed mirror. Finally satisfied with her appearance, she directed her attention to Eliza.

'I realise this might be a little awkward. As Alex no doubt has told you, he and I felt like we needed a break from one another. To renew our ... juices, so to speak. Relations were becoming humdrum, if you know what I mean.'

Eliza remained silent. What would be the right response under the circumstances? Instead, she tilted her head to acknowledge she was listening.

'Alex has always valued your friendship, so I'm not surprised he's reached out to you.' This statement was accompanied by a hand to Eliza's forearm and a smile that appeared genuine until you made eye contact. 'We agreed that during this time, we were free to see other people. I'm so glad it's you. You're like a favourite blanket to him – warm and cosy and entirely predictable.'

Eliza would have said one of her best attributes was her calm outward demeanour. Even when she was angry – like now – she worked at maintaining an impassive expression. Bec had on occasion criticised her for being inscrutable. Especially when she couldn't get her own way. But Queenie's *favourite blanket* analogy had her ready to smother the woman with her own fur trim. She was saved by Alex's reappearance and thankful for the speed at which he despatched Queenie and her reunited gloves.

Before she could say a word, Alex exploded, 'I have never invited Queenie to my suite. *Never!*'

She gave him a tight smile.

'And she left her gloves here in the lounge the night we broke up. I hadn't had the opportunity to return them.'

Glancing at her watch, Eliza realised her lunchbreak was well and truly over and thanked fate that Jenny was still on her honeymoon with Johnnie, and she didn't need any explanations.

'I've got to go. I'm late, and just lucky that Bec agreed to cover the start of my afternoon class. But her dance knowledge can only sustain the girls' attention for so long.'

'What did she say?' asked Alex in a steely tone.

Eliza considered his question. While she wasn't so green as to believe everything her newly anointed nemesis had revealed, she needed time away from Alex to reflect. 'I've got to go,' she repeated.

'Do not believe a word she says. She wants to poison our budding romance.'

'I'm late. You and Queenie have given me a lot to think about. I'm just not ready to talk about things until I have my thoughts in order.'

Alex growled. Eliza was startled into a chuckle and then a gasp as he lifted her hand to his lips and kissed the centre of her palm, closing her fingers over the spot. 'For safekeeping. Whatever Queenie said, believe me when I say I'm serious about you. And I'll do anything to make you believe that.'

Eliza nodded and stilled him as she rose. 'Stay here. I

don't need an escort. Will I see you tonight?'

'Try to keep me away. Remember, I love you. I no longer think it – I know it.'

Eliza nodded, robbed of speech. *Alex loved her. Had she heard correctly? Could he repeat it just so her head and her heart could be sure?* She tucked his admission away like a secret and fled down the stairs.

Damn! Damn! Bloody damn! Things had been going so well. Alex had never hated anyone as much as he did Queenie at that moment. He wished he could put her on the next train back to Sydney and ensure she never left.

Eliza's fledgling self-confidence was too new to withstand a targeted attack. And he had no doubt that Queenie's delivery would have been smooth. Conversational. He'd seen her in action before. He threw back the rest of his whisky, enjoying the warmth that spread through his chest. He called for another.

A small part of him – if he was honest – was also angry that Eliza gave any credence to Queenie's innuendos or outright lies. What hope did they have if she couldn't trust him? Yes, he had a reputation. But he'd told her he loved her.

After twenty minutes of brooding and a second calming whisky, Alex resolved to swallow his pride and take Daniel and Bec into his confidence. He needed reinforcements and this was no time to exercise reticence or wallow in his pride.

CHAPTER 33

Competition Final

A rampaging menagerie of critters had taken up residence in Eliza's stomach and all attempts to distract, dissuade, humour or calm them had failed. Wil was trying to exhaust them, having refused to allow Eliza to leave the dance floor for the last four sets. She was beginning to wonder if the competition had been changed to a dance marathon. Maybe that wasn't such a bad thing. In a state of exhaustion, she wouldn't be constantly reminded of Alex's words from earlier.

She'd arrived back at the Y to find a dishevelled Bec and eight mutinous young ladies. It had taken all her concentration and the rest of the afternoon to regain their full attention and enthusiasm. But once the lesson had finished, Alex's declaration had come storming into her head – much like the man himself. And although a cliché, seeds of hope had blossomed. Were still blossoming ... despite the critter gymnasts she was working to control.

'Enough,' she said, towing Wil towards the edge of the floor, as the band's tempo moved from a foxtrot to a

French tango. 'Mr B tells me it's normal to feel nervous,' she confided with a wry smile.

'I reckon we'll consider it a good omen, then,' said Wil, kissing the top of her head. 'Especially, since I'm thinkin' some of your animals have escaped and taken up residence in my chest.'

Eliza chuckled.

'That's better. I am the envy of every hot-blooded male here and I don't want people thinkin' it's a trial to be dancin' with me,' said Wil, his lopsided grin in evidence.

Eliza gave him a wide smile. 'I'm so glad that you and I met. You are the best dance partner any girl could wish for.'

'But not the best partner,' Wil said, turning down the corners of his mouth and pushing his bottom lip into a pout.

Eliza kissed his cheek. 'I wish I had a different answer for you ... but I don't.'

'We made it,' huffed Bec, landing beside Eliza in a flurry. 'I thought Christine's last customer was never going to leave.'

'But we are here, *non*?' said Christine with a nonchalant shrug. 'And this is ...'

'How rude of me. Christine, this is Seaman Wil Sanders, my long-suffering waltz partner. Wil, meet modiste extraordinaire, Christine Tailleuse.'

Christine openly studied Wil, then finally smiled in a way which suggested she liked what she saw. He later joked to Eliza he wouldn't have been surprised if she'd asked if he could strip for his measurements.

Excusing themselves, the three women hurried off to transform Eliza in preparation for the final.

Alex ran up the stairs of Birmingham's, surrendered his coat to the regular attendant and pocketed the ticket proffered. He paused a few feet inside the door, squinting against the glare of the chandeliers as he perused the dance floor and its edges. It was impossible to discern all but a few familiar faces since the floor was swirling with couples, many partnered with American seamen and officers. The edges were equally as crowded with those taking a break or waiting for an opportunity to slip into the whirlpool.

He'd hoped to speak to Eliza alone before the competition final but doubted his ability to find her among all these people. Damn! He should have got here earlier.

'Any sign of Eliza?' asked Daniel, arriving beside him, the question accompanied by a hand in the middle of Alex's back.

'No, and I'm unlikely given the crush,' said Alex, turning to greet his friend. 'Travelling solo?'

'Evelyn's got herself into a knot over your split with Queenie and is none too happy that I haven't severed our ties. She'll calm down, and if she doesn't, well ...' he shrugged, 'maybe it's time for a change.'

'Mmm,' Alex was only half listening. He'd spotted Wil in the middle of a scrum of blue jackets. There was a lot of backslapping, bumping and jabbing going on, but Wil's broad grin suggested it was good-natured. 'There's Wil at two o'clock,' he said.

'Let's secure a spot,' said Daniel, checking his wristwatch. 'It's about to start. Come on.'

They navigated their way slowly through the press of bodies – Daniel piloting a path and Alex drafting behind him. After what seemed like half an hour of tunnelling and zigzagging, they emerged on the edge of the floor. A few metres away, the band were readying themselves for the competition start.

'I'm impressed,' said Alex. 'You're a regular wombat.'

'Really? That's the best you can come up with. A wombat?'

'Who's a wombat?' asked Bec as she squeezed into a non-existent space on Daniel's left and offered a soft apology to a couple whose feet she'd just trampled.

'Never mind,' said Daniel, putting his arm around her waist and drawing her to stand in front of him. 'Stand here. Everyone will be safer.'

'How's Eliza?' asked Alex.

'Nervous. But she'll be all right once she's on the floor.'

A hush ran around the ballroom as a drum roll introduced Dick Birmingham and his wife, Nola, dressed in a gown resplendent with green glass beads, onto the dance floor.

'Very chic,' murmured Christine, who had appeared and taken up a position beside Alex. 'I love the draped cape back. And the shoes – notice the buckle matching the colour of her gown. It could almost be one of mine.'

Alex raised an eyebrow. Did the woman think he was interested in dresses and shoes?

She gave him a smug smile. 'Soon, you will see my gown for Eliza. It is much superior.'

Alex was much more interested in the woman wearing Miss Tailleuse's gown, but he merely nodded.

'Good evening, everyone. Well, what a fortnight it's been. My darling wife and I would like to welcome you to the finals of Birmingham's Fleet Waltz Competition,' boomed Mr Birmingham.

A round of applause greeted this along with a few admiring whistles.

Always the showman, he responded with, 'Thank you! But save your applause for my beautiful wife. Doesn't she look gorgeous tonight?'

More applause and many more whistles as Mr Birmingham stepped back and his wife dropped into a curtsy.

'Tonight, couples will compete for a purse of one hundred pounds. Each partnership consists of a member from the visiting American naval fleet and one of our own homegrown Melbourne misses.'

'Too much talk,' grumbled Christine to no one in particular.

'Ten couples were selected from a starting line-up of fifty couples. And the man responsible for that decision and for judging tonight's winners is the renowned British professional Philip Dickson. Please make him welcome.'

Debonair in tails and top hat, Philip strode onto the floor to stand beside Nola Birmingham, waving royally.

'And now, let me introduce our competitors.'

'No Queenie,' observed Daniel.

'Too bucolic for Miss Nolan, I understand,' said Bec, her dimple in evidence. 'Although, Philip Dickson's refusal to work with her again would have tipped the scales.'

'How do you even know that?' asked Daniel suspiciously.

'Jungle drums.'

Alex watched the exchange with amusement. Bec enjoyed exasperating Daniel, who as a typical engineer did not appreciate innuendo or any shade of *grey*. His 'pfff' summed up his thoughts on the matter.

'Miss Eliza Sinclair and her partner, Seaman Wil Sanders, from the USS *Oklahoma*.'

'Sensational ... stunning ... gorgeous,' were just some of the comments that Alex registered as he drank in the sight of Eliza as she bobbed a curtsy. He had prepared himself, based on Eliza's previous description of her gown, for acres of skin and an urge to punch anyone who looked at her with salacious intent ... or any intent! But the glimpse he'd seen as she'd glided onto the floor, and now, as she stood arm in arm with Wil, didn't even hint at scandal. Her arms were the most exposed, but this was offset by the demure neckline. Perhaps she'd elected to wear a different gown. He rolled his shoulders and settled in to enjoy the next forty-five minutes.

As the couples commenced their warm-up, he felt Bec and Christine cast curious glances his way. Surely, they didn't think he was so unhinged as to react to the sight of bare arms? He assumed his regular social countenance, pleased by thoughts of having muddled the two women's expectations.

Responding to a question from Daniel took Alex's attention away for a few seconds. Returning his focus to the tableau on the floor, he felt confused. Eliza ... he blinked. Yes, it was Eliza, and she was ... naked. At least to the base of her spine. Well, not completely naked, but those ties holding her bodice together didn't look too sturdy. He wasn't sure if they'd survive a vigorous spin turn, let alone a whole dance bracket. He continued his study. At least the skirt was full length ... until he realised that the roll of her hips produced a sensual display, emphasised by the web-like pattern of sequinned strings and small globes which appeared to hover and drift from her buttocks to her ankles as she danced.

'Beautiful, *non*?' Alex's jaw joined his cock, tightening in response to Christine's question. He hoped she wasn't expecting an answer. 'One of my best, I think,' she mused. 'No lines. The black silk underwear is very avant-garde.'

THE BATTLE FOR ELIZA

Bec clapped her hands, smirking as Alex swallowed hard and then cleared his throat.

Alex caught Daniel eyeing him. 'Game, set and match, I'm thinking,' his friend summed up the situation.

Through clenched teeth, Alex managed, 'I don't really care what you're thinking. I do care that Eliza is displaying parts of herself that I haven't even seen yet.' To his annoyance, Daniel merely grinned.

Alex regained control of himself by the end of the warm-up. That was, if he didn't count the three young men he'd threatened to decapitate, after the fools had tried to press slips of paper with their phone numbers to Eliza as she'd waltzed past. Or the growling sound that would automatically spring forth from his throat when Wil's hand drifted even a millimetre from its regulation hold.

Dick Birmingham had cleverly organised the finals into two parts. In the first half, all the couples would perform on the floor at the same time. But to make it fair, since there was only one adjudicator and it was difficult to assess all ten partnerships equally, in the second half, each couple would complete their routines without any other couple on the floor.

Alex only had eyes for Eliza, but Christine insisted on providing a running commentary of the gowns, which Bec punctuated with her opinion on the floor craft.

'Argh! How is it possible for a collision to occur? They have the whole damned dance floor!' Bec's hands shot up in the air in frustration.

'Such language,' teased Daniel, covering Bec's ears where she stood in front of him. 'Ow! What did you do that for?' he said, rubbing his ribs.

233

'An automatic reaction,' apologised Bec.

'That colour is too strong for that poor girl,' tutted Christine with a hand on Alex's arm. 'She even looks agitated and she's making me feel irritated.'

Alex quickly scanned the floor looking for the unfortunate gown. It was red. But at least it had all of its fabric intact. The only gown that was disturbing Alex was Eliza's. The bow-shaped brooch at the base of her spine kept drawing his eye. It was winking at him, taunting him.

As the final soulful notes from the saxophone echoed around the ballroom, the couples acknowledged the crowd's appreciation, which included foot stomping from an exuberant group in the far corner, before exiting the floor.

'I couldn't tell from Mr Dickson's expression who he scored highest,' groused Bec. 'They all danced well. Although, the girl in green looked a little fatigued.'

'Washed out,' agreed Christine.

Alex cocked his head and exchanged a bemused smile with Daniel.

'They're starting,' said Bec, standing on her toes. 'I wonder if there's any significance to the order they are asked to dance. Mr B is conferring with the judge.'

Alex watched Dick Birmingham nod and clap the other man on the shoulder before walking to the centre of the floor.

'I hope you enjoyed the first performance from our ten finalists. Each couple will now be invited back to the floor to demonstrate their skill and allow you to feast your eyes on the girls' magnificent gowns. Please make welcome our first couple, Miss Eliza Sinclair and Seaman Wil Sanders from the USS *Oklahoma*.'

'She looks nervous,' Daniel muttered.

As the couple waited for the introductory notes of the music, Alex watched Wil release one of Eliza's hands and place a finger beneath her chin. Whatever he said brought a brilliant smile to her face. They stepped back and then came together as one, just as the music settled into the three-four timing of the waltz rhythm.

Alex crossed his arms. He grudgingly admitted that Eliza and Wil danced well together. Suited in both height and stride length, they were graceful and elegant, flowing across the floor. Their steps, a combination of basic natural and reverse turns with several locks and spins, appeared effortless. But Alex was having a hard time concentrating on their dancing with Eliza dressed so sparingly. As they danced a spin turn out of a corner, he caught a flash of black-stockinged thigh. *All right, everyone has seen enough. Let's move onto the next couple, please!* yelled Alex silently.

He watched the other nine couples parade one by one around the floor. He knew most of the girls by sight, had danced with them – probably exchanged a flirtatious smile with a few at one time or another. But none engaged his interest or evoked his feelings.

When the last competitors quit the floor, Mr Birmingham returned to centrestage. He quipped at the challenge that awaited Philip Dickson to judge a winner and invited everyone to take a partner for the next bracket. He revealed that the champion couple would be announced in the next half-hour.

Alex's immediate thought was to engage Eliza, but it turned out that wasn't just his imperative, but half the male population of Birmingham's.

As if reading his mind, Bec grabbed his hand. 'Come on, it'll be easier if you have a partner to swap.'

Maybe they could become *mates*, Alex thought. Daniel, as a male of the species, did have limitations.

'Would you mind if I lead?' he asked politely as Bec's attempt to foxtrot against the line of dance threatened to have them expelled from the floor.

'By all means. Maybe the shortest route isn't the quickest ... or safest,' she agreed sheepishly as Alex deftly avoided another collision, apologised and redirected them safely in an anticlockwise direction.

'There she is ... eleven o'clock ... she's dancing with that dolt Derek Fisher.' Bec swung her head to keep Eliza in sight as Alex led them around the far turn of the floor.

'Well, she was ... someone's cut in. An officer, by the look of the uniform. And another one ...'

Alex frowned and revised his plan. He would have to whisk Eliza from the floor. After that he didn't have much of a plan, but he was sure he'd think of something.

'Prepare to jump ship,' he ordered Bec.

In later years, he might embellish the story of Eliza's abduction from the arms of her erstwhile admirers, for the snatch-and-grab manoeuvre proved comically easy to achieve and the feebly lit patio provided a discreet location for what Alex had in mind.

Eliza had been enjoying herself. Her ears were still ringing from the crazy compliments she'd received, and she was dizzy from the number of partners that had insisted on dancing with her. Wil's efforts to shield her had been ineffectual, especially in the face of the first person to cut in – one of his commanding officers. He'd shrugged apologetically and surrendered her reluctantly. She hadn't caught his name but could have listened to him utter nonsense in his deep southern drawl about how smart she was, how pretty and how sweet she was, all night. Apparently, *he was as happy as a clam at high tide*, which seemed nicer than the next seaman who butted in, who swore *he was happier 'n a tick on a dog!* As he was smiling when he said it, Eliza figured it was a good thing and smiled in return.

She still couldn't account for the exact moment that she found herself at the darkened end of the patio with Alex. He'd removed his coat and draped it carefully across her shoulders to ward off the cold Melbourne night air, maintaining eye contact the whole time. Using the coat's sleeves, he reeled her closer – until they were touching. Unable to maintain his gaze – or not without tilting her head at an odd angle – she'd closed her eyes and hoped the point of the exercise was that he would kiss her. She hadn't had to wait long before he bent and captured her mouth. It felt as if he was asking a question, as the kiss was neither comforting nor robbing her of thought.

Eliza sighed. She had no patience to examine whether his interest was the forever kind. He was here, with her – not Queenie – and she was hungry for him, enveloped in his smell and the warmth of his jacket. Boldly, she slipped the buttons of his waistcoat and ran her hands from his sculptured abdomen up to his chest. Two small points captured her attention and she circled them with the tips of her fingers. At Alex's gasp, she tweaked them between her thumb and forefinger. Fascinated, she leaned in and swirled her tongue around and over the left one, drawing back

VICKI MILLIKEN

slightly to study her handiwork. As she moved to lavish the same attention on the right nipple, she heard an anguished, '*My God, Eliza.*' It appeared her initiative had caught him off guard. His immediate response was to cradle her head in two strong palms and tilt it at the perfect angle for plundering.

Alex ravaged her lips and ransacked the inside of her mouth with the tip of his tongue. Eliza retaliated with an assault on his butt. She had mentioned at lunch it was her favourite part and she was determined to lavish attention on the taut globes. How many years had she waited to do this? Kneading and stroking. His cock pressed insistently against her abdomen and she giggled, feeling the urgency that had been building subside. Slowly.

Alex tucked her head beneath his chin and held her. She opened her mouth to speak, to tell him how much she loved him, but he quietened her.

'Shhhh. No words, there's no time to get them right,' he murmured, putting a little distance between their bodies and brushing the pad of his thumb across her lips.

'You're so beautiful. I've wanted to kill every man who's looked at you tonight, never mind those who touched you. That dress is very sexy.'

Eliza felt like a siren under Alex's gaze. He looked perturbed, not angry, just flustered, and bothered. And she was responsible. It made her feel strong and confident, she realised.

'Eliza, are you out here?' hissed Bec into the darkness from where she stood framed in the doorway to the ballroom.

'We're here,' responded Alex, before she could speak.

'Mr B's about to announce the winners, you'd better get in here.'

THE BATTLE FOR ELIZA

Alex kept a possessive hand in the small of her back as they walked towards Bec, only removing his coat from her shoulders as she stepped through the doorway.

Bec gave her a once-over, declared she'd do and swept her off in the direction of the assembled competitors.

Alex shrugged into his coat. Looking down, he smiled at the small wet patch on his shirt, before buttoning his waistcoat and concealing it. He rolled his eyes at the romantic notion of keeping it close to his heart.

He'd been curious as to how far she'd go and what form it would take – but was unprepared for the powerful jolt that had shot to his abdomen when her lips had covered his nipple and her hands had gripped his arse. *Where had she learned that? On second thoughts, I don't want to know.* When she'd cuddled closer and a series of moans had escaped her throat, he'd struggled to take back control. She'd appeared intent on monopolising their pleasure.

What wasn't in any doubt was he had an affliction, for which there was only one remedy. Whatever she wanted, whatever it took, he'd make Eliza his.

When Alex reappeared beside Daniel, Wil had Eliza tucked securely against his side.

Philip Dickson stepped forward and handed Mr Birmingham a slip of paper. Birmingham's patriarch read it and a smile spread across his face.

'I'm pleased to announce the winners are ... a drum roll if you please ... looking exquisite tonight ...' he paused for effect, '... and dancing fabulously ... Miss Eliza Sinclair and Seaman Wil Sanders.'

A loud cheer went up. It was reported in *Table Talk* that

239

the sound was so loud it could be heard by those as far away as the Princess Theatre in Spring Street. Balloons cascaded from the ceiling and those on and around the floor were engulfed in a web of streamers.

Both Wil and Eliza appeared to be in a daze – congratulating the other couples as if on autopilot – before another seaman propelled the couple onto the floor to shake hands with Philip Dickson. Accepting a cheque for one hundred pounds from Mr and Mrs Birmingham, Eliza had tears streaming down her face. Mr Birmingham jokingly complained to the watching crowd of a wet neck and the ruin of his suit.

'Thank you to everyone who competed. Congratulations to Eliza and Wil. A round of applause for Philip. And a huge thankyou to everyone for coming out to support the event,' roared Mr B over the noise, barely seeming to draw breath. 'But it's not over yet. The evening is still young. Art Bobbie and the Birmingham Syncopators are just warming up. Grab a partner and let's make this a night our American brethren will long remember.'

Alex watched as Bec and Christine ran onto the floor, seizing Eliza and dancing in a tight circle, refusing any intrusion from enthusiastic well-wishers.

'Shall we?' Daniel asked Alex with a lift of his brow, before shouldering his way through the crowd.

Alex followed, collected Eliza in his arms as she stepped out of her brother's hug, and in front of everyone, kissed her full on the lips. 'I'm so proud of you,' he whispered, ignoring those around him clamouring to congratulate her.

'Don't keep her all to yourself, ol' man,' drawled someone behind him.

Alex spun around to confront whoever had addressed him. Eliza was not a parcel to be passed from hand to hand.

'He's just a kid, Alex,' Wil stated calmly from beside a seaman who looked no more than seventeen. 'Just caught up in the excitement.'

Alex's chin rose a fraction and he considered the young man.

Wil clapped the boy on the shoulder. 'That ain't how you speak to ladies or gentlemen, Wallace. Now be off with you.' He turned back to Alex. 'I've come to collect my girl. They want to take some photographs of the winners and talk to some newspaper reporter.'

Alex nodded, although he was conscious Wil wasn't asking permission as he secured Eliza's hand and turned to burrow his way through those assembled. Eliza blew him a kiss as she hurried after Wil.

'Not your finest moment,' giggled Bec, looping her hand through the crook of his elbow and urging him off the floor. 'But sweet. It's obvious you love her.'

'Bec —' growled Alex.

'But don't ruin her night by threatening every man who wants to congratulate her or dance with her.'

Alex counted to ten. Bec had a point; this was Eliza's night. She deserved to bask in the attention. He just wasn't feeling social. The thought of the remainder of the evening spent watching her enjoying herself, or him making small talk with people he didn't care about and dancing with a bevy of admirers he no longer had patience for, stripped away his enthusiasm. And Eliza wouldn't thank him for standing around and brooding. He would speak with her, congratulate Wil, and then slip away. He suddenly felt every one of his twenty-six years. He'd also make sure Daniel was sticking around. Someone needed to keep an eye on Eliza and make sure she got back to the YWCA accommodation safely. Especially with the number of sailors on their last night of shore leave.

Eliza was buzzing. The competition result had been all that she'd dreamed of. And she couldn't remember her and Wil dancing so effortlessly – all their hours of practice had come together. They'd been inundated with well-wishers from the moment Mr B had announced their names. Wil had seized the opportunity after the *Table Talk* reporter had left them alone, to share a champagne toast, some quiet words and an enormous hug.

They still had an arm around one another when Alex appeared – the second time. He seemed calmer and sincere in his congratulations to them both. Wil excused himself, and she surrendered to Alex's fierce embrace.

Drawing away, he looked at her with eyes that resembled swirling pools of bubbling chocolate. 'I'm sorry if I embarrassed you before. But I love you.'

She nodded, believing herself finally able to give him her heart. They'd have to talk about limiting his possessiveness, but that was a conversation for another time.

The pad of Alex's thumb caressed her bottom lip. 'Let's talk tomorrow. All day if necessary. Without interruption.'

She smiled.

'You two look too sombre. Here,' Wil said, pressing a glass of champagne into both of their hands. 'Come on, the night isn't over yet,' he added, jerking his head towards a group including Bec, Daniel, Christine and a score of seamen. She didn't see Alex after that.

At the stroke of midnight, she ventured to ask her brother if he'd seen Alex. In her heightened state – two champagnes – she was boldly thinking that they might make their tomorrow conversation an early one and had sought him out without success. She was irritated to see Evelyn pasted to her brother like a pressed flower, an owlish look on her face. *One too many champagnes*, she thought uncharitably.

'Have you seen Alex?' she asked Daniel.

'Hmm. Went home. Getting too old,' he chortled.

'With Queenie,' mumbled Evelyn, blinking at her.

'No,' Daniel said emphatically.

'Yes,' she persisted. 'We were arriving as he was leaving.' She hiccupped. 'Queenie never made it up the steps.'

Eliza's heart sank and her stomach ended up somewhere near her knees. *He wouldn't*, she thought. *Would he?* He'd told her he loved her. She had been ready to tell him that she loved him … when he'd quietened her. She didn't know what to think. She mumbled something to Daniel and walked away, shocked. Bec found her five minutes later in a curtained alcove.

'Daniel alerted me,' she said by way of explanation. 'I don't believe it, by the way. Alex is wound up like a spring over you. If Queenie's with him, it was because she followed him, not by invitation. I could slap Evelyn.'

'Queenie told me they were having a break. That he'd only reached out to me because I was … that I was like a … a favourite blanket,' confided Eliza, biting her lower lip. 'You'd think I'd learn.'

'Fiddle-faddle,' spat Bec.

'I'm in love with him, Bec.'

'That's good because it'll make tomorrow's plan easier to implement.'

CHAPTER 34

Thursday 6 August 1925

The Departure

He'd be late ... she'd be gone ... and that Yank seaman would sail away with his most precious possession. Alex was sure if he were thinking clearly, he'd articulate that differently. Eliza would not approve of being anyone's possession. On the other hand, she could claim him all she liked!

Damn train. What was taking so long? They had only just crossed the river. He hung his torso out of one of the seven carriages bursting with sailors and young women intent on making the most of their final hours together. He had no doubt it was close to its crush capacity.

Finally, some speed. He pulled his torso back through the window and checked his watch – three-ten pm. *The Argus* had reported that the flagship Seattle and its three consorts, including the *Oklahoma*, were departing at eight pm and all crew were to be on board by four pm so that final preparations could be completed before sailing.

He'd arrived at the YWCA just after one, looking forward

to enticing Eliza to play hooky and join him in an intimate celebration of her success. Horn-rimmed Hannah had been guarding reception. He was surprised to learn that Eliza was not in today, but was offered no explanation as to why. He supposed he should commend the woman's handling of staff privacy, but it was damned annoying. Yes, Bec was on the premises, but in an interview for another half an hour. She reluctantly conceded he could wait and directed him to a chair.

Alex wondered if he'd forgotten Eliza wasn't working today. No, he was sure she hadn't mentioned anything. Maybe celebrations had finished late – or in the early hours of this morning – and she was still asleep. Although, he doubted Mrs Sinclair would entertain her daughter sleeping until lunchtime. Maybe she hadn't made it home and was still partying. His stomach tightened. Or maybe she was with that goddam Yank. He remembered seeing Wil with his arm around Eliza's waist, sharing a toast, just before he'd left. Damn, he should have stayed. What if —?

His manic thoughts were interrupted by the sight of Bec rushing into reception, dressed to ward off the Antarctic-fuelled winds battering the city and carrying a suitcase. She seemed unsurprised to find him waiting for her. *Probably alerted by horn-rimmed Hannah*, he thought.

'I suppose you're looking for Eliza. Well, she's not in, as I'm sure Hannah has explained. I'm in a bit of a rush, as you can see ... there's been a change of plans —'

'What plans?' Alex ground out, on his feet and striding towards her.

'Eliza's, of course ... so romantic ... and with Wil leaving tonight —'

THE BATTLE FOR ELIZA

'Where is Eliza, Bec?' Alex asked, trying not to loom over Eliza's best friend.

'At the pier. With Wil. Where else would she be?'

Alex could think of any number of places where Eliza should be. Here, with him, would top the list. 'Bec —'

'Got to run, Alex. The chaplain ...' The words were whipped away by the wind as she eddied out the door, down the steps and disappeared.

Alex blinked. Had Bec just declared that Eliza was tying the knot with Wil? He could think of no other explanation. He knew the *Oklahoma* had a chaplain – Alex had spoken to him at Jenny's wedding reception. But there'd been no time between last night and now to get a marriage licence – had there? Or had Wil secured one earlier in the hope that Eliza would say yes. The suitcase was undoubtedly hers from the bold lettering, *Miss Eliza Sinclair, Williamstown/Melbourne/Australia*. But she wouldn't be allowed to sail with him. He shook his head. Nothing was making sense.

He'd tried desperately to locate Daniel – Eliza's supposed chaperone last night. His had been the last assurance Alex had sought before heading home. But Daniel wasn't at work or at their usual lunchtime haunt. Alex had abandoned his search to travel to Port Melbourne to intercept Eliza.

Bending his head to peer out the window, he gauged that they were almost there as the train passed the North Port station sign. Another five minutes, if there were no further delays.

The train pulled into Port Melbourne station. Should he ride it to Princes Pier, the next stop, or leg it from here? It was three twenty-five pm. He decided to wait. The closer he

247

could disembark to the actual pier the better. The roads and foreshore were congested with an endless procession of cars and well-wishers.

Before the carriage wheels had stopped turning at Princes Pier, Alex squeezed around a sailor and his girl sandwiched beside him, offering a clipped apology. He opened the door, jumped to the platform and set off at pace.

Eliza and Wil stood on the outside of a group of blue jackets under the watchful eye of an officer. They, like Wil, had been given permission to step ashore one last time. Some were backslapping one another, delighted to be reunited after a fortnight apart partying – the air heavy with innuendo and male banter. Others had their arms around and lips locked with local sweethearts, sharing private endearments and soothing female tears. Music from the *Oklahoma*'s band floated across the pier.

Wil took Eliza's hands and squeezed them reassuringly. 'Any minute now, he'll come charging through the crowd. I imagine we'll see the smoke from his nostrils heralding his arrival.'

Eliza laughed despite the rolling of her stomach. 'You and Bec are awfully confident ... don't you mean *if* he arrives.'

'I've got a tenner on it. He'll be here. Safest money I ever laid. I reckon the thought of you marryin' me will undo him. He's takin' with you somethin' awful.'

'Ah, Wil. I'm so glad we met.'

'Me, too, honey. It's been crazy fun. I wish things had been different, y'know. I think we would have made a swell couple. Still time to change your mind.'

When Eliza tasted salt, she realised her eyes were wet, and

she probably had rivulets etched into her made-up cheeks. She gave Wil a watery smile and tucked her head into his shoulder as he gathered her close and took the liberty of painting warm circles on her back with the palms of his hands. Of their own accord, they started to travel further south, but Eliza was too miserable to care.

'She's ... mine ... take ... your hands off her.'

Eliza jumped at the sound of Alex's voice, turning out of Wil's arms with a dazed expression. *He'd come.*

'Eliza ... you ...' More deep breaths and unfinished sentences escaped as Alex appeared to be fighting to catch his breath, sucking in air at a rate of knots.

'Last call.' This from an officer brandishing a whistle – *Fweet!*

'Eliza, you can't. I won't let you.'

'Alex, I —'

'You're my —'

'Yes, I know. Your friend. Or is it your favourite blanket?' She narrowed her eyes in anger.

'What?'

'Yes. Queenie was very enlightening.'

'When? And why are you even listening to Queenie?' Alex asked, spreading his arms, imploring her.

'Were you with her last night?' Eliza asked, folding her arms.

'Absolutely not!'

Eliza stood motionless, trying to decide if he was telling the truth.

'She tried to waylay me as I left Birmingham's,' he admitted. 'But I brushed her off and told her she was wasting her time. I told her I loved you.'

249

Eliza looked away. The intensity of his gaze was making it hard to think.

'I went home. Alone. To bed.'

Eliza's gaze snapped back to his face. The raw emotion was unmistakeable. Alex seemed to sense her uncertainty. He stepped forward, reached out to capture her hand and pulled her towards him, step by step.

'And dreamed of you. All night.' When she was inches away from him, and her skirts were flirting with his legs, he whispered, 'Please believe me.'

Eliza parted her lips, and he leaned forward to brush his lips over hers. Careless to the wolf whistles and claps from the crowd, Alex kept on exploring – the corners of her mouth, her cheekbones, the delicate skin beneath her eyes.

He drew back and kissed the tip of her nose. 'Don't do it. I want all of you, forever, every day. You can't marry him. Not without giving me a chance. I love you.'

There it was again, that marshmallow feeling in the pit of her stomach. Did she dare trust that he genuinely loved her? Eliza's resolve was melting. Soon Alex would be kissing a puddle if this continued.

'Ahem ... sorry to break up this very touching scene, but I have a ship awaitin', and last call was a few minutes ago,' interrupted Wil.

At the sound of his voice, Eliza started. Alex's arms were locked around her and he hadn't turned a hair at Wil's announcement, content to nuzzle her ear. She rather thought he'd happily ignore Wil altogether if she didn't act.

'Alex,' she admonished him. 'Release me so that I can say a proper goodbye.'

Unperturbed at her tone, he turned her slowly within the

security of his arms until she was facing Wil. He ensured she maintained an arm's-length distance.

'I guess this means we won't be gettin' hitched,' said Wil, a twinkle in his eye.

Eliza braced herself as Alex lunged towards the sailor, almost knocking her over in the process.

Wil put his hands up in defence, a grin splitting his face.

'I won't let her marry you without a fight.'

'Oh, stop it. Both of you. Wil's only joking,' said Eliza, shaking off Alex and moving forward to give Wil an extended hug.

'Only half joking,' he whispered in her ear. 'Take care.' This he said in a voice loud enough to extend to Alex. 'And if this jackass don't treat you right, wire me, you have my address. I'll marry you in a flash.' Matching his words to his actions, he made a reluctant show of releasing her, trailing his fingers down her arms to gently squeeze her fingers.

Stepping up behind Eliza, Alex anchored two arms across her hips and pulled her back against him. 'Your departure can't come soon enough,' he growled. 'Safe passage ... bon voyage ... have a good life.'

Wil blew her a kiss and saluted Alex's scowling face, before he turned in the direction of his ship. Johnnie met him at the bottom of the gangplank, throwing an arm across his shoulders as they made their way onto the ship. Once on deck, he braced himself against the railing, blew her another kiss, and with a final wave disappeared from view.

Eliza realised that she was watching the tableau around her as if from under water as Alex's handkerchief was pushed into her hand. It had only been two weeks, but she missed Wil already. She didn't want to marry him, but he'd been a lot of fun. Deep down, she knew he wasn't serious about her. Not in a way that mattered.

'Don't cry. Please, don't cry,' said Alex, turning her so she could hide her face against his chest, where she continued to quietly sob.

Alex ran his hand through her hair, cupped the back of her head and began massaging the knots at the top of her neck. He was struck with a surge of protectiveness, followed closely by a desire to consume her, one kiss, one caress at a time.

After jumping from the train, he'd battled the crowds for close to half an hour, trying to find her. He'd been elbowed, pushed, shoved, and nearly had his eye taken out by a miniature flag and streamer thrown at close range. Resorting to unorthodox means, he'd climbed a girder for a bird's-eye view. And then he'd seen her. Wrapped in Wil's arms. He was not afraid to admit he had been panicked.

Eliza had his heart and he wasn't allowing her to give hers to anyone else without a battle – of epic proportions.

He heard her hiccup, then in a hesitant voice she asked, 'Is there anything I can do to help?'

Unsure he'd heard her correctly, as her nose remained buried in his coat front, he placed a finger under her chin and lifted her head. Better. Although, her eyes refused to meet his.

'What did you say?' he asked softly, smoothing her bottom lip with the pad of his thumb.

'You know, with that ... him ... you know ...'

Alex suppressed a smile. His cock was somewhat more optimistic than he was at this point – eager for a formal introduction. He shifted to relieve the pressure, mortified. What must Eliza think of what appeared to be his

THE BATTLE FOR ELIZA

uncontrolled physical urges.

'No, I don't think I do,' said Alex slowly. 'Can you be more specific?'

She lifted her gaze and he saw his reflection in two green pools, before Eliza stared intently at his chin. 'Well, we haven't been introduced, so I don't know his name. But he seems a little ... restless.' A giggle, then a hiccup. 'I was just wondering if there was anything I could do to help. Like before.'

Alex choked out a laugh, startling her into looking directly into his face.

'There's only one thing that would help. But given we're in the middle of a crowded pier, overlooked by thousands of America's finest, I'll just have to grin and bear it.'

Tipping her head to the side, she regarded him.

'Maybe we could get out of here. To have that talk, in private,' said Alex. 'Or do you want to watch the ships sail?'

She shook her head. Looking down, she skated her fingers across the visible bulge. 'Let's ... talk,' she agreed, smiling at his quick inhalation of breath.

'You are a minx. *My minx*. Come on, before I spill in my pants.'

For once she didn't argue, and he took advantage of her acquiescence to turn her and fight the throngs of people trying to secure the best vantage points for a view of the departure. They were in the minority when it came to crowd direction. It would be another thirty minutes before they arrived at the Port Melbourne station, but each step put distance between Eliza and any temptation offered by the American contingent.

CHAPTER 35

Later

The return travel time to the city was quick, by comparison with the outward journey. Alex would have preferred more time to sit cradling Eliza, her body tucked against his side, head resting on his shoulder, the smell of her hair teasing his nostrils. But the transportation gods had other ideas.

As Eliza dozed, Alex contemplated his next move. They couldn't talk at Eliza's house or at a public coffee house or bar. He made up his mind. The Federal. Would it be too forward to take her to his suite? He wanted her to himself, without interruption. But what did she want?

As the train rattled across the Sandridge Bridge, Eliza woke, giving him the befuddled look of the newly awakened. He kissed her lingeringly, playing with her bottom lip. A habit, he realised. A sniff and cough behind them reminded him of where they were. Public affection was still considered the actions of the immoral in many quarters.

'Let's go,' he said, grabbing her hand and pulling her from the carriage. 'Do we need to tell Bec?' he asked. At her puzzled look, he continued, 'About your change of mind.

254

She was taking your suitcase to the pier.'

Eliza shook her head, a smile hovering across her lips. 'Single females aren't allowed on board, nor the suitcases of single females.'

'So, how were you planning to … does that mean you're already … is it too late for an annulment?'

'Goodness, Alex, one minute you're seducing me, the next infuriating me with lewd suggestions.'

'But I thought —'

'There's the answer. Stop thinking,' Eliza flung at him as she flounced up the stairs to the hotel's foyer, pausing to survey the clientele reclining in overstuffed chairs.

With a hand in the small of her back, Alex steered Eliza up the central staircase and from there to a secluded alcove. He watched as she threw herself into one of the two leather armchairs. He could tell from the muted reflection of the lights along Collins Street that she had got herself into a high dudgeon.

Screened from prying eyes, a glass of champagne in hand, Alex was relieved to see the colour fade from Eliza's cheeks. But over the flute's rim, she was watchful. As usual, he found it hard to unravel what she was thinking. Inscrutable. Unsure as to how or where to start, he decided to be honest and figure it out as he went along.

'I'm new to this, so bear with me. But know that I love you something fierce, so some of my comments and questions will be borne out of … well, out of jealousy,' he said, waving a hand in the air.

She continued to watch him without comment as she sipped her drink.

'Firstly, believe me when I say Queenie and I are finished.

I'm not seeing her or even thinking about her, apart from wanting to throttle her for putting doubts in your mind.'

'She said that you two were taking a break. To spend time with other people. To spice up your relationship. That she was glad you'd reached out to me – as a friend.'

'Utter nonsense. The thoughts I entertain about you are not the least friendly. They're steamy and sensual,' Alex dropped his voice an octave, 'and one-hundred-percent carnal.'

Alex was happy to see Eliza take a hurried gulp of her champagne. Good, she wasn't unaffected.

'And I have no intention of straying ... or sharing. So, if you've made any commitment to that damned Yank, please tell me.'

'How could you think that, knowing how I respond to your kisses ... and other things?' exclaimed Eliza.

'Bec intimated ...' Alex began and then stopped. 'The suitcase, her talk of changed plans, romance ... none of it was true, was it?'

'I haven't made any plans with Wil, if that's what you're asking. I couldn't even consider him seriously, as you kept invading my thoughts. Every time I closed my eyes, I saw your face.'

'Only when you closed your eyes? What about in between lessons? On the train?' Alex leaned closer, resting his chin on his hands.

'Sometimes. But it was worse at night ... I dreamed about you. You ruined my fortnight!' Eliza accused.

Alex smirked. 'I'm glad. My equilibrium has been upset ever since I realised that I wanted my best friend's sister ... but that she only saw me as an adopted big brother ... and decided that she would practise all the things that I was willing to teach her with someone else.'

At each admission, Alex's voice became lower.

Eliza smiled. 'Not everything. There were some things I only practised with you.'

Uncaring as to any consequences, Alex scooped her from the chair, deposited her in his lap and wound his arms around her. 'That's better. You were too far away. I don't think I want to hear about anything other than what we practised.'

'Alex! You're going to get us kicked out,' protested Eliza.

'I live here, remember. They can't kick me out. And they wouldn't dare kick you out ... as my future wife.'

'A little presumptuous, aren't you?' she chided him, crossing her arms.

'I prefer to call it ... optimistic,' he said, placing languid kisses along her jawline. 'What were your plans for the rest of the evening?'

'That depends.' She gasped as Alex lapped at the sensitive spot behind her ear.

'On?'

'What's on offer ...'

'Oh, I think you have some idea of what's on offer. Or would you like me to spell it out for you, here, in the lounge?' Alex asked.

'No!' she squeaked. 'I have no plans that I can't change.'

'Good answer,' he breathed into her ear. 'Would you like to finish your drink?'

'Maybe ... for courage.'

'Sweetheart, you won't need courage. Do you trust me?'

Eliza nodded, wide-eyed.

'Come with me. Will you walk or will I carry you.'

'Alex!'

He grinned, unrepentant, as he stood and slid her down his body, maintaining a tight connection until her feet touched the carpet. 'It's time for some overdue introductions.'

Eliza swallowed. She was nervous and excited. What if she was hopeless? She was lousy at sports, apart from dancing ... although that was more an activity than a sport. She wasn't sure if her thoughts were helping or making things worse.

As if sensing her unease, Alex kept a hand at the base of her spine as they walked across the lounge and waited for the lift that would take them to the top of the five floors reserved to accommodate guests and residents. Once the lift doors closed, he backed her against one wall and caged her with his arms.

'I know you're nervous,' he said gently. 'I am too. The first time may not be mind-blowing, but we'll take things slowly ... until you get your confidence.'

'That's a relief as I have zero experience.' She laughed to cover her embarrassment over the admission.

'I'm glad for your lack of experience,' he said fiercely, before crushing her mouth and driving all thought from her mind.

'I'll think of it like a new dance,' she said as the lift bumped to a halt and they exited, then turned left down a shadowed hallway.

Stopping before the door to his suite, Alex pulled her in for another explosive kiss. Eliza caught herself thinking she'd seen fireworks and rolled her eyes at the cliché.

Entering his suite, she had a brief glimpse of a living room lit by the muted glow of a single lamp, before Alex pulled her through an open doorway into what must be his bedroom. She approved of the richly decorated wallpaper, the warm mahogany tones adorned with a peacock-feather-fan motif, which on closer inspection was studded with small metallic dots. They caught the light and twinkled like faraway stars.

'Like a dancer's costume fan, against a night sky,' marvelled Eliza. 'So beautiful.'

'But not as beautiful as you,' said Alex, pulling her gently into the circle of his arms. 'You can't imagine how difficult it has been to exercise restraint during your tuition over the last couple of weeks.'

'Maybe we should just get this one time over and done with, then,' said Eliza, tucking her hair behind her ears.

'We won't be rushing, Eliza. I've spent weeks imagining your body twined around and under me. We're going to make up our own steps, to our own beat. And if at any stage the tune doesn't suit, I want you to tell me and we'll change it.'

She nodded, watching as his eyes darkened to the gooey chocolate colour she loved.

'Just kiss me, won't you?' she asked.

Alex needed no further encouragement. His plan was to take things gradually, but he'd reckoned without Eliza's response, amplified due to her nervousness. She launched herself at him, nearly knocking him backwards, and then plastered herself hip to chest.

'Easy, sweetheart, we've got hours.'

Cradling her head, he alternated between taking long sips from her mouth and nibbles at her bottom lip. She gradually quietened and he deepened the kiss, invading her mouth until she was clinging to him, fingers tangling in his hair.

Widening his stance, he traced the line of her body from her hip to her shoulder, his hands restlessly bunching and smoothing the material of her dress. On its first foray, his fingers encountered and despatched the sash tied at her hip. On its second, he caught the sides of her asymmetrical skirt and drew the garment up her body and over her head, the butter soft velvet making no sound. He loved that the latest fashion eschewed buttons.

'No hiding.' Alex drew her arms away from her body where they'd rushed as air had hit her skin. Her blue silk camisole veiled her peaked nipples and hinted at a trim waist.

'But it isn't fair, you're still fully clothed.'

'And why is that, Eliza? Don't you wish to see me?'

She reacted to his droll self-mockery as he'd hoped – with a glint in her eye. She'd always had a competitive streak. He was surprised though at her choice, expecting her to divest him of his shirt first. She must have decided equality of states would be arrived at quickest if she stripped him of his trousers. She reached for the waistband of his Oxford bags and made fast work of the buttons. As they fell to his ankles, Alex stepped out of the wide leg, dispensing with his shoes at the same time and standing proud, his cock eager for introductions, straining through a pair of white boxers. The drawstring tie proved no match for industrious fingers, and his boxers soon joined his trousers.

Cupping her palms around the head of his penis, she rubbed her thumbs across the velvety tip, before she stroked down to its base. Alex sucked in a breath. Eliza raised her eyes and smiled serenely. Minx. Her exploratory fingers set up a rhythm as she watched his face carefully.

'Enough, sweetheart.'

'Am I doing it wrong?' Eliza asked, her fingers now circling his landing gear.

'No! It feels fantastic. But your first time shouldn't be against a wall, which is where I'll take you if you don't stop.'

Eliza removed her hand, but only after trailing it back up the length of his now rampant erection, and caressing the tip, as if in reluctant farewell.

Two could play that game, Alex thought, bending his head to suckle the crests jutting from the opaque material of her undergarment. She moaned and clawed at the buttons of his waistcoat and shirt. With a shimmy of his shoulders, he dispensed with both. Her fingers were everywhere as if on urgent reconnaissance.

His hands travelled to her waist, to the top of her knickers. Circling her belly button with the thumb of one hand, he undid the ribbon drawstring with the other and they slid to the floor. Lifting her from the debris of clothing, he sat her on the end of the bed and knelt between her legs. Securing her with his hands, he suckled her naval. His mouth moved lower, raining kisses over her mound and the inside of her thighs.

'My God, Alex!' she cried, squirming.

'Shhhh, sweetheart. Relax.'

'That's easy for you to say,' she panted. 'I feel about as relaxed as a nun in a brothel.'

Alex grinned despite himself, then spread her legs a little farther apart to position his mouth over her most sensitive part. And then he began lapping.

Eliza bucked, instinctively closing her legs. He placed his shoulders between her thighs and settled down to some serious loving. Taking the hood of her clitoris between his index and middle fingers, he teased it, lightly at first and then with more pressure as he felt Eliza's arousal build.

'I can't take this much longer,' Eliza sobbed, grabbing at the counterpane.

'Yes you can.' Alex maintained his intensity, his attention worthy of any vocation. It was taking all his willpower to remain where he was and continue to pleasure her, but he wanted to make this first time special.

'Alex!'

'Soon, sweetheart,' he soothed, applying a little more pressure. With his breathing coming in pants and his heart drubbing, Alex felt as if he was rafting a rapidly moving river.

Eliza arched her back and cried out, and Alex tasted the wetness streaming from her.

'Beautiful,' he breathed as he climbed up her body, nestling the head of his cock where his fingers had been moments ago and then sliding into her. He was caught between a sense of coming home and nervous anticipation. He felt her brace herself but continued to kiss her and tell her how many times he'd dreamed of this moment. Any physical resistance was brief.

Fully seated, Alex began to move, slowly grinding up and down on the same spot he'd kissed and caressed. Eliza locked her legs around him, pulled him closer and hung on.

'More.' He heard her whisper frantically.

Alex was barely in control. Eliza's responses were like an aphrodisiac, spurring him as he ground his pubic bone into her and then thrust. Harder, faster, stronger. He was

THE BATTLE FOR ELIZA

glistening with sweat. They both were. She was so close, he hoped he could hold on. And then finally, she was thrashing and convulsing. He buried himself in her, losing his breath in a final blatantly possessive kiss as he pumped into her ... before he collapsed on top of her.

CHAPTER 36

Much Later

Alex awoke with a sleeping Eliza tucked against him, a cock stand and the incessant ringing of the telephone. What to attend to first? It seemed when the telephone quietened that it was in accord with his own preferences and he set his mouth on an exploratory trail of Eliza's shoulder.

Eliza sighed and rocked her derrière backwards, eliciting a groan from Alex. Wondering if she knew what she was doing or whether she was dreaming, he levered himself on one elbow and caught the flicker of her eyelids closing.

'Minx. Actions have consequences,' he whispered into her ear, before he expertly rolled onto his back and took her with him, so she was perched atop him.

Shyly, she ducked her chin and burrowed into his chest.

'None of that, sweetheart. Unless you regret the experience.'

'No! Do you?'

'Can you feel me, Eliza?' At her cautious nod, he said, 'This tent is pitched for you and only you.'

She giggled. 'Who knew camping could be this much fun,'

THE BATTLE FOR ELIZA

she said, as she came up on all fours, effectively caging him on the mattress where he lay, her lips over his before she bent to kiss him.

Alex hoped she wasn't feeling too sore as he wanted Eliza something fierce. He set about stoking the fires of her desire.

The shrill of the telephone startled the couple into an awareness of life outside of Alex's suite and bed.

'Careful, sweetheart,' cautioned Alex as Eliza's thigh connected with his aroused member in her attempt to sit up.

'Sorry,' she said, dropping a quick kiss onto his penis, much to his amusement. She was a curious mix. One minute reserved and reticent, the next whimsical and playful.

Snaking an arm around her waist to prevent her escaping, he answered the phone.

'Hello ... yes, this is Alex. Tell him ... all right, switch him through.'

'Who is it?' whispered Eliza.

Alex replaced the receiver before he turned towards her. 'Daniel and Bec are in the foyer and are refusing to leave until they speak to me. The front desk is patching them through.'

At the news, Eliza drew the sheet up to cover her breasts. 'What are you going to tell them?'

Alex tugged the sheet back down and grazed both nipples with his tongue, before he closed her mouth with another heart-stopping kiss. 'The truth, of course.'

'What?'

'Well, not the whole truth. But I'm not going to lie as to your whereabouts. They've already guessed anyway, or they wouldn't be here.'

The phone rang again.

Eliza cuddled in close and Alex held the receiver far enough from his ear so that she could hear both sides of the conversation.

Daniel was upset, and after Alex acknowledged that they were together, demanded that Eliza appear in the foyer immediately. Alex diplomatically suggested that that may not be in everyone's best interests, and Daniel became incensed, informing Alex that he was coming up. Alex had never heard his friend speak with so much anger.

Eliza wrested the receiver from Alex's fingers and spoke calmly but firmly.

'Daniel? Oh, it's you, Bec. I'm fine. Do you think you can keep Daniel contained for half an hour? Good. Alex and I will meet you in the lounge on the first floor in about thirty minutes. Bye.'

Handing the receiver back to Alex, she smoothed his questioning brow and placed a finger across his lips. 'We can spend the next half-hour talking or you can teach me to ride.'

It took but a moment for Alex to catch her meaning. He wasn't going to waste precious minutes arguing.

CHAPTER 37

The Proposal

'Eliza.'

She'd turned from dressing to find Alex, in all his naked magnificence, on one knee.

Securing her hand, he entwined their fingers. 'No one could love you more than I do,' he said. 'Will you marry me?'

Eliza thought he looked a trifle self-assured, so she hesitated – naughty of her – but she'd briefly entertained the notion that perhaps he thought her a pushover.

'Eliza?' he'd prompted.

'I'm thinking.'

'Please ... marry ... me,' he implored. 'I want to spend the rest of my life with you. You have become as necessary to me as breathing.'

'Are you sure? Deep down I'm shy, and ... and I can be stubborn. Are you sure you can settle for just me?'

'To me you're just the right mix. Temptress with a splash of reservedness and a dash of humour. And from your responses earlier, you are a siren in the making, luring me with untapped depths.'

She quite liked the sound of that.

'But I will not share you. My stomach is in knots just thinking about anyone dancing with you, flirting with you, or touching you, however innocently. You may find me a tad possessive,' he said with wry smile.

She brushed his hair from his temple. 'We may need to temper that with a pinch of trust.'

His brown eyes darkened. 'I won't make any promises.'

Eliza smiled at his fierceness.

'And I have no intentions of straying. I won't deny that I haven't been exclusive in the past. But that was before I realised that you were the one.' Alex kissed the back of her hand. 'I'll do whatever it takes to keep you satisfied ... both in and out of the bedroom.'

This last had been said with a wink, but Eliza had watched the uncertainty invade his face and she knew he was not as self-assured as she'd first thought.

'Ask me again.'

'Eliza Sinclair, will you do me the honour of becoming my wife and my waltz partner for life?'

Leaning in, she kissed him, pouring all her emotions into her acceptance. The words, 'I will', confirmed her commitment.

The duty manager informed them he had discreetly directed the gentleman and young lady to one of the private first-floor rooms, understanding their need for discretion. Alex thanked him and ordered a bottle of champagne and four glasses to be brought in to toast their upcoming nuptials. Clearly relieved there wouldn't be any trouble, the manager congratulated them and assured Alex the champagne would be delivered in the next few minutes.

As they opened the door, Daniel reminded Eliza of an angry cockerel they'd had as children, strutting around the room, chest out. In contrast, Bec was seated on the opposite side of the room, feet tucked up beneath her skirts, reading. At their entrance, Bec jumped up to embrace her and quiz her in hushed tones, while Daniel moved forward to confront Alex and demand an explanation. Even before the door had closed.

'Now see here, Alex —'

'Eliza and I would like you both to be the first to congratulate us,' Alex interrupted smoothly, grabbing Daniel's hand, raised in accusation, and pumping it firmly. 'Eliza has accepted my proposal of marriage.'

A look of delight crossed Bec's face and she hugged Eliza tightly. 'Oh, Eliza, I'm so, so happy for you,' she whispered before she leaned away to study her face. 'You look ...' and her eyes grew wide, 'sated ... oh you wonderful, wicked girl.'

'Yes, well, things moved along quite quickly after we arrived here,' whispered Eliza, her crimson-coloured face managing an impish grin.

'I'm not judging, my friend. Alex is looking equally satisfied.'

Turning, she was relieved to see Daniel engaging in some backslapping and a man hug with Alex, who despite the attentions was watching her intently ... hungrily, if Eliza wanted to be fanciful about it. She shivered.

The arrival of the champagne brought Alex back to Eliza's side, the air visibly crackling between them, raising Daniel's eyebrows and bringing a smug look to Bec's face.

Eliza was worried when the topic of their departure from

the hotel to their respective homes arose.

'I'll see my fiancée home safely,' Alex insisted, wrapping an arm around Eliza's waist.

Daniel countered strongly with, 'I don't think that's a good idea,' adding with a meaningful look at his friend, 'Under the circumstances.'

Both men glared at one another, seemingly unprepared to budge.

'I'll spend the night at Bec's place,' said Eliza with an enquiring look towards Bec. At her nod, she continued, 'Daniel, you can tell Mum it is so the two of us can catch up after the whirlwind fortnight. We have so much to talk about.'

'Not everything, I hope,' Alex murmured for her ears only.

Eliza's mind flicked back to the images of the last couple of hours. Those of Alex, his attention, his loving – their loving. 'Not everything,' she agreed with a smile, tucking those images away for examination at a more private time.

CHAPTER 38

Friday 7 August 1925

'You have that stupid grin on your face again,' remarked Bec conversationally from beside Eliza as they stood, pretending interest in the crowd circulating the dance floor.

Eliza had been marvelling at how easily under Alex's gaze she felt fascinating, compelling, attractive and intriguing. She smiled at her use of the same words Bec had flung at her just over three weeks earlier, before she turned to face her friend.

'You know, since everything that's happened, I haven't thanked you for all your help.'

'You just needed a push and an occasional reminder to keep you tracking in the right direction. Luckily, those skills I have in abundance.'

'Yes, you do.'

'And don't forget Wil.'

'I can't forget Wil. He did wonders for my self-confidence. *Cain't never could*, he said. And he was right. Don't mention that to Alex, though, he gets a steely look in his eye whenever Wil's name is uttered. Sometimes he even growls.'

Both girls shared a smile.

'Did you hear about Queenie?' asked Bec.

Eliza shook her head.

'She's sojourned to Sydney. Left this morning. Apparently, a little birdie hinted that her behaviour during the fleet's visit had become wild. Her aunt spoke with her parents and agreed she'd spend some time with them, back home.'

'I'm not concerned by Queenie, despite her past with Alex,' said Eliza, surprising herself, and Bec. 'Alex was furious when I told him about her intimations and insinuations to me. And I believe it when he says he loves me.'

'Well, I've been told on good authority, the little birdie fitted Alex's description,' Bec said, nodding at the man under discussion striding towards them.

Later that evening, Alex danced Eliza out onto one of the balconies overlooking the gardens. As the heavy velvet curtain fell back into place, cocooning them, he gathered her close.

'God I've missed you today,' he whispered. 'I couldn't concentrate and my boss even threatened to send me home.'

'Really? I'd barely given you a thought,' she teased, filling her hands with his arse.

Alex growled, kissing and caressing her until she was boneless, plastered against him and wantonly asking how long before they could leave.

'That's more like it,' he murmured.

Raised voices reached them from a balcony around the building's corner.

'I thought I was helping.'

'I didn't and don't need your help.'

'Truly, Bec? He was all over you. From where I was standing, you were being attacked by an octopus.'

Eliza stifled a chuckle into Alex's shoulder. Daniel had never been known for his thoughtful choice of words.

'Argh! That's offensive. I'll never be able to look at him the same way now.'

'Good. I'm glad.'

A pause and then Eliza heard lips meeting lips, the sort of meeting that would be better described as a continuation of an argument, but without words. She frowned, cocking her head to one side and listening intently for further sounds.

Alex was less interested in the goings-on between Daniel and Bec than he was in the opportunity that it presented to maximise his time with Eliza. Alone and uninterrupted.

He'd promised his best friend and soon-to-be brother-in-law that he'd be discreet. He would never lie if asked a direct question, he'd told him, but stopped at refusing to entertain unavoidable subterfuge during his and Eliza's engagement. He just wanted her so damned much. So damned often. And if he wasn't mistaken, and after all this was an area of prowess for him, she was likewise afflicted.

He nibbled the side of her neck and ran his palms over her ribcage to cup her breasts.

'Alex, we can't. Not here ...'

'If I learned one thing from your naval swain, it was *cain't never could*,' he said hoarsely, capturing her lips and effectively preventing any further argument, and assuring her surrender.

AUTHOR'S NOTE

This book is a work of fiction; however, the backdrop and setting are inspired by real events and places woven into the story. I realise not all of you will forgive my decision to delay the fleet's departure from morning to evening, although Alex was certainly grateful.

1920s
LANGUAGE

Bo Mate or pal.

Cain't never could A saying from the south of the United States of America. Cain't is a combination of Can't and Ain't. It means if you don't try, you'll never do it.

Knows her oil Someone who knows how to be 'entertaining' on a date.

Pegity A boardgame where players insert coloured wooden pegs into a punch board.

The glad eye Look at someone in a way that shows you are sexually attracted to them.

278

ABOUT VICKI MILLIKEN

After a lifetime in the corporate sphere, from oil to beer, Australian author Vicki Milliken, opted out to follow a passion to write. *The Battle for Eliza* is her first historical romance.

When not writing, Vicki spends her time cycling, ballroom dancing, travelling, reading and drinking chai lattes.

She is looking forward to the day her writing keeps her in champagne.

vicki@vickimilliken.com

www.vickimilliken.com

ACKNOWLEDGMENTS

To my husband, Andrew; to those friends and family who encouraged me; to my editor, Alexandra Nahlous, and coach, Julie Postance; to others who guided my steps along the way and offered feedback.

Thank you!

CPSIA information can be obtained
at www.ICGtesting.com
Printed in the USA
LVHW111113161120
671798LV00005B/470